Caravan

Caravan

Dorothy Gilman

LARGE PRINT BOOK CLUB EDITION

DOUBLEDAY

NEW YORK   LONDON   TORONTO   SYDNEY   AUCKLAND

This Large Print Edition, prepared especially for Doubleday Book & Music Clubs, Inc., contains the complete, unabridged text of the original Publisher's Edition.

PUBLISHED BY DOUBLEDAY
a division of Bantam Doubleday Dell Publishing Group, Inc.
666 Fifth Avenue, New York, New York 10103

DOUBLEDAY and the portrayal of an anchor with a dolphin are trademarks of Doubleday, a division of Bantam Doubleday Dell Publishing Group, Inc.

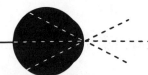

**This Large Print Book carries the
Seal of Approval of N.A.V.H.**

Printed in the United States of America

to
Hilary Richardson Butters

Book 1

one

It was Mum who kept trying to make a lady of me through all my growing-up years but it was Grams who taught me her magic tricks and how to be a pickpocket, and of the two of them I have to say that Grams' lessons certainly proved the more valuable to me in my life.

"Head up," Mum would say. "Shoulders back, Caressa, never say ain't, watch your manners, be a lady and learn to roll with the punches."

Grams, bless her, would only laugh and say, "Waste—all waste!"

Much to my amusement I have at last become a lady, quite elegant and proper in these later years, and if I take up my pen to write of the strange events in my past I do this because they've been kept secret for too long. I indulge myself: the time has come to place on paper who and what I have truly been—and what I have seen— and to record all that happened to me during those years when I was young and counted dead by the world, my bones assumed to be whitening under the desert sun with all the others who were murdered. To speak of those years becomes important, too, because of the stranger who came to my door this morning asking to see Lady Teal about a certain *antiika nahet* with a green stone in it that came from a queen's tomb in the Sahara. What memories that brings back! I'm sure Bertram thought him mad—Bertram is a very proper butler—but he carried the message to me faithfully. The stranger was being discreet, of course, for *antiika nahet* means in Arabic a sculpture, very ancient, and it was only decades later that I discovered the green stone to be an emerald of much value. He was speaking of the tomb of

Queen Tin Hinan, officially found south-west of the Hoggar Mountains in 1925 by Reygasse and deProrak, but how the man had learned of the existence of the little stone figure that I took from the tomb, or for that matter of my own existence I don't know, for I've had many names and it happened so long ago, when this century was not many years old.

I did not see the man; I told Bertram to say I was indisposed . . . an interesting word. Still, I've lived a longer life than most, and if I should die next week, the prehistoric carving ought to be returned to the country it came from, and Deborah should know why. A pity I'll not be able to see her face when she reads what I write now. Only two people know of my past and both of them are dead, but Deborah always assumed her father was the man I married; it will be one of those shocks that have to be endured when Truth is laid out as bare as the naked lady at Mr. Laski's. As for Mum, if she happens to be looking over my shoulder from that Heaven she always believed in, I'd like her to know that I really learned to roll with the punches—a few too many, I might add—and became a lady after all, with a capital L at that.

Lordy, she'd say—but just listen to me, slipping back into how we talked in Oklahoma, when this is 1980, and I long ago learned to speak what Linton called Impeccable English and have known my share of prime ministers and ambassadors, a dull lot usually, but how easily the mind slips into the past at my age. I don't tell my age now, and I don't look into mirrors either. Beauty is beauty and I had it in abundance, but whether it was a curse or a blessing is not for me to say. Grams told me it was my fate, and "look at the lines in the palms of her hands," but Mum's lips would only tighten and she refused to look, saying stubbornly, "She'll do fine if she's ladylike and learns to roll with the punches."

When I was young I told people I came from a circus family but that was long ago and only half-true because after my father fell from his trapeze and missed the net, dead on arrival it was said, Mum and Grams left the circus to begin their own plunge down, which ended in their being carny folk—big-time and then rag-bag—where Grams told fortunes in the mitt camp and Mum was in the cooch show, although later, no longer so young, she was the headless woman. If I close my eyes and listen hard I can hear the sounds now: the steam organ on the calliope pumping out its rollicking music, the screams from the Loop-o-plane, the shuffle of a hundred feet tramping the midway, the smell of sawdust and hot grease and popcorn. I can hear the talker shouting his come-ons, the grinders and openers shouting their spiels to the tip: "See the tattooed lady! the sword swallower! Only a nickel to see real, live, man-killing snakes! See the contortionist—the geek! Thrill a minute, folks, thrill a minute. . . . Step up and try your luck at the Cat Rack . . . at Spin the Arrow . . . a prize every time! . . . the bucket game, skillo. . . . Win a doll, win a teddy bear . . . !"

And since the carny was usually full of strong games, and the fuzz paid off, I would be mingling with the crowds, no longer in boys' overalls but an innocent child with a ribbon in my hair and a few ruffles and a washed face, and a vast number of pockets inside my dress for the wallets and bills I collected during the night, handing them to Grams in her tent when my pockets grew stuffed.

I had good fingers for a pickpocket, Grams told me, long and tapering, the first and middle fingers nearly the same length, and she made me take good care of them and rub glycerine or petroleum jelly on them every night. With constant practice I learned all the tricks. It was like conjuring, Grams emphasized, not so different at all from palming coins, needing keenness of eye and quickness, and two strong supple fingers. Picking a pocket was easy enough at the carnival when a mark was intrigued by a game and reached into his pocket for money, advertising where he kept it, but as I gained in skill Grams saw to it that I practiced now and then on the streets in a village, with her observing from a distance and me carrying a cape or sweater over my arm to conceal what my fingers did. I would bump into a man and apologize or brush against him or inquire directions of an amiable-looking one, or in similar manner distract while my two fingers slid into his pocket to open like a pair of scissors and extract what it contained. Later I went to the streets alone; it needed experience to know just how firmly to grasp a bulky wallet without losing it, and without thrusting too deeply into that pocket. Oh, I was good, I really was.

Would Linton call this "emotion remembered in tranquility?" I never knew whether he actually loved me but he made an honest woman out of me—a titled one at that—before he had the tact to die. But I was useful to him, and I was still beautiful when he died, not an aging woman with arthritic knees, although thank God my fingers are still supple and I can wear all my rings . . . strange unusual rings, museum pieces now, probably, coming from such faraway places.

If the stranger returns will I see him? What would I say to him, what would I admit? It suddenly brought too much back to me, the nose-quivering smell of the dried cheese they called *tikamarin,* and the gruel —*assink*—they fed me; the beat of drums can still do this—bring it all back, and too much at once.

What I didn't know in those contented carnival days was how determined Mum was to make a lady out of me, and why she squeezed every penny until it screamed. It was not enough for her to see me stand up straight and say please and thank you; she had A Plan. Over the years, moving from place to place, she'd taught me to read and write and do sums; presently, between shows, she began to dress up in her best clothes, ask her way to a public library and smuggle out books that she never returned, and suddenly I must learn history, spelling and geography. When I was fourteen her Plan was divulged: I was to go to Boston the next year to a school for young ladies, an expensive one called Miss Thistlethwaite's Finishing School for Young Ladies. Worse, I had already been accepted.

"But why, Grams, why?" I cried.

"It's her dream," Grams said, brushing my hair. "People need dreams, there's as much nourishment in 'em as food."

"But what about *my* dreams?"

She smiled faintly. "And what might your dream be?"

"I can be a magician," I reminded her.

"You're already a magician, and you'll always be a magician."

"Then make her stop, Grams," I

pleaded. "Even the name Thistlethwaite sticks in my teeth. I don't want to leave you or the carny, this is home."

But Grams only shook her head. "It's not just her dream, it's more than that."

"What, then?" I asked stormily.

"It's fate working through her," she said. "It's the beginning."

But of what I didn't know, nor could Grams, but a beginning it was, yes.

Fabrics and paper patterns were ordered from the Sears catalogue, as well as cutting shears and thread, and an orgy of sewing took place all through the winter. I shudder even now at what it cost Mum and Grams in money and stamina, because the carny rarely stayed more than four nights in a town, and the sewing had to be done on trucks or during train stops, or early mornings before the shows began. They had settled it between them that by making my everyday clothes they could afford one Thistlethwaite uniform, a navy blue jumper with insignia that cost a frightening $10; I helped do what I could but I was all thumbs with a needle. By summer when the carny headed north there were three ankle-length skirts, four shirtwaists, a cape cut down from Mum's black winter coat, and Grams had trimmed one of her old hats for me with a velvet ribbon, and one of Mum's straw hats with flowers. The Fat Lady took up a collection for a pair of bright new kid boots for me that cost all of $1.50, the first I'd ever owned that weren't cloth, and the sword swallowers' wife came to our tent one morning with a handful of ribbons and lace for my shirtwaists. I thought I was already a lady when I looked at the clothes I'd take with me in the old straw suitcase the Tattooed Lady contributed.

There was no holding back September, though, and one rainy day—an omen, I thought—I was put on a train for Boston to enter Thistlethwaite School, a huge Gothic mansion not far from the Boston Common. There was a lawn with flowers, and dozens of girls as pretty as flowers and wearing beautiful new clothes, and bells rang for each class. The stair railings were solid brass and there were ferns and jardinieres everywhere. The classrooms were downstairs, the rooms for out-of-town students upstairs near the attic, but most of the students were the daughters of

Boston doctors, lawyers, ministers, judges and businessmen, and went home every night.

What can I say of Thistlethwaite? My clothes were all wrong and badly made, my yellow kid boots were too bright and my two hats out-of-date. It was only when one of the girls saw me absently palming a coin that I achieved visibility. Or notoriety. Otherwise those early weeks were lonely and homesick, and Mum's ambitions felt very cruel to me. All I could do was study hard so that her hoarded money would not be wasted. Even the $1.00 spending money Grams sent each month was a sacrifice, I knew this, and knew I had to earn good marks so that I'd receive an engraved certificate after two years and magically be a lady. What this would bring me had never been defined, and I had never thought to ask. After all, I was living out someone else's dream, which is never easy, and the staid atmosphere in which I had to live it thoroughly depressed my spirits.

Until November.

I had dyed my bright yellow kid boots brown and I had solved my embarrassing clothes problem by wearing the school uniform every day, but its serge by this time was almost shiny enough to reflect a face. Worse, Christmas was coming and I was determined to send Grams and Mum a gift. I had been very well behaved for two and a half months but now I needed money: it was time to revert.

I practiced first by picking Jennie Todd's pocket of 50 cents and returning it to her, saying the coin had fallen from her pocket. I filched the janitor's key without his feeling the slightest whisper of two fingers invading his pockets, and thus reassured that I'd not lost my touch, I set out for the park one crisp and sunny Saturday afternoon to look for more fruitful possibilities than Jennie Todd and the janitor, glad to be free of Thistlethwaite's virtuous and stifling ambiance for a few hours.

two

———～———

I sat in the park on a bench and watched people passing by, observing each one closely in order to choose the easiest and best mark. I saw a few grand ladies in furs who looked profitable, but out of honor to Mum and Grams I wasn't going to take anything from a woman. Then I saw a man strolling toward me who looked just the right sort of person: he gave the impression of being a professor, for certainly he looked preoccupied, his thoughts entirely elsewhere, but what was best of all he wasn't wearing an overcoat but a belted

Norfolk jacket half a size too small so that I could see the bulge in its right-hand pocket. He was neither young nor old, with a stern pale face that was rather long in shape, and dark, melancholy eyes. Definitely he looked easy prey and my spirits rose at once. I stood up and began strolling behind him while I studied the shape of his pocket and its contents, and then I drew abreast of him to pass, and a second later I was slipping his wallet into my own coat pocket.

Two seconds after that I was stunned by an arm shooting out to grasp mine; the man swung me nearly off my feet. "Young lady," he said sternly, "you have just pocketed my wallet."

I thought of Mum telling me to roll with the punches and I couldn't think of any way out of this because his grip was strong and the evidence on my person, so I gasped and said bravely, "Yes, sir, I did."

"Hmmmm," he muttered, staring down at me. His eyes examined my coat, which was not threadbare as he'd probably expected, and my face, which was trying not to look frightened, and he said, "Why?"

"Well," I began, "I wanted—" But I wasn't going to tell him, I made my lips thin and shook my head.

"Hmmm," he muttered again. "And very cleverly it was done, too; in fact if I'd not traveled widely and learned to recognize the—" He glanced down at his jacket and nodded. "But very careless I was today, yes. Where did you learn the trade? Come, come," he said with a faint smile. "If you tell me I'll not turn you over to the authorities, I promise."

It was at this point that I began a real struggle to free myself; if I'd had my wits about me I would have shouted for help, due to appearances being entirely in my favor—a grown man hanging onto a schoolgirl—but having never been caught before, and being thus in a panic, this didn't occur to me and I could only struggle wordlessly. What he did next was pin both arms behind my back and march me toward the nearest shop, which happened to be an ice cream parlor, and once inside he edged me into one of those little round chairs with wire legs, sat me down, took the chair next to me and bid the waitress bring us two ice cream sodas. Vanilla.

"Chocolate," I said.

He corrected the order and looked at me. "So—you prefer chocolate to vanilla and you pick pockets. How old are you?"

"S-s-sixteen," I stammered. He had begun to look less severe and I was ready to admit that much, quite proud that I'd left my fifteenth year behind me a week ago.

He glanced thoughtfully at the blue of my Thistlethwaite uniform with its insignia prominently outlined in gold braid; before I could draw my coat closer to hide it he said, very calmly, "And now you will tell me—in exchange for one chocolate soda and no recriminations—how a pupil at Thistlethwaite, and a very properly dressed young lady—"

Mum, I thought, would be pleased to hear this.

"—learned to steal with such cleverness."

"Not so cleverly," I told him sulkily. "You caught me."

He smiled, which made him look quite kind. "Ah, but you didn't know that I'm a man who has developed a sixth sense. I have learned from two trips to the Middle East to beware of any person passing me so closely when there is space all around. It is, as I say, an awareness grown in me from the rapaciousness sometimes found in foreign climes."

"Is that what you mean by sixth sense?" I asked, growing interested.

He nodded. "I can assure you, young lady, that if you'd chosen any other man on the street you would not be here—ah, thank you," he said to the waitress. "Would not be sitting on that chair, about to tell me your name, I trust, and to imbibe an ice cream soda. Now may I have my wallet, please?"

Reluctantly I dug in my pocket and placed his wallet on the table where it lay between us, bulging obscenely with crisp paper money. Watching me he said, "I see my mistake . . . I am not dealing with a pupil at Thistlethwaite but a street urchin." Picking up the wallet with long pale fingers he extracted a ten-dollar bill and placed it on the table. "Earn this," he said, adding dryly, "Did you steal the uniform, too?"

Ten dollars and an ice cream soda were a better bargain than the police and being sent home in disgrace. I shook my head.

"Then where did you learn such a skill?"

"In the carny," I told him, picking up the spoon to eat the ice cream before it melted into the syrup. "Carnival, that is."

"I see," he said, staring at me. "Well, well, so you visited a carnival? No," he added thoughtfully, "a visit wouldn't do it, who taught you?"

"Grams." Sucking the straw made a great deal of noise and so I returned, lady-like, to the spoon.

"That would be a grandmother?" When I nodded he said, "And was she a pickpocket, too?"

"She's a magician and fortune-teller." I wasn't about to betray Grams. "She's a juggler, too."

"And your mother?"

"Right now she's the headless lady."

Soon enough he was extracting the story of how I came to Thistlethwaite School and asking a great number of tiresome and silly questions. "Because," as he said at last, "I am by way of being something of an anthropologist, as well as a linguist and scholar, and—" He frowned. "I wonder if a paper on the language of the carnival might be in order for the Society? Fuzz, for instance, what is that?"

Since I didn't know what either anthropologist or linguist meant I very kindly told him that "fuzz" meant police.

"I see," he said, nodding. "Yes, that could be useful, very useful. You haven't told me your name, by the way."

"Caressa."

He winced at that. "Caressa what?"

"Caressa Horvath."

He slid the ten-dollar bill across the table to me. "And my name is Jacob Bowman, but before I leave I want you to pledge, on your honor, that you do no more stealing. You must know it's dishonest, illegal and highly reprehensible."

I'd never thought it more than a game, frankly. Carny folks are a tight-knit people, with a family closeness bred of late hours, constant movement and a struggle to survive, while townies came from a world of nine-to-five jobs, regular meals and real houses, church on Sundays and baths on Saturday nights in real metal tubs. They came to the carnival for thrills, practically being asked to be tricked, and they were as alien to us as foreigners from another

country. If Gus Fritz was waiting to whee-
dle a mark into betting on slum skillo, a bet
the man could never win—not with Gus'
foot on the pedal under the boards—what
was a little wallet-lifting? Nevertheless, I
looked at this man and gravely admitted
that it might be dishonest, yes. What I really meant was that I understood—with fi-
nality—that I was a member of the other
world now, where the fuzz had not been
paid off and there could be trouble. This
was obviously part of learning to be the
lady Mum wanted me to be, and ladies did
not indulge in picking pockets. I promised.

"A sheep led astray needs some
shepherding," he said firmly. "It is the duty
of any good Christian to give aid to the
transgressor. I shall stop in on occasion at
your school—I live nearby, and they know
me—and inquire of your progress. Have
you read the Bible?"

When I shook my head he said, "I will
bring you a Bible."

And that is how I met Jacob Bowman.
He was a strange man: he arrived on the
next visiting day carrying both a Bible and
a copy of Shakespeare; he lectured me
again about Honesty and pressed a five-

dollar bill into my palm as we shook hands at his departure, so that I now had Mum plotting my future as a lady, and Mr. Bowman working hard at shaping my character, and Thistlethwaite trying to shape my mind with classes in English grammar, literature, the French language, mathematics and history. It was all very well in its way but it was surprising how tiring it was, and how captive I felt.

A few weeks later Mr. Bowman received permission for me to visit his home for a day, and I began to acquire a clearer picture of him. For one thing, he was rich. He lived in a large mansion, dark, with stained glass windows and brown woodwork, and with books everywhere. It was astonishing: there were books piled on the floor, books on tables and books on shelves. There were old swords and daggers hung on the walls. Rugs were hung there, too, with bizarre designs woven into them. There was a glass cabinet in his library with a display of gold coins—unfortunately it was locked—and a glass case of fossils and of weird little figures of people carved out of stone. And dictionary stands in every room except the kitchen.

Whatever wall space wasn't crammed with books, rugs, pictures or daggers held maps of just about every country in the world. He was certainly an odd one. There was a housekeeper named Mrs. Briggs, and a Mr. Briggs who did all the heavy work, stoking the furnace and what he called yard-work, and I learned what a linguist is because Mr. Bowman was studying all sorts of foreign languages and showed me their dictionaries.

There was someone else in the house with him that winter, a young man he called Sozap. It seems that Mr. Bowman had been learning a language called Tamahak, spoken in North Africa by a people called the Tuareg, but during a summer trip to Maine he'd found Sozap, who was a full-blooded Abenaki Indian and still knew the language. He'd borrowed him at once to bring home with him and had put aside the Tamahak to study Sozap's language, presumably so that he could write a Paper on that, too. Sozap occupied a small room with a desk, and looked depressed when I first saw him. We regarded each other with interest, each of us being new to this strange house, and of nearly the same age.

He was much more attractive than Indian Joe at the carnival, who did war dances with piercing shrieks while he waved a tomahawk, but then of course Indian Joe wasn't a real Indian, he was Italian.

Sozap joined us for lunch and I was surprised to find that he spoke English. It was a strange lunch, with only three of us seated at a huge mahogany dining table, and Mr. Bowman jovially trying out his new Abenaki vocabulary. "Caressa," he said, "today is *Kadawasanda,* am I right, Sozap?"

"Saturday, yes," Sozap said politely.

"And the month is—no, don't help me, Sozap—*Peb—Peb—*"

"Pebonkas."

In an aside Mr. Bowman said earnestly, "It's so extremely interesting to learn that the word for good-bye in Abenaki is *adio.* . . . When you recall—as I'm sure you must—that the Spanish for good-bye is *adios,* and the French for farewell is *adieu,* there is a fascinating connection worth tracing if I have the time."

But time was something of which Mr. Bowman never seemed to have enough; he was planning a third and more intensive trip to North Africa at some future date; there were languages to learn, and Papers to write for his mysterious Society, but each Saturday he would appear at Thistlethwaite and escort me to his house for the day, and give me $5 when I left. That was a lot of money in those days when you could buy a sewing machine for $12, a silk petticoat for $5 and a dozen oranges for 20 cents. Each week I sent three of the dollars to Mum and Grams, I saved up and bought a new school uniform, and quieter kid boots, and put aside the rest for what Mum said always lay ahead for everyone: a rainy day.

At Christmas Mum and Grams sent me a present of three wooden eggs with a small, slanted hole drilled in each. On one of them Grams had glued a moustache and a beard of black thread, and she'd painted eyes, nose and eyebrows to make a wonderfully humorous face. With it there was a note whose words I cherished for a long time and have never forgotten:

Put these on your fingers,
Not diamonds, it is true,

But diamonds aren't a fun that lingers
And we must all make do.

To this had been added, *We miss you, dear, leaving tonight for Kansas City, we both thank you for warm sweaters and chocolate. Bless you. Love.*

The holes in the wooden eggs just fitted my fingers and I really loved the one that Grams had painted; when I was lonely I'd insert him on my index finger and talk to him, or sit in front of the mirror and have him talk to me. I named him Mr. Jappy, and as soon as I had the money to buy paints I created faces for the other two, a clown with a huge red smile and sad eyes, and a girl with a cupid's-bow mouth and yellow hair. I'd fit them on my fingers when I was alone in my room, and our conversations were lively and of much more interest than Mr. Bowman's talks on his travels and the Papers he was writing about them.

It was because of Mr. Jappy that I became better acquainted with Sozap. I was wearing the puppet, if he could be called that without insult, after lunch one day at Mr. Bowman's, and Sozap giggled when he saw him.

"Thou has a funny man on thy finger!" he said.

"You like him, Sozap?"

He made a face. "Please, my name is Joseph really. Mr. Bowman insists on Sozap but it is strange to me."

This was interesting. "Why?"

"He wants me always Abenaki," he said simply. "And Joseph in Abenaki is Sozap."

"Do you like teaching him the language?" I asked.

He sighed. "It is, to be frank—in my language the word is *pizwi*. It means—" He frowned. "It means senseless. What does he want with it, I ask? Most of my people don't even know or speak the language now. He pays me good money and dresses me in good clothes, but it is *pizwi*," he said firmly.

"He gives me money, too," I told him wistfully but I had to admit even then that Mr. Bowman gave me much more, because of the books. Aside from lunch, which was always a treat, and the $5 I was given each week, there wasn't much to do at Mr. Bowman's and I'd begun to look at the books on the shelves. Even before

Christmas I'd discovered Gene Stratton Porter's *Freckles, Little Lord Fauntleroy* and *Robin Hood,* and then had moved on to *The House of Seven Gables* and a few sips of Shakespeare. These had already brought me the companions I would never have at Thistlethwaite School, and after catching up with books I'd never read as a child I'd begun some real explorations. Mr. Bowman, for instance, had several translations of Omar Khayyám's *Rubáiyát,* none of them matching, and I loved "Good friends beware! the only life we know Flies from us like an arrow from the bow, The Caravan of life is moving by, Quick! to your places in the passing show." I memorized that one as well as "Set not thy heart on any good or gain, Life means but pleasure, or means but pain; when Time lets slip a little perfect hour, O take it—for it will not come again."

The words had begun to stir in me a desire to find my own place in the passing show, and to not let slip a little perfect hour that wouldn't come again, except that I didn't know how. I was captive at the school learning how to be a lady, and the only life at Mr. Bowman's seemed to be found in book-words.

Or perhaps in Sozap. I looked at him more closely, standing near me in the library and watching me. He was really very attractive: his black hair was like dark water full of lights, his brown skin was taut over very high cheekbones and his soft eyes were looking at me with much interest, too. Very slowly, as if drawn by magnets, we moved closer and abruptly he placed his arms around me and we stood like that, so close I could feel his heart beating fast under his shirt, and although I didn't know whether Indians kissed with their lips or rubbed noses like Eskimos, I lifted my face and pressed my lips to his, and apparently he knew about kissing because we kissed for a long time, his tongue pushing its way through my lips to meet my tongue, which made me feel very warm inside, and then hot in a strange new way to me. When we separated I felt breathless.

"Miña," he murmured, eyes closed. "More—again!"

But hearing Mr. Bowman's step outside in the hall we leaped apart, Sozap to begin idly twirling a globe of the world and I to open a book. Mr. Bowman had come to ask if I was ready to play a game of checkers and I meekly followed him out of the library, feeling that checkers couldn't possibly measure up to kissing Sozap.

The next weekend I had to study for my exams; I did not at any time neglect my studies, always aware of Mum's hopes for me, and the following weekend Mr. Bowman sent word that he and Sozap had come down with influenza. This was a disappointment, because having received very good grades on my exams, on topics heavily researched by me, I'd been looking forward eagerly to research of another sort with Sozap. And so for two weeks I was kept waiting and forlorn.

This took us to early April and spring, which is a risky time for such experiments, with the sap running in the trees, and the forsythia buds glowing gold and all the world loving a lover. I found Sozap looking pale after his bout with influenza, but there was nothing pale about the ardent look he gave me, and following lunch a subtle jerk of his head directed me to the library.

We met there and moved at once toward each other, our kisses becoming more and more passionate, so that it seemed only natural, in the heat of this new discovery, for Sozap's hands to move to my breasts and begin caressing them, when—"Sssst," I hissed suddenly, sure that I heard Mr. Bowman in the hall. We jerked apart to stare at each other, all flushed and gasping, and were relieved to hear Mr. Bowman call out to Mrs. Briggs from the dining room. Only then did he make his way down the hall to the library, to find Sozap again toying with the globe of the world, and myself running a finger down the page of a book and looking very studious indeed.

That Mr. Bowman had seen us after all, and had retreated tactfully to the dining room before approaching the library again, was not evident until the following Saturday when I came to the house.

Sozap was gone.

"But—where?" I faltered.

Mr. Bowman seemed incapable of meeting my eyes; his gaze had dropped to the floor where he appeared to study the intricacies of the Oriental rug on which we stood. "To use the vernacular," he said dryly, *"Môjo wigiidit*—he is on his way home." Still not looking at me he added firmly, "It was time that I returned to my study of Tamahak."

Two months later, just before classes ended, Mr. Bowman asked me to marry him.

three

⌒‿⌒

Mr. Bowman had not confided his plans of travel to me but I should have guessed that plans were being consolidated because of the crates that had begun to fill the library, very efficiently roped wooden crates labeled—now that I looked more closely—MEDICAL SUPPLIES, CLOTHES (cold weather), CLOTHES (hot weather), FOOD, AMMUNITION. I had assumed for some weeks they held only new books for his library.

"No," he said gravely, "I am planning another trip to North Africa, this time to experience the Sahara, and I would like your company on this trip very much, Caressa."

I looked at him blankly. He knew very well that I was returning for the summer to Mum and Grams, to be followed by one last year of schooling.

"I dislike the thought of leaving you," he continued, "for your youth and inexperience render you vulnerable and you need looking after." He gave me a glance that told me he was referring here to Sozap. "I am considerably older than you, but I would consider it an honor if you would marry me so that I may take care of you, Caressa."

As I write these words so many years later I cannot help but regard them with irony when I consider what followed some months later, but that is how he proposed marriage to me and no doubt Grams would have told me that it was already written in the palm of my hand. I was certainly astonished by his proposal and idiotically blurted out, "I'd have to ask Mum and Grams."

"But of course," he said. "I will not ask how tenderly you regard me. Many marriages are arranged ones, in other countries at least, and love has a way of blossoming later. And you will be very well provided for," he added tactfully.

The blossoming part didn't move me in particular but I suddenly realized what the words "provided for" meant. I could repay Mum and Grams their investment in me, and become a grand lady all at once, as well as have a chance to see the world. After all, that caravan of life was moving by, I was already sixteen and mustn't let slip a perfect hour. There was that Shakespeare line I'd memorized, too . . . about a tide in the affairs of men which, taken at the flood leads on to fortune and, omitted . . . well, I was not one to prefer being bound in shallows and in miseries.

How could I say no?

Mum and Grams were over a thousand miles away that month, doing shows in Colorado, so it was impossible to speak to them face-to-face. In his letter to Mum, Mr. Bowman described his pedigree, his history and his plans, listed his education (Harvard and Brown universities), his clubs, his published articles, omitted his age but artfully enclosed a bank order for $1,000.

Of course his age had been well-es-

tablished in my letters to them. When I finally heard from Mum she wanted to know
if I loved Mr. Bowman, and rather wistfully I
remembered how she'd fallen in love with
my father the first time she saw him in his
spangled tights mounting the ladder to his
tightrope. Grams' letter was more confiding: she wrote that Mum was upset because, although she'd never wanted me to
marry a roustabout or a snake-eater, she'd
never dreamed of my marrying a man so
"above my station" in life, and twenty
years older. She didn't write what *she*
thought but I don't suppose it would have
changed much. At sixteen my future didn't
look very promising; I didn't seem to fit in
anywhere, and here was Mr. Bowman
shepherding me and promising Blossom-
ings. In any case, by the time Mum's letter
reached me I was already Mrs. Jacob
Bowman, and struggling to call him Jacob.
The ceremony took place in the library, between the box labeled GUNS and the box
labeled AMMUNITION, with Mr. and Mrs.
Briggs as witnesses. The wedding night
proved of little interest to either me or to
Mr. Bowman, and was not what Omar
Khayyám would have called a perfect hour.

Technically I lost my virginity, but Jacob
was apparently so appalled by the process
that he put aside all thoughts of repeating
it, and returned to his own bedroom, to his
plans and his lists. In retrospect I think—
and this was not unremarkable—that just
as I looked upon him as a father figure (although not aware of this at the time), he
looked upon me as a daughter, which I
was certainly young enough to be, and a
whiff of incestuousness attacked his con-
science and made him impotent, which I
did not know enough to realize at the time.
Poor Jacob.

The result of becoming his bride was
that I was instructed each day on the exciting trip we were about to undertake. We
were to cross the Atlantic to Southampton
in England, and then proceed by train to
Marseille, where we would board a smaller
ship for Tripoli. There we would spend a
month or two collecting documents, arranging for guides, buying protection and
finding camels to take us into the desert in
October, when the heat had diminished.
He was not without a goal: during a previous trip to North Africa he'd spent an interesting evening conversing with a White Fa-

ther named *Père* Arnaux, on leave from his missionary station at Ghadames, and it was *Père* Arnaux whom we were to visit, bringing to him Bibles in French. To reach him, explained Mr. Bowman, we would travel for a week or so across the sands and I could only assume that still another paper was to be written about this for his Geographical Society. I was told that such a trip had once been impossible because of certain nomads in the desert called the Tuareg, but after a number of pitched battles the French army had subdued them. Nevertheless, he'd been learning some words of Tamahak, which was their language.

"And I'm confident," he said complacently, "that if we should meet any Tuareg, my being able to speak a few words to them in their own language—as well as our being well-armed—will suffice to render any problems minimal."

I looked up Africa in Smith's *New Geography,* where it said it was noted "for vast burning deserts, for the dark color and barbarous character of its inhabitants, and as the ancient seat of the arts and sciences"; it added that this "land of mystery" was almost unknown to geographers, who might, with good reason, place elephants in all the gaps. In its map this was true; the desert was colored pink, with a camel pictured, and an ostrich, but no elephant. But then Jacob pointed out that I was looking at a geography book published in 1860, and digging out more recent maps he showed me Tripoli, and roughly where the oasis of Ghadames could be found, and there were so many towns and cities along the coast of the Mediterranean that it all looked very civilized. I began to look forward intensely to our traveling, gripped by a strange restlessness, only vaguely aware—unadmitted, of course—that Saturday visits to the dark mansion had been very different from occupying the house for seven days of the week, and that I had only exchanged one bondage for another, being now in a different sort of school. There was very little for me to do. Jacob's passions remained with his studies, and the Briggses managed the house, and so, feeling a lonely need to keep in touch with Grams, I retreated more and more to the little room that Sozap had occupied, to read or to practice sleight-of-hand or juggling and all the tricks of magic I'd learned. These I had concealed from Mr. Bowman—Jacob, that is—lest he disapprove, finding them as inappropriate for me as picking pockets. And so, into the small trunk I was given for our travels, I packed my few clothes, my finger puppets, a number of bright coins and white handkerchiefs for palming, and a small English dictionary so that I could translate the long words Jacob used.

On July first I sailed with Jacob on the steamer for Europe. There were no signs or omens to tell me that I would never see Mum or Grams or the United States again. As Shakespeare said, "There's a divinity that shapes our ends, rough hew them how we will . . . ," although there were moments when I felt it was the devil shaping my ends. At such times I tried to roll with the punches and to remember the words in the *Rubáiyát:* " 'Tis nothing but a magic show, played in a box whose candle is the sun, round which we phantom figures come and go."

I had been positively prescient, however, in anticipating travel, for I learned a great deal during the two voyages that took us to Tripoli: I learned first of all the vastness and moods of the Atlantic Ocean, and I learned that I was beautiful, being told so by a surprising number of young men whom I attracted aboard ship—until, that is, they discovered that I was not Mr. Bowman's daughter but his wife. Even then several dashing young men persisted so that I was made much of during the voyage to England. From Southampton, without pausing, we caught the train to Marseille and there we boarded a battered but seaworthy little ship that would take us to Tripoli. This was even more exciting, for we dined at the captain's table with the son of a maharajah, an Egyptian rumored to be a spy, a mysterious Bulgarian, and— oh, best of all—Miss Isabelle Stanhope, related in some manner to the Vanderbilts. Dear Belle! She was bound for Cairo, where her brother held a diplomatic post, and she traveled with a dragon of a chaperone who was overtaken by seasickness as soon as the *Valeria* headed into the Mediterranean. I really believe that if her chaperone had been present we would have exchanged only pleasantries, for certainly Isabelle would never have been allowed to become intimate with anyone as gauche as I. Isabelle was four years my elder but so friendly, and I so awed by her generosity, that she became my first true friend, almost instantly obliterating all the hurts I had suffered at Thistlethwaite. Within hours we became Belle and Caressa to one another, and deeply attached. Even when I confided to her that I came from a "family of circus people," as I chose to put it, she was not shocked.

"Most people are so boring," she explained simply, "and one meets the same ones over and over in Newport and Boston and New York.

"But what a pity you go to the desert," she said, shaking her head over me. "With a face like yours—it's perfection, Caressa—what a waste to hide you! I'm sure you would be a sensation in Paris, New York or London. We *must* speak to Mr. Bowman about your coming to Cairo before you return home."

And with sparkling mischievous eyes she added, "I would give a ball just for you, Caressa, and see myself put in the shade for that evening. Only once, of course. A real sacrifice on my part, I assure you."

"Oh Belle," I said, "it would be wonderful to see you again, but as for beauty—you embarrass me."

"You didn't know?"

And this was true, I hadn't. Once Grams had said that when I shed my rough and tomboy ways I would be pretty, but when I had looked in a mirror I'd seen only two dark eyes, a nose, a mouth, a chin and long dark hair; I'd not realized that features in a face could be arranged in such juxtaposition as to spell beauty. Thus it was that I began to notice that a nose could be too long to suit a face, or the chin too sharp or too small, or eyes too close together and lips too thin or too wide. I really grew quite elevated from this, and asked Mr. Bowman —Jacob, that is—if he couldn't buy me a new dress when we docked in Tripoli, for I was still wearing schoolgirl clothes, shirtwaists and long drab skirts, and except for the dress I'd been married in—Mrs. Briggs had seen to it that I wore a silk blouse and skirt—Mr. Bowman had not thought to add to my wardrobe. Now he brushed my plea aside, reminding me that in one of his steamer trunks there was a long divided skirt for me to wear when I rode a camel, and that Tripoli was not a place to enlarge a wardrobe, being a Turkish outpost populated by Berbers and Arabs and only a handful of Europeans. Perhaps, he added more kindly, seeing my face fall, perhaps on our way home a few more mature clothes could be found for me in London.

With this I had to be content, although I continued to passionately envy Isabelle her many changes of frocks during the day, from her simple morning dress to a tea gown, and silk or velvet at dinner. Belle, noting my envious glances, only laughed and said my face was enough to capture everyone's attention and my modest clothes only enhanced it. I did not for a moment believe her.

We were only four days aboard ship together, which is a measure of how many hours we spent in confiding, talking, laughing and sharing far into the night, so quickly did we become friends. When we parted at Tripoli it was with tears and embraces and with an exchange of addresses, hers in Cairo, mine in Boston. Lest I lose this treasured slip of paper, I memorized her address and spent many a later night repeating it to myself and composing letters to her that I would write from Tripoli and then from Boston upon our return.

I was not without consolation, however, for we had at last reached North Africa.

four

———～———

The city of Tripoli hugged the shores of the Mediterranean in a blaze of color: of yellow sand, dazzling white walls, dusty green palms, gold-tipped minarets and bright flags, all set against the rich blue of the sea and under the clear golden light of the African sun. As our ship steamed past a lighthouse set on a rocky point I saw that crowds of people lined the shore to watch our arrival. Most of them wore long robes —*barracans,* Jacob told me, handing me his pair of binoculars, and peering through them I discovered the faces were of colors ranging from white to ebony-black. All the tedium of our long voyage left me, for this was certainly very different from Boston!

We were taken ashore by launch, our trunks and crates to follow, and once on land were the object of much curiosity, for tourists were unheard of at that time and very few travelers stopped at Tripoli. At first glance I was disillusioned, I confess, for I was new to the Oriental, and the paradise I had seen from the ship proved on closer inspection to be overlaid with a patina of shabbiness, dirt and age. But Mr. Bowman—Jacob, that is—explained to me that Tripoli was a province of Constantinople and that Turks were indifferent landlords and that the shabby arch standing not far from the waterfront had been built in A.D. 164.

We were met by the British Consul, with whom Jacob had corresponded during the previous months. It was said that an American Consulate would be opened soon but at that time there were only British, French and Italian consuls in residence. Many orders were issued; a two-wheeled, gaily painted little horse carriage was waved away and a hansom with two horses summoned, and with our trunks to follow we set out for the consulate at number 27 Shar'a al-Kuwash, where we would stay while arrangements were made for our trip into the desert, there being no hotels in the city. I was still much daunted by the sight of the city. The arch that Jacob had pointed out might be the Arch of Marcus Aurelius, built in A.D. 164, but small shops had become attached to it like barnacles, and the streets were full of rubbish: fishbones, egg shells, fruit peelings and dung, yet before many yards had passed I began to feel exhilarated. The streets were narrow and teeming with life, it was like the carnival with its tumultuous background of noise—how tired I had grown of the silence in Mr. Bowman's house! We passed veiled women carrying earthen water jars, old men with soft eyes in long white robes, and in turn we were passed by a flock of goats and once a camel that approached us silently on padded feet, then gave a terrible groan at sight of us so that we must turn into a side alley to allow him passage. The longest walls were scalloped with arches under which men crouched, pounding metal or weaving rugs or sound asleep.

"Well, Caressa?" said Mr. Bowman, smiling at me benevolently.

"It's wonderful," I breathed.

"I'll engage a guide for you," he said, nodding. "I myself will be too busy with preparations but it will be very educational for you to view the antiquities; you will learn almost as much as you did at Thistlethwaite."

It was at this moment that it first occurred to me, unholy thought, that Mr. Bowman was not a man for joy but must reduce all of life to an education of the mind. It was only a passing thought, to return at a later time, but it was perhaps the first discerning perception of my new life. We continued on past mosques and markets, and reaching Shar'a al-Kuwash, I found it no different in character at all, in fact we made our way past loaves of bread that lined one side of the street, tossed up from an open-air oven below ground. Having been told that the Consulate had once been a great palace I could scarcely believe it when the hansom stopped at a small door in a high wall not far from the ovens, but when the door was opened to us we walked into a splendid courtyard with a broad staircase that led up to an open gallery, and at the stairs were posted guards in uniform, so that we ascended with much pomp.

We were soon settled, although not unpacked. In those first days Jacob spent many hours with the consul, gathering information on caravan leaders and suitable guides and provisioners. It was now that I learned why he had chosen Tripoli rather than Algiers for our departure to Ghadames; such desert travel was forbidden by the government in Algeria, at least for all Europeans, and we were ungraciously lumped with Europeans. But permission from Constantinople was also needed for us to leave from Tripoli, and much to Jacob's dismay it had not arrived yet, which sent him almost every day to the Pasha at the castle in Tripoli to press for response. When not busy at this he had begun his interviews, so that it was a rare day that he wasn't deep in conversation in the courtyard with a man wrapped in a soiled barracan, swarthy of face, and speaking in harsh gutteral language with many gestures, a startling contrast to Jacob's short stature and fastidious Western clothes.

In the meantime—surely with some irony—the consul produced a guide for me so that I could be educated in the history of Tripoli, as well as in the intricacies of climbing on a camel. Considering that fewer than two dozen people in the city spoke English, finding this guide was miraculous. It must also have been a matter of desperation because the choice, as I soon realized, was exceedingly strange: he was described to me as an Arab merchant so that I couldn't but wonder how such a man had been persuaded to guide a young woman, and a nonbeliever at that, and how on earth he came to know English.

His name was Mohammed and he was a man well into middle age, old enough to reassure Jacob who came to look him over, no doubt to be sure he was not another Sozap. His face was dark, with a stubble of gray beard, a wispy gray moustache and shrewd eyes set under thick brows. Introduced to him in the courtyard, I saw him inspect me from head to foot with much curiosity—this Christian female whose face was not hidden behind a veil—and although I now put up my hair, as befitted a married woman, I must have looked very young to him, as indeed I was. His inspection was thorough and for this I respected him; there was nothing sub-servient about him, he wore dignity like a cloak, but I could swear that I saw a look of mockery in his glance before he left, saying that he would return for me the following morning.

And so, without a chaperone, but from necessity, I was delivered to Mohammed so that I might not languish in my room.

At the appointed hour Mohammed called for me, carrying with him the List of Things to See that Jacob had presented to him, written now in Arabic. We set out on foot because the Gurgi minaret was not far, and then, if I had not tired, he said, we might proceed to the waterfront to observe the sponge divers. For me it was a great relief to leave the Consulate and venture into the city itself. I found my eyes and my senses dazzled by the brilliance of the sun-light slanting across white walls, by flat roofs, narrow, shadowed alleys and by the sound of music from an unseen source, a wailing poignant melody to stir the blood. We had scarcely gone far when I realized I had allowed myself to become too dazzled, for the Shar'a al-Kuwash was a busy thoroughfare and Jacob had given me a wad of Turkish lire that I had stuffed into a button-bag tied to the sash around my waist. When I stopped to watch the bakers drawing their round yellow loaves of bread from the oven I became aware that someone in the crowd around us stopped, too. Glancing behind me I saw a barefooted man wearing only a pair of cotton trousers and a turban with a cloth bag slung from his wrist by a string.

We had resumed walking when it happened: out of the corner of my eye I saw the flash of a knife, and so quickly and skillfully was it done that if I had not taken notice of the man earlier I would never have felt the loss of my silk bag. He did not even trouble to run but merely passed us without a glance, my tiny bag apparently tossed into his greater one.

To Mohammed I said, "Quick, have you a knife?"

Startled, he reached among the folds of his barracan and produced a dagger, saying, "For what do you need—"

But I had snatched it from him, too angry at my carelessness and at being preyed upon to speak. Racing ahead I overtook the thief and slashed furiously at the strings by which he carried his sack. He turned in surprise, staring at me with outraged bloodshot eyes, and snarling words I couldn't understand. My knife had severed only one of the two strings but this had caused his sack to drop open and hang from his wrist. Ignoring his half-crazed eyes I plucked my silk button-bag from the interior of his bag, nodded politely to him and retreated. He would have followed me if he'd not seen Mohammed, who had stopped in his tracks, watching in astonishment. As I joined him, the thief gave me one last vicious glance and vanished into the crowds.

Mohammed said sternly, "Little Bowman, what is this? What kind of person can you be?"

"He cut loose my purse and stole it," I told him.

"But how did you know? The thieves here are cunning."

"I knew, that's all," I said stubbornly, tight-lipped.

"You were mad to follow him—*mad*—

for he was full of hashish and his knife sharper than mine."

At this moment it occurred to me that I had not behaved like a lady and I said politely, "I'm sorry if I embarrassed you."

He suddenly laughed. "You speak the lie, little Bowman, you are not sorry. It is I who did not see clearly, thinking you unformed and a mere stick, like so many foreign ladies. Come, let us buy you a barracan," he said. "I will show you many things, little Bowman, for I love this city, but you will attract much attention as you are. If you wish truly to see my city, you must be as one of us and wear a barracan and cover your face."

We turned a corner and plunged into a narrow alleyway where I could hear the sound of shuttles at work. Stopping at a stall piled high with silk-and-camel's-hair robes, Mohammed began an interminable ritual of greeting the merchant, followed by an interminable bargaining over price. At last he turned to me. "I have made good price for you, little Bowman, show him your lire."

Unwrapping the barracan, he showed me how to distribute it so that it covered all

but one eye, and thus, as a happy partici-
pant in a masquerade—for it pleased me
to shed my identity—we resumed our
walk, and it was pure delight. We wandered down sunless narrow alleyways under pastel-colored arches into patches of
brilliant sunlight, and then into shade
again, always to a cacophany of street
cries, the braying of donkeys, shouts of
passersby and the pounding of metalwork-
ers shaping silver and gold into armbands
and bracelets. It was like a splendid carnival midway except that instead of walking
on sawdust we walked on sand, stepping
over the litter of discarded vegetables,
bones and dung, the smell of decay growing denser as the sun climbed high at
noon.

Each morning Mohammed would call
for me now in one of the gay little carts
called an *araba,* drawn by a horse strung
with little bells, and there he would present
me with my barracan, which I would wear
over my own clothes. Presently the araba
would be dismissed and we would walk,
rubbing shoulders with ragged-looking
Turkish soldiers, black Sudanese, pious
men in skullcaps and in tarbooshes, but

most mysterious of all were the men I saw one day in blue robes, proud and aloof, their faces veiled so that only their eyes could be seen.

"Who are they?" I asked Mohammed when they had passed us.

"Desert men called Tuareg," he said, "and never to be trusted."

"Tuareg!" I exclaimed. "But Jacob says they were tamed by the French, and he must be right if they walk the streets of Tripoli."

"Tamed?" echoed Mohammed. *"Tamed?* They enter the city, yes, to sell their camels and buy silver but they come too as spies."

I frowned. "Spy on what?"

"The Tuareg call themselves 'People of the Veil' but Arabs call them Tuareg, meaning 'abandoned of God,' " he said, and repeated firmly, "They're desert people, not to be trusted." And he would say no more.

But if he would not speak again of the Tuareg he had many other stories to tell. We stood one day and looked at the Jam'a Gurgi, with its beautiful spire, and he described to me how it came to be built.

Years ago, he said, there were two devoted friends, one the son of the Pasha and the other a sealord named Mustafa Gurgi. One day they stood on the shore watching the return of the Pasha's fleet as it sailed into the harbor, and the son of Ahmad Pasha said that as a token of his friendship he would give his friend the last ship in that convoy of eight. This was customarily loaded with the lightest of cargoes, the articles of real value always stowed in the leading ships. Much to their surprise, when the fleet anchored, the last ship turned out to be a captured pirate ship loaded with treasure of gold and silver, tapestries and teak. Mustafa Gurgi, overwhelmed by such riches but not wishing to lose the friendship of the Pasha's son, drew on the ample funds from the pirate treasure and tactfully built a mosque.

"It's a very lovely mosque," I said politely, my voice muffled behind my wrappings, "but how is it that as an Arab you speak English so well?"

He smiled; his teeth were dazzling white against his dark skin, but he did not answer. "Come, there is more to see, and another story."

His next story was about the Jam'al Kharruba, which he said meant the Mosque of the Carob Tree. "Named for a *tree?*" I said disbelievingly.

"Yes, little Bowman, a most significant tree." It had been built, he said, following a great plague in the city long ago, when the poor devils infected had been banished outside the city walls to die. No food was given them, and they had to eat what they could find, and what they ate were the fleshy pods of a great carob tree growing wild beyond the gates. And the carob cured them, and they did not die. And because of this, out of gratitude, the mosque was built where the old carob tree had stood.

"Yes," I said smiling at him, "but you've still not told me how it is that you speak English in Tripoli, where so few do."

He only laughed.

I grew even more curious when this rough but kind man guided me to the Arch of Marcus Aurelius. Looking at it I said cautiously, "I hear it's terribly old."

Mohammed smiled a little and closing his eyes said, much to my surprise, "Whatever may happen to you, it was prepared for you from all eternity, and the implication of causes was from eternity spinning the thread of your being."

That sounded spooky, and under my wrappings I scowled. "You made that up? It sounds like Grams."

"Grams?" He turned and looked at me. "Those be the words of Marcus Aurelius."

"Oh," I said.

"You do not know of him?"

I shook my head. "Is he like Omar Khayyám?"

"Ah—not so ignorant after all," he said, regarding me with a smile.

"Ignorant!" I sputtered, insulted.

But he only laughed.

I did not see him every day, for Friday was his holy day, the *yaum al-jum'a,* the day of gathering together, he said, and Sunday was the Christian Sabbath. On our walks together he was a popular man, too, and the Arab greetings were time-consuming, making me impatient and angry until I learned some of the words myself.

A bearded man would stop, seeing him. "Ya, Mohammed!"

"Alaaaan," Mohammed would say.

"Ahlan wa sahlan. Kaif haluk, bahi," would exclaim his friend.

And so it would go: How are things? Fine, how are you doing? Very well, thank God . . . until at last, Peace be with you, *adieu* (the *adieu,* I felt, would interest Jacob) and we could go on, with me following a step behind him like a proper Muslim woman, but when I asked Mohammed indignantly if he'd cloaked me in a barracan to save himself the embarrassment of walking beside me, he only smiled. I loved these mornings spent with him, when for an hour at a time we might watch the sponge divers make their precarious descents underwater, or we would stop at a suk to watch a boy fashion pottery, or a man carving ivory. At every call of the muezzin Mohammed would join the others in the *tashah-hud,* their profession of faith, while I waited in the shadows, watching, and each day after combing the city on foot he would return me formally in an araba to the Consulate. I would remove my barracan and step out, thanking him with a conspiratorial grin, and enter the door in my Western clothes. I was being educated but not precisely as Jacob had expected, of this I was sure.

And at night I would go alone to the rooftop of the Consulate and look up at the deep velvety sky and see more stars than I'd ever seen in my life, and feel the enchantment of the city enter my heart. It was because of Mohammed that it became forever engraved there.

And each day I would ask Mohammed, "How is it that you speak English like this?"

One day he said, "Come, I show you something."

This time we took an araba to the waterfront, and dismissing it walked through a labyrinth of alleys until he stopped beside a small door. Turning to me he said, "This is my home."

I was deeply touched that he was about to allow me into his own life, which I felt the highest compliment he could give me. He opened the door and we strolled into a courtyard, open to the sky but with brilliant passionflowers overhead that filtered out the sun like a lattice and splashed the floor with shadows. Leading me across the courtyard we entered a room so dim that I was at first blinded, but as my eyes adjusted to the change in light I saw that it was filled with leather cushions and low tables. At one of them sat a plump, middle-aged Arab woman with sewing in her lap. He spoke to her in Arabic, she nodded and went out, giving me a curious but friendly glance. Gesturing to a mound of pillows for me to sit on, we waited in a silence that was interrupted by the woman bringing in a tray with tiny cups of coffee.

"This is my wife Asma," he told me, and gestured to her to join us. I nodded politely and when she smiled I smiled, too.

"Now I will show you something," he said, and rising he brought from a corner of the room a small packet wrapped in exquisite silk. From it he drew out two books, very worn, their pages curled as if they'd been drowned and then dried under a hot sun. He placed them in my hands. They were a small Bible—in English—and Marcus Aurelius' *Meditations.*

"You learned English from these two books?" I said in astonishment.

He shook his head. "These books

were in my pocket when I was found in the sea, half-dead and clutching a plank of charred wood that only a little made me float. I was brought ashore and nursed back to life by her family." He nodded toward his wife. "When it happened I was no older than you, little Bowman."

"But—then you're not Arab or Turkish at all," I stammered. "You may even be English!"

He shrugged. "I remember nothing even to this day. All I know is that English was the only language I could speak. Everything else was knocked from my head. *Everything,*" he added firmly.

He said that last word too quickly, so that I knew this wasn't true but that I would hear no more.

I said, "And the consul learned this?"

He smiled. "A clever man, the consul, yes a clever man. I deal in esparto—the wild grasses of the desert sent to Europe for paper-making—and one day he and the vice-consul had come to watch the esparto baled for shipping. In my presence he spoke of business matters to his companion—in English, you understand, and hearing his words I explained the matter to him more clearly—in Arabic, you understand, but"—he smiled faintly—"what an expression on his face! Later he sent for me and said, 'You understood our English!' So I told him. He is the only European to know."

"And now I know."

"And now you know, little Bowman. You have asked and you have asked, and now you know how I come to speak English."

I said softly, "And for this I thank you, Mohammed."

He nodded, and rising easily to his feet from the floor, said, "Come, you have not yet seen the desert, and next week you learn the camels. You have completed the coffee? I have shown you the Mosque of Sidi Hammuda, the Jam'a an-Naqa, the Jam'a Gurgi, the markets, the castle and the suks. Before I return you for your Sabbath tomorrow it is time you see the desert."

For this trip we rode again in an araba, with its tiny bells jingling merrily, but this time to the fringe of the city where we made our way on foot through narrow lanes where the sand lay a foot deep and the mud walls confined us on either side. At last we reached the final wall, met with a few palm trees and then abruptly all trace of the city ended; we stood at the edge of such space as I had seen only once before, on our long voyage across the sea. The earth stretched out flat and tawny—into infinity, surely—until it met and became one with a yellowing sunset sky. At my feet the ground was dusted here and there with bleached dried grasses, but not one of them was high enough to quiver in the wind that I felt upon my face, full of freshness after the heat and smells of the city. Far away I could see a line of dark shapes moving across the scrub, camels or goats, but otherwise there was only the spellbinding silence and a vast emptiness.

Mohammed, watching me, said, "Well?"

I drew a deep breath and nodded. "Yes," I said.

"You will travel many days by camel to reach Ghadames."

I felt no sense of foreboding. I was

only sixteen, after all, and on Monday I would learn to ride a camel. I made no reply, and after a few minutes we left and I was returned to the Consulate.

five

~

I had always assumed, and my geography class at Thistlethwaite had done nothing to dispel this, that a desert was made entirely of sand, but Mohammed laughed at that. "There is not so much of it as people think, little Bowman," he said. "The great sand hills are called *ergs,* but there are many miles of gravel-wastes, or *regs,* and in the Sahara tall mountains of stone."

In my geography class I had also been given the impression that camels go for weeks without water, but Mohammed told me this was exaggeration; I had also as-

sumed camels were fast and covered
many miles a day, but Mohammed only
smiled at my naïveté, saying the best
speed of a riding camel was four or five
miles an hour, and that of pack animals
even slower, and yes there were tales of
camels covering incredible distances in a
brief time, but no one added that on the
next day such camels often lay down and
died of exhaustion. I then announced that
I'd heard camels made people seasick,
whereupon he assured me that this too
was rare, it was more likely I'd be rocked to
sleep, which was far worse and more dangerous, so that altogether I was being
stripped of all my conceptions and left curious as to what the truth of it might be.

Since Mohammed was a prosperous
esparto merchant he owned his own camels, two of which he had selected for my
Camel Day. These were waiting for us outside the city walls as well as half a dozen
ragged, cheerful boys. Jacob did not join
us, indeed he seemed at this time a man
demented; his letter to the Grande Portale
in Constantinople, applying for a passport,
or *furman* as it was called, had still not arrived to give us permission to travel, and

now, besides making arrangements to leave, there were desperate visits to the Pasha at the castle to persuade him to issue the furman instead. Jacob had come too far to be balked; I'd not realized the importance of this trip for him, or his stubbornness, either. I guessed that the paper he planned for his Society was to be a culmination, a crowning glory, his entry into the world as adventurer and globe traveler, but he had not confided his dreams to me, in fact I saw so little of him that I wondered often why he had married me.

The camel I was given to ride on this day was a sand-colored mare and I had looked forward to making friends with her, much as one did a horse, but this too was a mistake as I immediately learned. When I approached her, lifting an arm to stroke her long throat, Mohammed shouted, "NO!" and I stopped, confused. The camel glanced down at me from a vast distance, bared her huge yellow teeth and with a look of contempt spat a stream of saliva at me. This camel was therefore not a horse, and was only to be ridden, but she was also very high and I was very small beside her. With shouts and sticks the boys prodded the camel into a crouch, I was inserted upon what felt a very unsteady wooden saddle, the camel was prodded to her feet and I fell forward; she gave a great tired sigh as she reached a standing position and I fell back, desperately clutching the saddle horn.

Off we went, a boy walking beside my camel with a lead rope. I assumed this was to prevent the creature from running away, which seemed inconceivable because her pace was so slow. Even this assumption was an error: each time we passed a few blades of grass or thorns we came to a halt, the camel lowered her head to examine and then eat, at which point I once again came near to sliding over her head to the ground. Transferring the greenery to her great maw of a mouth, she would chew, belch, bray pitifully, while I slid back again on the saddle. I began to understand that a camel was a very eccentric animal and I could not understand why nomads sang love songs to them.

We did not ride far on this first lesson, for after a few minutes Mohammed called out, *"Gibleh!"* and pointed to the horizon, which was becoming blurred by a yellow cloud. "Back—*yuaf!*" he shouted, and with much prodding turned his camel around. Having no idea what a "gibleh" might be, I experienced a sense of alarm made greater by the stubbornness of my camel, which was talked to, shouted at, prodded and thumped until, much against her will, she too was turned around. The sky was still vividly blue but the heat seemed to have gained weight and intensity and the wind was rising, bringing with it skittish swirls of sand and dust so that by the time we reached our starting point my lips were gritty with sand that stung my eyes and clogged my nostrils, and Mohammed's face had become a white mask.

"What," I demanded crossly, "is a gibleh?"

"The wind blowing north out of the desert," he told me. "It lasts until the wind changes. How did you like your ride?"

"I will do better tomorrow, you'll see," I promised him.

He said carelessly, "Someone else will teach you tomorrow."

Startled, I said, "What do you mean?"

He turned, giving instructions to the boys in Arabic, and they led the camels away. Mohammed and I walked to the pair of donkeys on which we'd ridden out of the city; they waited among the palms, tied to a tree in the lee of the wind blowing in from the desert, and as I untied mine I said, "What did you mean, Mohammed, someone else tomorrow?"

He gazed at me soberly over the shoulder of his donkey. "I must leave tomorrow—on your Sabbath—to go to Misurata, little Bowman."

Stunned I said, "Oh, Mohammed, truly?"

He nodded. "It is for the sake of my business I abandon you, it cannot wait longer."

I looked at him in dismay. "But I'll see you when you get back, won't I? Is Misurata far? Jacob is hopeful about a furman in a few days, but even so the consul insists we wait and join a caravan from Benghazi that's not expected for a few weeks. Will you be gone that long?"

His smile was wry. "He will get his furman, but I do not think your husband a man to patiently wait for any caravan, little Bowman."

"But—but I will miss you," I stammered, and then as I realized what he'd said my cheeks flamed. "Oh Mohammed, I'm sorry, I didn't think at all about the business you left to be my guide. Did the consul force you?"

He shook his head. He said gravely, "You know I study Marcus Aurelius very much, little Bowman. He has written 'the universal cause is like a winter torrent carrying everything along with it.' I have thought on his Meditations much, and on doing what is woven into the thread of one's destiny." He said simply, "It was my duty to show you my city."

I stared at this man who for so many years had lived his life in the company of an Arab wife and Marcus Aurelius.

"But I am also an honest man," he added with a sudden smile," and I wanted to be your guide, for if I am English—if I *should* be English—I might have had a daughter just like you."

I was deeply touched by this. "Oh I would have liked that very much," I told him warmly. "You've been so kind to me, Mohammed."

He nodded. "I will be kind even more and say something else, little Bowman. It is well that your husband has chosen Edrasi as leader of your caravan, but I hear he also chooses Umar as guide for your journey."

"Yes, do you know him?"

He shrugged. "A good guide, Umar, but there have been rumors lately in the suks, little Bowman, such as the consul may not have heard. If you have influence—"

"What rumors, Mohammed?"

"You think I wish a knife in my back some dark night? There are whispers of greed, of his being too friendly with—but I say no more. If you have influence—"

He stopped, and although I pressed him he would not say more, but I did not like the sound of this.

We mounted the donkeys—such amiable creatures after my spitting hostile camel—and plodded through the sand-filled lanes until we reached the streets of the city, and then the Consulate. Dismounting at the doorway Mohammed said, "I have something for you, little Bowman."

It was a Hand of Fatima, carved of solid silver, and small enough to fit into the palm of my hand; this shape hung over every house and suk in Tripoli as protection against evil. His gift brought tears to my eyes. "It's beautiful, Mohammed, thank you," and with a wry smile I added, "Does Marcus Aurelius have anything to say about good-byes?"

There was an appreciative twinkle in his eye. "He has written 'how ridiculous and how strange to be surprised at anything that happens in life!'"

"Well," I said stubbornly, "I shall still hope to see you again."

"That," he said, "rests in the hands of both our Gods." He bowed to me, touching his hand to his lips and to his forehead, the traditional mark of respect; I did the same, although I would have preferred to hug him. Grasping the lead ropes of the two donkeys he led them down the street; I watched until he turned into an alleyway—he did not look back—and vanished from my sight.

His words remained with me, however, for I trusted Mohammed, and I felt much unease, not knowing what he had meant about this Umar, so highly recommended by the consul. I determined to learn something of Jacob's decisions and plans.

The gibleh blew all that night and the next day, a hot and sickly wind, very strong and so dry that it was hard to swallow food, which in any case held the grit of fine sand, no matter how carefully protected in the kitchen, for the wind and the dust crept in through the walls and deposited a film of white on steamer trunks, bedding, crates, tables, chairs and floor. Held captive by the persistent gibleh I dreaded the next weeks without Mohammed's company, for everyone at the Consulate had work to do and Jacob spent long hours going over and over the supplies for our journey, checking and rechecking them and not at all inclined to talk. I expressed my feelings to Mr. Jappy but unfortunately his painted smile was fixed upon his wooden head and he could give no counsel. I practiced the words of Arabic and Turkish that I'd learned from Mohammed; I wrote a long letter to Belle Stanhope, and was infinitely relieved when, after two days, the wind ceased its savagery from the south and we were restored to the glorious breezes from the Mediterranean.

It was on this same day that the Pasha in Tripoli took it upon himself to issue the furman to Jacob, no doubt to be rid of his tiresome daily visits, and it was that evening that I saw Jacob, the vice-consul and a lean man in turban and barracan walk into one of the rooms off the courtyard and close the door behind them.

I opened the door and walked in.

All three men turned in surprise. Jacob said sharply, "Caressa, we are busy. Later, please."

I stood my ground. I had been silenced before, but there was a distraughtness in me now, it was not a concern for my safety but something deeper that was in revolt. Too many sudden changes had been hurled at me in the last year and I had submitted to all of them because in Jacob's world I had been a child. But we were no longer in Jacob's world. A very different Caressa had been alive in another world for fifteen years before meeting him, a Caressa who was the daughter of a trapeze artist and a headless woman, and it was this Caressa who demanded audience. "Mr. Bowman—Jacob," I said, "I want to know the plans."

Shocked, he said, "Caressa—"

In a steady voice I told him, "There are two of us, Jacob, I'm going with you and I want to know."

I had deeply embarrassed him but he carried it off smoothly, with only a small look of reproach. He said as if to a child, "Then you may sit in the corner, but be very *quiet.*"

I sat quietly and listened. What first startled me was learning that Umar did not always understand Jacob's Arabic; it was the classical Arabic that Jacob had studied, not the colloquial, so that it was necessary for the vice-consul to interrupt frequently and explain to Umar what was being said. I began to wonder just what communication would be possible out in the desert, with no vice-consul to interpret. Then Umar moved into the light so that I could better see his face, and something in me did not like this much either. He was certainly impressing Jacob with his quick laugh and dramatic gestures but I thought his eyes too close together. He reminded me of Sharkey Bill, one of the talkers at the carnival who had a wondrous spiel to pull in the townies but who Grams said had the heart of a snake.

Sitting there in my corner I realized that in spite of all Jacob's wealth and the learned papers he wrote for his Society, he'd never learned much about people. He couldn't see the mockery gleaming in Umar's eyes as he bowed and charmed this infidel. I was sure that Mohammed had been right about this man and that he was demanding of Jacob ten times the money he would ask of any Arab merchant traveling to Ghadames. I did not know whether to be the more indignant at Umar or at Jacob, who so prided himself on his astuteness yet failed to see that in this country his wealth was as juicy a target as a stuffed panda in a game of slum skillo that had been rigged from the start.

Well, I thought, *if he is to be fleeced he at least can afford it, and he will not look kindly at my confiding these thoughts.*

With this I returned my attention to the conversation among the three men. They had already discussed the safe-conduct money paid to the Ajjer Tuareg, through whose territory we must pass. Their talk now concerned the caravan that was reported to be on its way from Benghazi. I listened closely, for from Mohammed I had learned much of such matters. He had told me that once Tripoli had been a starting point for almost all of the caravans setting out to cross the desert from north to south, and on a map he had traced the routes they would take, some heading for Murzuk in the Libyan Fezzan, some to the salt mines of Bilma, others to Lake Chad, to the Sudan or to the Niger River. But times had changed, he'd said, because the British and the French had established colonies below the Sahara, and now they moved their goods to the Ivory Coast to be shipped by steamer to Europe. It was rare these days to see a caravan in Tripoli, and the Turks who ruled were content to let the country grow stagnant.

"Where the Turks walk, no grass grows," Mohammed had said, and he claimed there was still a prospering slave market in Murzuk in spite of the trade being illegal now. The slaves, he said, were brought there to be smuggled off to the harems in Constantinople.

What was being discussed now was just how long it would take the caravan from Benghazi to reach us. Now that Jacob had received the furman he was impatient to know; what's more he seemed impatient to leave.

"It's ridiculous to wait," he scoffed.

"But safer," pointed out the vice-consul. "The larger the caravan the safer your travel."

"But for heaven's sake, it's only a three-week jaunt to Ghadames," complained Jacob. "You speak as if we were heading for the Sudan or the Niger, halfway across Africa. Already we've been here six weeks and no one knows when this Benghazi caravan will reach us; they may not even have started out yet. Does anyone *know?*"

"Lah," said Umar, shaking his head.

"Well, then . . ." and Jacob shrugged. "Why not go? We've paid the blasted Tuareg their tribute money, the camels are ready, our provisions packed, you've told me I've the best of leaders in Edrasi, and Umar will guide us. We've cameleers, I've hired guards and we have weapons. We're wasting time."

The vice-consul smiled a little. "In this country one learns patience."

It was at this point that I crept away, not wanting to hear any more, for I was remembering what Mohammed had said: "I do not think your husband a man to patiently wait for any caravan, little Bowman." He was right, of course, and I knew that we would soon be leaving and our sojourn in Tripoli ended.

six

Three days later we left Tripoli.

Our caravan was to set out from the fonduk, the caravanserai where travelers from the desert found safety for the night behind its thick walls and massive gate, sleeping among their goats, sheep and camels. We came to it in midafternoon to watch the last of our camels being loaded, for we were to leave before sunset. I had followed Mohammed's advice as to my clothes, which irritated Jacob greatly, for although I wore the long divided skirt he'd ordered for me, I had abandoned the prescribed leather riding boots for a pair of soft felt Turkish boots and around my neck I'd hung a pair of desert sandals, called *naïls,* which Jacob looked upon disparagingly. Mohammed had said there would be a goatskin of water, more precious than gold, a blanket or two, and the rest was up to me—I had learned much from him since I reached Tripoli—and so I refused to wear either petticoats, waist cincher or cork hat. He had warned me, too, that many layers were needed against the heat of day and the cold of night, and that wool was best, so I had secretly wrapped my woolen barracan inside my blanket roll and I insisted on a turban for my head, with a straw hat perched on top of it. Because I was cautiously emerging from Jacob's domination, I had sewn pockets into the divided skirt and inside the barracan, and in these I carried the silver Hand of Fatima that Mohammed had given me, a few coins for palming and my three finger puppets—the clown, the golden-haired Isabelle and Mr. Jappy.

As for Jacob, he looked like a stern riding master in khaki, riding boots and pith helmut.

I was astonished to find that so many

camels and so many people were necessary for a 300-mile ride across the desert, even though it would take three weeks by caravan; I'd forgotten the crates of supplies that had surrounded us in Jacob's library and that had occupied an entire room at the Consulate. Edrasi and Jacob had accumulated sixty pack animals, groaning and grunting under their loads and ranging in color from beige to brown to pure white. The riding camels were common *jamal,* but from somewhere Edrasi had secured a *mahari* for Jacob, sleek and elegant and graceful.

Entering the crowded fonduk I found myself regarded with much astonishment and curiosity, a female in such a place and a "European" at that, and longed for the disguise with which Mohammed had protected me from this mix of curiosity and—surely hostility as well? I stood in a corner attempting to identify those who were there simply to watch, and those who were to go with us. I counted twenty-six cameleers; I found Edrasi and Umar and the eight armed Turkish soldiers who would provide military escort for us until we reached Mizda (leaving us then to the mercies of Allah) and there was Jacob, now rushing about and shouting orders, tight-lipped and cross lest these Arabs not respect his sense of time, which they never did.

Nevertheless, by sunset it was announced that we were ready to go, and there was a flurry of excitement to which I was not immune myself. I mounted the straw-filled sack lying across the rump of my *jamal;* a cameleer applied a stick to the poor creature who began an intricate unfolding of knees and joints until he stood, as disgruntled and wary as I. At this moment a bale of fodder dropped from one of the baggage camels behind me and I had to sit, feeling a mile high, while ragged men swarmed around the animal to bring him to his knees and reload him. Beyond the walls of the caravanserai the sky flamed red and gold, squandering its brilliance in an eruption of color before withdrawing its light. Camels brayed, roared and dropped dung; small boys shouted words at me I couldn't understand; Jacob, Edrasi and Umar stood together directing the stowing of the last pack, and then with a shout the camel was whipped to his feet, Jacob mounted his *mahari* and the gates of the caravanserai were opened to us so that we might ride into the rapidly fading sunset.

I had been shown our route—south to Mizda and then southwest to Ghadames—but we were not to go far this night; the first leg of the journey was to be short, to test both us and the camel loads, but it would be midnight before we halted. Soon enough the sun set, draining the sky of color and robbing us of the day's heat. As the moon rose in the West, a chill descended as cold as the moon's pristine silver, but I did not mind for we rode under a velvety dark sky glittering with stars, and once the shouts and laughter of departure died away we settled into a silence broken only by the soft swish of camels' feet and the creak of wood and leather.

At midnight we stopped to make camp, which seemed a great waste of time until Jacob explained to me that we would be on our way again long before dawn, and would not stop again until midday when the sun was at its peak. Nevertheless, it was a shock to me to find that every single pack camel was to be unloaded again, and fed and watered for these few hours, so that it was I who had to swallow impatience now. This making of camp led to a bedlam of roars from the camels and shouts from the men. A fire was kindled, creating a circle of gold that turned the stars pale and the faces of the men chiaroscuro as they sipped tea, hobbled the camels and moved back and forth in the flickering light. Somewhere among all the packs and crates there was a tent for Jacob and me, but in the semi-darkness it couldn't be found and I could hear him shouting angrily that it had not been packed on the animal selected for it.

"Does it matter?" I asked wearily, for I was already stiff and sore from riding.

"You don't understand," he flung at me curtly. "We shall lose face with these men if I don't assert control in every way. They're working for me, it's I who pay them."

Once the bales had been assembled in a loose circle a few of the men abandoned the fire to scoop hollows in the earth to fit their bodies. Seeing them lie down to sleep I wrapped myself in a blanket and followed suit, finding the earth still warm from the sun. I lay drowsily watching the flames of the fire rise and fall, no more than a twinkle under the sky, and Jacob still rushing from bale to bale to look for his tent. Soon my eyes closed and for the scant four hours allowed us, I slept.

We were like a small enclosed world moving slowly across stony ground toward the low bare hills of the Gharyan, riding eight and ten hours of the day and sleeping fitfully at odd hours. At first there were knots of wild flowers, olive trees and fields of esparto, but soon the vegetation thinned and we traveled a treeless dreary waste, dun-colored at first light, amber by noon, bronze by twilight, with only a few soft hills and sand ridges to ease the monotony, or a Bedouin camp glimpsed in the far distance. In Mizda we stopped for two days to buy more provisions and to rest, but Mizda was a cheerless village of stone houses and here we lost our escort of Turkish soldiers. When we left Mizda it was to head southwest, skirting the Hammada al-Hamra—the red stone desert—our destination Ghadames, and nothing between it and Mizda but long hours of riding and one solitary oasis.

Mohammed had been right about a camel's pace threatening a person with sleep. It was not until we were into our second week of travel that I recovered from a terrible drowsiness brought on by the deadening monotony of long hours in the saddle, the searing heat by day, the bone-chilling cold at night. Of the crates of food Jacob had brought we listlessly opened only one small case that yielded sardines and canned peaches, and these I ate, over and over. The cameleers marveled at this, having never seen sardines before, and much preferring their millet, dates and cups of tea thickly laced with sugar. This tea was a ritual at every halt; Jacob would shout at the men, his watch in one hand, his compass in the other, pointing out that camels still had to be loaded and our departure was already late. Watching him I began to learn a little patience, seeing how little his tirades accomplished.

One morning I woke from sleep to find myself anticipating the day ahead of us, suddenly aware of the freedom of caravan travel that was not so unlike carnival life. I began to see the wisdom of walking for a few hours at a time, my camel on a lead rope; I liked it when things went well and the men sang. Once there were rumors that a gazelle had been seen and Jacob and Umar rode off with rifles, and although they returned empty-handed the hope of meat had revitalized everyone. I also began to know some of the men, to smile and nod at the deaf-mute who rode a donkey, and Edrasi was particularly kind; it was possible that Mohammed had spoken to him of me in Tripoli, for he took time to occasionally ride or walk beside me and describe the wonders of Ghadames.

"The most beautiful oasis Allah made," he said, speaking a mixture of Arabic and French, but somehow we came to understand one another's words, and I to learn new ones. Although it was Umar's job to guide us, and Edrasi's to manage the cameleers and the camels, Edrasi had made this trek many times, he said, and he pointed out nearly invisible landmarks of the trail we followed: the occasional fossilized camel print embedded in a rock, a small rise in the earth off to our left or right, the bones of a camel that had long ago died on the way to Ghadames.

We were a five days' ride from Ghadames when Jacob lost his compass and with it his temper, and it was now that everything began to go wrong. He was furious at not finding his compass and spent his midday rest in retracing with Umar a few miles of our route, which seemed very foolish of him because the noon sun was merciless. He returned pale and defeated to furiously pry open crates in an attempt to find another compass, so that he took no rest or sleep at all and we were late in getting underway, and Jacob still without his compass. No sooner had we set out, however, than from the head of the caravan Umar shouted, "Gibleh! *Subka!*"

In a frenzy the camels were couched, and bales and crates dragged from their backs. There was scarcely time to hobble them before the brassy smudge on the horizon rose with frightening speed into great towers of sickly yellow cloud that blotted out sun and sky. The storm hurled itself upon us with the velocity of a tornado. The roar of the wind sounded like the scream of a thousand devils—a bale of precious fodder blew past me and then an acacia tree from heaven only knows where, followed by a tent pole. I wrapped myself in my barracan and huddled close to my camel, the heat suffocating, and sand and dust penetrating even my cover. Worse, I might be surrounded by men and animals but I could see none of them nor be assured that I was not alone. For comfort I brought out Mr. Jappy and talked to him in a most demented way until, after an hour, I uncovered my head to find that I was nearly buried in sand, and had to dig myself out.

For two more hours we endured this attack of nature, and when at last it stopped it was night; and a night without stars. We had lost two camels to the storm and three goatskin bags of water, and it was another hour before the camels were loaded again. It was Umar's advice that we travel all night to make up for the lost hours and this we proceeded to do.

It was not until the sun rose the next morning that we discovered we'd been traveling in the wrong direction all night, heading to the south instead of to the southwest. Jacob's temper, not yet re-

paired, was lost again, and he flayed Umar
with his anger at such a thing happening.
This was also when two Tuareg rode
across the reg toward us, hungry and asking for food. Seeing them I thought how
Joe Laski of Laski's Traveling Shows
would have loved to capture a Targui for
his carnival: they were incredibly tall and
incredibly spooky with their faces veiled in
black and only their kohl-rimmed eyes
showing. Each of them wore a dozen or
more amulets strung around their necks:
tiny leather sacks, bits of silver, snips of
feathers, and their swords were sheathed
in leather with red and green designwork.
The rifles they carried were old-fashioned
ones, not at all like Jacob's 12-bore shot-
gun or 450 Cordite Express.

"Well, give them something," Jacob
said crossly, interrupting his talk with
Edrasi and Umar, "and then for heaven's
sake let's retrace our route. My God, we
must have traveled 30 or 40 miles off
course. Umar—" Realizing that he'd spoken in English again he upbraided the
guide in Arabic. Whatever he said I
couldn't understand, but Umar looked sul-
len. The pair of Tuareg asked for tea and

sugar, which were absentmindedly given them, and while Jacob and Umar argued over what to do next, the Tuareg looked us all over and rode away.

"If I'd not lost my compass—" snapped Jacob.

Umar interrupted him to say he knew of a shortcut to the north if he could find it, and suggested that he ride to the sand ridge a mile away and look for landmarks. I watched his camel diminish in size, struggle up the hill and disappear. It was dull waiting, and I risked bringing out my finger puppet again to amuse myself until presently a party of men appeared over the sand ridge farther south and began riding toward us.

Jacob, lifting binoculars to his eyes, began to swear. "Not Umar. Tuareg, a dozen of them."

Next to him I heard Edrasi murmur, "I do not like this, sir."

The Tuareg headed directly toward us, their figures changing shape and shimmering in the desert heat but as they drew nearer not only their shapes changed but their number: I counted twenty against our thirty. Edrasi's hand moved to the revolver tucked into his belt and we waited.

This time as they reached us I saw that their swords were not sheathed. The leader of the party glanced at Jacob, but it was to Edrasi he spoke. He gave the Arabic greeting: *His peace be with you,* to which Edrasi, eyes narrowed, replied, *Peace be to you. No evil,* said the Tuareg. *No evil,* said Edrasi, followed by *How are you? . . . No evil, thank God. May you and yours be safe, no evil, thank God.*

All this with Edrasi's hand on the revolver in his belt and the Tuaregs' swords unsheathed.

Jacob, struggling to gain control of this situation, recalled his study of Tamahak and stepped forward. *"Matulid,"* he said to the Targui, and to Edrasi, "Tell him we've paid tribute—*mouna*—for safe passage and received the *ghefara* from his tribe to travel here."

The Targui ignored Jacob's Tamahak greeting and spoke directly to Edrasi, who translated. I caught the words *sukkar* and *shayy, bundegeeya* and something else.

Edrasi explained, "They want tea and sugar, rifles and two camels."

"They want *what?*" said Jacob incredulously.

"*Attini,*" said the Targui, holding out his hand for gifts. "*Attini.*"

I looked at Jacob, who had lost his compass, his sleep, the trail to Ghadames and was struggling against heavy odds to seize control of this confrontation. To my astonishment I saw that he was livid with anger as he faced these tall skeletal men in their outlandish veils and robes with their old flintlocks and swords at their side.

"Tell them to go, they'll get nothing," he said furiously, utterly blind to the fact that we were outflanked. "This is piracy, I won't have it, I won't have it."

Caressa, I thought, *this is what you get for marrying above your station, he must think these men are Halloween trick-or-treaters, for heaven's sake. The man has no sense.* He looked very small, too, next to the Tuareg astride their camels and he wouldn't be liking that either, I thought, and—*Oh damn, he's going to try and prove himself—all those colleges, all those blasted papers for his Geographical Society—*

Edrasi said patiently, "They wish tribute, sir. Rifles, a few camels, tea and sugar."

"Ridiculous," scoffed Jacob. "We gave food to three of them who came begging only hours ago."

"Sir, Tuareg do not beg."

"No?" said Jacob, amused.

Edrasi shook his head. "They demand."

"Demand!" sputtered Jacob, outraged, and he drew his revolver out of its holster. "Unspeakable affrontery! Damn it I paid a small fortune in safe-conduct money for passage through this territory."

Vehemently Edrasi shook his head. "No sir, you pay *Ajjer* Tuareg, these be *Hoggar* Tuareg. *Mukh-ta'lif*— Give now, I beg of you."

"Bloodsuckers and blackmailers," snapped Jacob, waving his revolver wildly. "Tell them they get nothing more from me, tell them to be off or I'll shoot."

I shouted to him lest he not understand, "Jacob they're a *different tribe,* give them what they ask!"

"Never," he shouted.

I heard him release the safety catch on

his gun and I thought, *He's gone mad, he's really gone mad.*

Edrasi screamed, "*Lah! Hayir, hayir! No!*"

But it was too late. Jacob—angry, stubborn Jacob—pulled the trigger and fired three times.

Three of the Tuareg fell, one clutching his stomach, barely alive and making strange keening sounds, the other two dead as they hit the earth.

There followed an unearthly silence and it seemed to me that even the Tuareg were in shock, never expecting this. Behind me one of our caravan men struggled to dismount from his camel but it was too late, it had been too late the minute Jacob's finger pulled the trigger. The silence ended with a great angry cry, a lashing of camels, and the Tuareg moved among us with infinite skill, their swords flashing in the sun. Heads literally rolled, and Jacob's was the first.

I stared in horror at his head lying in the sand, his eyes still wide open. The sounds of carnage were hideous: shouts, screams, camels roaring in fright; others were falling now, too. I was stunned by the sight of steam rising from the severed heads, sickened by the reek of blood sending the camels into panic, but there was no time for thought, I was still alive beside my camel and it was my turn.

It was damnable not to see his face, only those fierce kohl-rimmed eyes blazing at me. As he lifted his bloodstained sword with both hands I could see his muscles straining for the blow that would end my life and instinctively I shrank back, lifting my arm in a foolish, useless attempt to shield my head, scarcely aware that when I lifted my arm a finger of my right hand still wore a puppet.

The sight of the clown's face on my index finger startled the Targui. *"Ugarra,"* he snarled, taking a step back, and lowering his sword he called to a companion who came to his side. There was pointing at the wooden face on my finger, words were exchanged and then to my relief there came a fresh shout and they turned away for the moment to the men who were rounding up the camels.

It had been cruel enough to face my own death but it was even crueler to look around me now and learn that I was the only living person left from our caravan. In the space of five minutes everything I'd known was gone: Jacob, home, past and future. Every man of them lay dead, some decapitated like Jacob, others lying on the earth with crushed skulls. A great nausea rose in me but I swallowed the vomit in my throat, determined to show no weakness. It was all of it beyond understanding until a terrible thought occurred to me. I left the shelter of my camel and began a walk among the dead, kneeling beside those who had fallen to check each face, and when I had identified each man—avoiding poor Jacob—I knew that Umar had not returned from the sand ridge and was not among them.

Not so long ago Mohammed had said to me in Tripoli, "There are rumors in the suks, little Bowman, that the consul may not have heard." Of greed, he'd said, and then he'd stopped.

How naïvely I'd assumed that Umar would only charge Jacob ten times the price. Now I knew it had to have been Umar who betrayed us to the Tuareg, wanting some of Jacob's wealth for himself and cunningly removing himself once he'd led us into the trap. How fortuitous that sandstorm had been for him, and the disappearance of Jacob's compass, which I had no doubt was in Umar's pocket all the time. Standing there in the midst of this carnage I swore that if I lived and met with Umar again I would kill him. It was a vow that was enough to sustain me, as anger so often will, and I needed that anger as I faced my situation, which was death by sword, captivity or worse. I threaded my way among the bodies and found the deaf-mute's donkey and seated myself upon it, for a donkey had little value, it was the camels they would prize. I would sit here, hard-faced, and wait for them to decide my fate.

Still, remembering that something about my finger puppet had preserved my life a little longer, I drew Mr. Jappy from the pocket in my barracan and inserted him into a finger of my other hand. I did not look again toward Jacob, it was as if the months I'd known him had been severed from me as neatly as his head had been severed from his body; indeed I *dared* not think of Jacob, for it was his obsession with writing papers for his Society that had brought us to this terrible moment. I thought instead of the father I'd never known who had walked a tightrope night after night, and how Grams had said it was a thing of beauty to see him in his spangled tights so high above the spellbound crowds. It was after he'd fallen to his death that Mum had learned to roll with the punches, Grams said, and "What doesn't kill you makes you strong."

Well, they've not killed me yet, I thought, and certainly as I looked out at the empty scorching desert I could see how strong I was going to have to be. I watched as three shallow graves were scratched in the gravel, three Tuareg placed in them and handfuls of stone and rock found to cover each one. There would be no graves for the others, and already the vultures were circling. I watched as packs were ripped open and the French Bibles Jacob had brought for the White Father scattered across the ground; Jacob's rifles were distributed and ammunition unwrapped. Camels that had wandered were led back, Jacob's beautiful white *mahari* among them . . . these Tuareg would leave rich in animals and weapons. I watched a caravan slowly take shape, the packs reloaded, men shouting, camels barking and groaning. When they were ready to leave the Targui who seemed to be their leader walked over and looked at me: I stared back at him without expression. His eyes fell again to my fingers and he scowled. After a moment he reached for the donkey's lead rope and led me and the donkey silently toward the caravan. I was to go with them.

given or assigned to a woman named Marsaya and her family. Marsaya was not young and so far as I could see she was a widow, for the man who slept behind the partition in the tent appeared to belong to her daughter. The flesh on Marsaya's face had slackened, finding a new existence in folds and sharp lines between nose and lips, but once she must have been as sleek and doe-eyed as her daughter. From head to foot she was swathed in black that matched her thick eyebrows with their twin frown lines between them. Her eyes, set close under her brows, were thickly fringed with lashes. Her voice could be sharp or gentle, but I could see that in her tent, in the whole encampment, she was treated with respect.

There were four of us in the tent that night, one of them a child, but in the morning the man left with the other men, who took all the camels with them leaving only the sheep and goats. I watched the caravan move out, watched it for a long time until it shrank in size and disappeared, heading back in the direction from which we'd come, but there was no one to tell me why or where they were going.

seven

—⌣—

I would learn later how uneasy those two finger puppets made them, for they feared I might be a wizard or sorceress and dared not kill me. Apparently they talked seriously of changing their route and taking me to Murzuk to sell to a slave-dealer, a good way to be rid of me without bringing evil spells upon themselves, but their route lay directly to the south, and then west over the Tassili n' Ajjer massif, and Murzuk was too far to the east. It was hoped they might instead meet with a slave caravan on their way, or so decided their chief, the *amrar.*

It was merciful that I did not know this, for my thoughts were dark enough as the long line of camels made its way south that day, with me at the end of it leading the donkey, choosing to walk most of the time with nothing to look at but the dung dropping from the camel ahead of me. Despite my hopelessness—and setting up a merry conflict—I knew I must stay aware and not be careless. . . . *Careless,* when I scarcely cared whether I lived or died? There were moments that day when I'd gladly have ridden off into the desert to end it all, and other moments when my anger climbed so high I wanted to scream at these people at the cost of my life. These moments came and went, leaving me trembling and the worse for them, until it came to me slowly that if it's not written in the palm of one's hand to die young, as Grams might say, then it can be as hard to find a way to die as it is to live in misery.

And so I plodded on, hour by hour, hungry and thirsty, until near dusk I sensed a quickening in the caravan, heard voices and laughter among the men, and peering

ahead I saw half a dozen low tents in a cluster against the dunes. Much to my surprise I could see women there as we drew nearer: it was a Tuareg camp, and I realized this terrible day was about to end; I would soon learn what my fate was to be, and whether death with Jacob would have been kinder.

That evening I knew they spoke much of me around the fire because of their frequent glances seeking me out in the shadows of the tent. What surprised me was to see the women sharing equally in whatever arguments took place; I had supposed that being Muslim they would be hidden away and mute, but this was not so. Nor did they wear veils as their men did. On that first night it wasn't known to me that Tuareg women are given much power as well as leisure, and blessed by chivalrous songs and poems composed in their honor. Not then: it needed time for me to realize the women did not intend a captive roumi to share a bed with any of their men or boys, which I only began to understand later by their gestures, and the way they kept me near them.

I was moved that night to another tent,

In Marsaya's tent I was treated as half-servant and half-guest, an inconsistency born of a certain unease because of the word *ettama,* a word I heard about myself often enough to recognize it, and which I came to realize had to mean magic power. Yet I was also a convenience and not to be wasted. It was astonishing to find that all the Tuareg had servants, called *imrid,* but I could still be useful, and if the imrid built the fires in the morning I was often the one to carry tea to the others, and my eyes were useful in guarding the little boy against scorpions and snakes outside the tent while the women chattered, which they did much of afternoons.

But the words hurled at me that first night were, *"Attini, attini . . ."* with Marsaya's daughter pointing to the wedding ring gleaming gold on my left hand.

Intimidated, I made an attempt to slip off the ring, feeling my life still precarious, and then in the light of the fire a long shadow fell across me. It was Marsaya, standing erect and looking very commanding. "La," she said sternly, and the others were silenced. More words followed, one of them *ettama,* repeated twice. Eyes widened and it was then that a bowl of gruel was brought to me which I later learned was called *assink* in their language, as well as a piece of hard dried cheese called *tikamarin* that smelled so dreadfully I put it aside as discreetly as I could.

But not speaking their language was a hardship—that language that poor Jacob had begun learning but was never to use— because I did not know whether they regarded my "magic" as dangerous to them or not. They had not killed me because of it, or so I thought, but whether out of fear of me or for some future usefulness was unknown, so that for many days I could not take my survival for granted. By sign language and by repeating words we communicated. Marsaya's daughter one morning pointed to herself and said, "Fadessa," and hearing her called this later I understood that it was her name. Her small son was made much of as he crawled naked around the tent, and I deduced from hearing it often spoken that his name was Sebeki, and later that the name of his absent father was Yunis.

But I soon discovered that I was not allowed to touch the child Sebeki. On a day that I tried to take him into my arms the women froze. Marsaya called out sharply, "La! La!" and Fadessa rushed to the boy and took him away, giving me a frightened, reproachful glance. Again I heard the word *ettama.* They did not know what to make of me, or perhaps what to do with me, and one day when the finger puppet Mr. Jappy fell from the pocket in my barracan a hiss like a snake issued from their closed lips and they stared at him almost with terror. *Ettama,* I thought, plucking him from the mat and returning him to my pocket. Their eyes watched him disappear and then rushed to my face to scrutinize me carefully.

"Attini," I said, the only other word familiar to me, but if it meant "give to me," or "I want that," it was near enough.

After six or seven days, when I saw that I was not going to be killed—not now at least—my thoughts turned to the future and to thoughts of escape: I wanted to escape, longed to escape, dreamed of escape, all the while knowing that I was captive not only of these people but of the desert surrounding me, this great and dangerous tableland stretching to the horizon

with its treacheries of heat, cold and thirst.
It went hard for me to accept my helplessness and in the end I refused it; there grew
in me the thought that if I carefully ob-
served and learned what the Tuareg knew I
might one day find a way to both escape
and to survive. How I would do this without
compass, map or camel I had no idea, but
it was this that steadied me, and this that
gave my days some purpose. I began to
study and memorize the stars and their po-
sitions each night. I watched one of the imrid cure a goatskin, waterproof it with a liquid made out of acacia bark and fashion a
waterbag or *guerba,* as Edrasi had named
it. I could not save food because the mats
were swept and turned each day and anything hidden under them would have been
found; I would have liked to save pieces of
the cheese called *tikamarin* but its odor
was so potent the smell would have preceded me anywhere.

Feeling as much a slave as the imrid, I
began to watch them and was sometimes
allowed to help: to hand them the twigs or
dried camel's dung with which they fueled
the fire, to watch how they made it flame
by rubbing a green stick, sharpened at one

remained puzzled she went and fetched a beautiful dagger. "Enaden," she said, and made motions with her hands of shaping it, after which she walked to Yunis' spare saddle hanging on the tent pole and patted it. "Enaden," she repeated.

Apparently they were people who made things, and later I walked to the edge of the tent and in the distance, quite removed from the camp, saw a new cluster of tents, three in number and small. I was curious: this at least was something new and I needed things to think about, my life being so confined and domestic. I wondered, too, about the black boy, for the others with whom he'd arrived had copper-colored skins. It needed another day for me to learn why they were regarded with uneasiness, and much to my surprise the word repeated over and over about them was *ettama,* the same that had been applied to me.

Well, well, I thought, *we have something in common, then, and I must find out what magic they use to be so feared.*

The next day when Marsaya, Fadessa and the child visited friends in a tent not far from the camp of the enaden I wandered after them, trying to be inconspicuous. It was as if the boy had been waiting all this time for me, because suddenly he was at my side.

Beaming, he pointed to himself. "I," he said.

I looked at him in astonishment. "You?" I said stupidly.

"I Bakuli, Jesus-boy."

"You speak English?" I gasped. I could scarcely believe this.

"Yes, Missy, most good, and Jesus-boy, too."

"A Christian?" I said blankly. "But—how is this?"

He thought a moment and I despaired that I might have heard the last of his English, which hearing was like a miracle. But he had more to say and had only needed time to find the words. "White Jesus-man my friend, he die of sleep sickness," he said. "In my village." Turning he pointed south across the lonely desert. "When he die, Bakuli stolen by bad men. Many moons we walk, Missy, to North Star, and many die. One day I choose better to run and die but the good Jesus save me." He pointed to the tents of the enaden. "They

find me all dead in desert and give water."
He thumped his chest triumphantly, grin-
ning his huge and radiant white smile. "I,
Bakuli, *live.*"

I smiled back at him. "You live, yes—
and speak *English.* You were stolen by
slave-traders?"

"Yes, Missy."

I shivered. "Then are you happy with
the—the enaden, Bakuli?"

He thought about this and at length
his face grew somber. He said simply, "I
grow sick for trees." He glanced up at me.
"And thou, Missy?"

Abruptly someone from the tents
shouted, "Bakuli? Bakuli!" With a last
glance at me, filled with meanings I
couldn't read, he turned and ran back into
the enaden encampment to leave me
standing there homesick, astonished and
lonely at having heard English words spoken. Before the day ended I couldn't believe it had happened and I began to measure time by how long it would be until I
could speak to the boy again. It was not
easy. Certainly it should have been, because I caught glimpses of him every day,
but I had to conclude that desert people,

surrounded by empty land, never found it comfortable to be alone.

But there was so much I wanted to know, and he was the only one who could tell me.

It seemed that he was as curious as I, for when at last we met again six days later —an eternity of waiting—he looked at me with a troubled face. "Missy," he said, "you have magic *munwe?*"

"*Munwe?*"

"Bemba word," he mumbled, and scowled; holding up one finger he stared at it. "Ah—finger!" he said, and looked at me. "Missy, what be this? You tell?"

From the pocket inside my barracan I drew out Mr. Jappy, and when I placed him on my finger he shrank away from me. "*Iyo, iyo,*" he gasped, "you be *ndoshi?* Oy Yesu!"

"Bakuli, not to fear," I protested, quickly removing it. "It's called a puppet— for fun, for play."

"Not magic?"

This I did not want to deny, but I insisted he touch Mr. Jappy, which he did reluctantly, and only out of a wanting to know me, I could tell, and then I placed Mr.

Jappy on my finger again and talked to him, telling him he was meeting Bakuli, with whom I wanted to be friends. Mr. Jappy nodded and spoke back in a different voice until Bakuli laughed excitedly, no longer afraid, the child in him responding.

It was now that I learned from him why I had been spared, for he spoke enough Tamahak, their language, to have asked questions as to who I was. I learned too that these Tuareg came from the Hoggar Mountains in the middle of the Sahara and that months ago they had assembled a caravan of camels to trade and sell in Ghadames, where prices were higher than among the Turks; it was in Ghadames they'd heard of a small rich caravan due to arrive soon—Umar, I thought darkly—and they had decided to further enrich themselves by raiding us.

"And that is it," said Bakuli. "That is all."

"No, tell me about the people you live with, the—they're called enaden?"

He nodded, and I was silent as he searched for an English word to explain. "Smitts," he said at last, and stretched out both his hands, turning them over for me to see.

It was my turn to shrink away, for the palms of his hands were filled with raw ugly blisters, and scarlet from burns. "Oh, Bakuli!"

"Much fire to make spears," he agreed. "Me, I learn hard."

"Blacksmiths, then," I said, and nodded. There had been gypsies from time to time in the carnival and the enaden seemed much like them in the carelessness of their dress and a certain independence that was different from the others. But I wished I knew a way to heal his terrible burns. "Why are they feared?" I asked.

"Oh, they know magic, Missy. Make spells, give amulets."

So that was it, they could put spells on people: desert magic. . . . It was time to part before we were noticed but I had one more question to ask. I said, "Bakuli, when Marsaya sings of an evening she often sings the word *tinanin.* What does it mean, do you know?"

He laughed and gave me his former radiant smile. "That be lady, Missy, big mama of all Tuareg, she be Queen Tin

Hinan—white lady from north like thou, Missy." He added mischievously, "Ataka and Bukush think thou art her spirit come back in new body."

"She's dead then?"

"Oh yes, Missy, long, long ago, her grave—" He stretched out his arms to the desert and shrugged.

Not a word, then, but a person, and a queen at that. I felt more kindly of my captors for having a queen, although I found it surprising. As for Bakuli he had given me much to think about, which I had needed; best of all, I felt I might have found a friend in this fellow-exile, and this too I had badly needed.

All that night camels kept arriving in the camp, and although I didn't stir from my mat, as Marsaya and Fadessa did, I slept little from the noise. When I woke from a last fitful nap it was to a silvery predawn light, and sitting up I saw the shapes and shadows of couched camels where once there had been empty desert. Creeping out of the tent I heard shouts from the north and saw more camels on their way to us, all of them heavily loaded, and as this last group drew near I saw Jacob's mahari among them. The men were returning.

All day the ensuing bedlam lightened my boredom until I learned that on the next day we were to break camp and leave, and at this my heart sank. My one terror at hearing this, a greater fear than the un- known into which I must plunge next, was that the enaden might be left behind and I never see Bakuli again or hear English spo- ken. Recklessly I ran to where he was help- ing unload the camels, and asked.

He beamed at me. "We go, Missy, much big work not done. We go, yes."

Relieved, and filled with a pleasure that surprised me, I returned to the tent to help with packing, and that night when the sun had set in a blaze of lemon and or- ange, many fires were lit and sheep were killed for a feast, or a *tafaski* as Fadessa called it. Marsaya made music, her face strong and dark in the light of the fires as she picked out sweet melancholy notes on her *amzar,* but it was after the feast that I learned what magic the enaden pos- sessed, if what they did could be called magic, for it was painful to see. Into the fire went shapes of iron, and when they shone nearly transparent from heat and fire the men took them into their hands and with a weird half-dance of twists and turns they held the flaming pieces of iron against their bodies without flinching and then against their heads until smoke rose—*and they were not burned.*

I had seen swords swallowed and fire eaten at the carnival, and both were dangerous enough, but after overcoming his retching a man could safely swallow a sword once he learned the right path into the esophagus; as for fire-eaters, the moistness of their mouths was protection for them, and for so long as they slowly exhaled their breath the flames would not be drawn into their lungs to explode. This was a new kind of magic to me, however, I was seeing it for myself and there were no explanations possible. For many days I would think about this, slowly agreeing with my first instincts that a strange kind of Mind-knowledge had to be involved to inure them to pain.

There was real power there, I thought, and wished I might learn it.

In the morning the tents were struck, the tent poles and mats tied up with palm lacings, beds taken apart and loaded on baggage camels, pots and gourds tied to saddles, and guerbas filled. Prayers were made by a withered old man called a *Marabout* and after interminable delays the stream of camels and people set out, and I among them, sometimes on the donkey, sometimes walking, occasionally seated behind Marsaya on her camel, and knowing only that I was moving farther and farther away from Ghadames and Tripoli and deeper into the desert.

eight

———⌣———

What can I say *now* of our crossing of the Tassili n' Ajjer mountains? Like strong brandy thrust on a child for medicinal purposes, the effect at the time was searing enough to bring tears to the eyes and to burn the throat but what lingers to this day is the memory of what my eyes saw, and no longer the terrors or hardships.

Picture if you will a great and towering wall of rock, rising out of the sands like an impregnable fortress with seemingly no way to penetrate that unforgiving stone until, drawing near, there is a seam that has been stripped open by erosion and storm, a cleft strewn with rubble and so narrow that its passage admits only one camel, one person at a time. A whole caravan climbs skyward in single file, on a winding trail over heights where a miscalculation could send man and beast crashing to their death. There is no water except what is carried in a goatskin bag, no food except what can be eaten while walking, and everyone walks. The camels labor, they groan, a camel slips, stops, his load must be shifted and everyone waits. The climb goes on all day until suddenly a corner is turned and like a mirage—but not a mirage —there is a valley in the heart of this massif, a long green valley holding in it like a jewel a pond of water as blue as the sky, with bright primroses along its banks and an enormous ancient cypress tree beyond it. Over it stand walls of rock that must still be climbed before reaching the great plateau at the top, but here is a paradise of color and softness—and there are *birds.*

I had forgotten the miracle of birds. And of cool clear water to drink, unflavored by goatskin or tar. Into this paradise we descended. Loads were dropped from the backs of the camels and left where they fell, the camels turned loose to drink and graze, a fire built and tea set over it to boil. As the sun's rays sank toward an unseen horizon, they flooded one wall of the cliff with a brilliant gold that slowly faded into lemon, changed into mauve and deepened into purple until night arrived as abruptly as a cloak flung over the valley. With our surroundings obliterated we became only a tiny circle of bright fire under a ceiling of stars.

I slept deeply that night, waking at dawn to cliffs flaming with color again: peach, apricot, pink, gold. I had begun to notice how gently the Tuareg treated their camels, we were to linger here for a few hours to rest them, to treat their saddle sores and examine their soft padded feet for cuts from the rocks. Seizing upon the moment to gain privacy I wandered off among the rocks, drawn to a shadowed opening among them beyond which I could see splinters of sun. Climbing over rubble I entered this narrow passage and emerged into an open space to gasp in astonishment.

Behind me, following, Bakuli said, "Missy?"

"Look!" I cried. "Look, there are drawings on these rocks." I counted a gazelle, a giraffe and an ostrich, all rendered in joyous lines of ocher.

Whistling softly through his teeth he clambered over rocks to touch the lines with his hands. "Oooo, many peoples here."

"No, there are only animals so far as I can see."

He shook his head. *"Peoples,* Missy, thou feel them?"

I looked at him curiously. "What do you mean, Bakuli, ghosts?"

He didn't recognize the word and walked back to me, thinking deeply. "No, Missy, spirits. *Myeo."* He lifted his arms in a gesture that encompassed the cliffs, the sky and the earth. "There be spirits in trees, in stone, in mountains, and sky. These stones speak, thou not hear?"

I admit that in my arrogance I nearly laughed. Recovering I said solemnly, "And what do the spirits here tell you, Bakuli?"

But he must have sensed my amusement for he only shrugged. "They be very dead now, long ago. No speak."

I looked again at the gazelle leaping so gracefully across the surface of the cliff, every line in motion, like a song, but the only message I drew from it was that someone had once been very happy here, and I sighed.

Bakuli said anxiously, "Missy? Thy eyes sad, thou not feel good?"

I turned from the drawings and we exchanged a thoughtful glance, examining each other very seriously, with no falseness, weighing the matter of trust between us, two captives of different age, race, country and culture. For a long moment it was in balance and then I said simply, "I want to escape, Bakuli."

He laughed uncertainly, not sure whether I was joking or not.

"I want to go *home,*" I emphasized.

Politely he said, "Where be home, Missy?"

"The United States."

"Is this far?"

It was my turn to laugh, but it was a bitter laugh. "Very very far."

"I do not think good, Missy, there be one big desert to kill thee."

"I was hoping you might want to escape too, Bakuli."

He looked shocked. "Oh, Missy, Bakuli want to stay live, this Jesus-boy almost die once in desert." He shook his head vigorously. "Bakuli no."

"Very understandable," I admitted with a sigh, "but still I have to keep hoping it's possible, except without a compass—"

"What be a compass?" he asked.

"It's a—" I could find no words to describe it so I applied a stick to a bed of sand between the rocks and drew a large picture of one. "It always points north and south, to keep a person heading in the direction they want."

"But there be stars, Missy."

"Yes," I said, "but they shine only at night."

"This big shape work in sun?"

"Yes, but not big," I explained, and made a circle with two fingers. "Like this."

He nodded, frowning and regarding the drawing with surprise. "Com-pass," he repeated, and then, "Best go now, Missy, or they beat me."

I felt a sadness to hear this for at least no one had beaten me, not yet, and compared to his lot mine was easier. But I could not find any comfort in what lay ahead of me, for my disadvantage lay in knowing better, in remembering cities and streetcars, books and trains and such things as would find me called a madwoman if ever I tried to describe them.

I stopped him between the two rocks through which we'd entered the cleft. "You will not speak of this to anyone, Bakuli?"

"No," he vowed, and made the sign of a cross. "Thou be *friend,* Missy."

I took one last glance at the strange pictures on the rock wall and then returned with him to the camp where I was given sharp glances and where Bakuli was beaten, but not for long because the camels were nearly loaded and it was time to go.

It was wise that I'd renewed my sense of purpose, having never had a purpose all my own before. A part of me knew that escape was impossible but another part of me knew that without hope I might not survive either; it seemed a matter of weighing different kinds of death. It was wise, too, because the journey now grew harder: when we left the fertile green valley it was to climb higher and higher over more rocks and shards, until we reached a sheet of black hammada as slippery as glass. Here we lost a camel; it fell, breaking one long slender leg, and had to be killed with the ruthless thrust of a knife, its blood spurting out sickeningly. We ate its flesh that night, the second meat I'd eaten since I was captured.

It was in the morning during the usual bedlam of loading the camels that Bakuli suddenly appeared at my side. "Missy?" he whispered.

The camel meat had not gone down well and my stomach was still queasy, so I didn't understand why he was holding out one hand to me. "Take," he said, beaming at me.

I looked into his hand and gasped in astonishment. "Bakuli, where on earth— this is a *compass!*"

He nodded proudly. "They throw to desert, Missy, they not know. My peoples take to hide." He beamed at me. "When you draw picture, Bakuli know."

I kept staring at it, telling myself that

all compasses looked alike, and yet the dull pewter-silver of this one—I turned it over and saw why it had seemed familiar, it was Jacob's compass with his initials engraved on the back: JLB.

I turned from Bakuli so he wouldn't see my face, which I knew was suddenly convulsed from remembering Jacob, remembering Tripoli and Mohammed with his Marcus Aurelius, while beyond this waited memories of Mum and Grams, the carnival and even Miss Thistlethwaite's School.

"Missy?" Bakuli sounded anxious.

I bit my lip and turned back to him. "It's all right, Bakuli, it's just that I knew the man who owned the compass. He died back there in the desert."

His eyes were soft. "Thou love man?"

The instant sympathy in his face made me honest and I shook my head. "I was careless," I said. "No." I took a fleeting glance back at that Caressa who had been so careless, and did not like her much.

Bakuli looked sad for me. "Jesus-boy full of love. You know Jesus, Missy?"

"I've heard of him," I said cautiously,

thinking it just my luck to meet a missionary's convert.

"No read Bible? About God—Jesus's
papa—and Little David and big man
named Go-lie?"

I had to shake my head, feeling just
plain godless and obviously reduced in
Bakuli's eyes, so I picked up some smooth
stones and palmed them, causing them to
disappear and reappear just to reassure
myself that I was still Caressa Horvath, or
Jacob's widow, or whoever I was. Except
that whoever I was had begun turning into
a puzzle, because to be stripped, as I was,
of accustomed clothes and background,
shorn of all that was familiar—name, language, people, family—was a shattering
attack on identity. Who *was* I, now that I
was thousands of miles from home and
sleeping in a Tuareg tent pitched on a desert under a blazing sun, the desert white at
noon, silver at night, eating dates and
tikamarin and millet? Only my youthful optimism could preserve me but since it was
precisely that youthful optimism that had
seen me marry Jacob and arrive in this situation, I felt it very suspect, and had to
wonder how this would end. . . . In this I

was thinking of Grams, who used to say that everyone's life was a story but it was clear to me now that some stories could end early and violently, as my father's had ended, and Jacob's, and who was I to expect more chapters when no one knew where I was, or even that I was alive? This latter thought had not occurred to me before, but I saw that of course news of Jacob's death would eventually reach Tripoli and then Boston, too. With only bones— and all those Bibles—strewn across the sand who would know that I wasn't dead, too? I was no more than a ghost, a wraith . . . I no longer existed.

I decided in a panic that it was time for that youthful optimism after all, no matter how treacherous. I had a compass now and someday there would simply have to come a way to escape; it was either that or spend the rest of my life wearing a bathrobe and washing my hair in camel's urine.

I watched Bakuli's hasty retreat, his dark legs flashing, his *naïls* kicking up clouds of dust. He looked very small beside the camel he was about to lead, and very small to burst with such enthusiasm over his papa-God and Jesus but I wondered at his not seeing what a hard and luckless life his God had given him.

It took us five frigid nights and six scorching days to cross the Ajjer. When we stopped for a day to water the camels at a well they called Zaoatallez, it was to look across a desolate, sun-baked plain to a pale frieze of mountains that punctured the sky with sinister peaks and towers.

"What are they?" I asked Bakuli, pointing.

"Tassili Hoggar," he told me.

The Hoggar Mountains . . . I remembered that to these people the Hoggar was home, and therefore would have to be home to me, too. It did not look a hospitable place, not even softened by distance.

nine

~~~~~~~

I was to live in the Hoggar Mountains with the Tuareg for a length of time that I could only guess to be six or seven months. There were neither calendars nor clocks for telling time, nor familiar seasons to judge it by, except that by desert time the dry season was nearly upon us when everything would soon turn brown and sapless and the men move the animals north to pasturage.

The Hoggar was a wild place, a true witch's lair with its tortured rocks and black volcanic peaks—black like mourning, like widows weeds, like hell, or so I thought at first, although later we camped more sensibly (but only briefly) in a valley where patches of *alwat* had not yet withered, and my eyes drank in color as thirstily as water, which there was not much of either in the dry season. Still, as I learned more words of their language, I understood the Hoggar to be like a fortress for these people, and this I could certainly believe. But I never stopped feeling dwarfed by the towers of stone around me, no matter how grateful for their shade, nor cease being startled by the explosive shattering of rocks as the temperatures sharply dropped at night and rose again in the day.

If I was to survive and remain sane the adjustments needed were unending and I had to lean heavily on Marcus Aurelius. Over and over I muttered, *How ridiculous and how strange to be surprised at anything that happens in life, how ridiculous and how strange to be surprised at anything that happens in life,* but the sorest loss was my hair. I could tolerate the fleas that lodged in my barracan but the lice in my hair were a constant torment and not even camels urine discouraged them for long. Seeing me scratch my head until I drew blood Bakuli urged me to have it shaved.

The enaden, it seemed, were also barbers.

Thus I was taken to his master Bukush and my head shaved, for which service I paid with my abundance of hair, which must have made a fine pillow when sewn into leather skins. It scarcely altered my appearance since I could wear a headscarf, as all the women did, but its loss affronted my vanity. Still, this was assuaged by the crusts on my scalp healing and by the absence of lice, so that my period of mourning was brief.

There were small groups of the Tuareg living all through the valleys of the Hoggar, and the enaden, or blacksmiths—Bakuli among them—frequently moved their tents to another camp to work but mercifully they always returned. Once in a while our camp was visited by neighbors for what was called an *ahlah,* and at such times I found myself eyed covetously by the young men and again feared my future. There were no mirrors but I could see from my hands and arms that my skin was a deepening brown and not so different from Marsaya's, but she kept a strict watch over me, and apparently it was explained to them that I was not a Targuia, and that they had yet to learn whether I was a danger to them.

It was Bakuli who told me of this. From speaking English with me he had begun expanding his sentences more confidently, which was ironic because as his sentences grew longer mine had grown shorter to accommodate him until I was flinging away adjectives and adverbs and reducing my speech to nouns and verbs. What he had to tell me, however, was all too clearly expressed.

Very solemnly he explained that of course I possessed magic, the Tuareg knew this because I had two wooden fingers with faces, but if it turned out that I practiced *bad* magic they would abandon me to the desert or simply kill me in an unpleasant ritual way.

I protested this vigorously. "They wouldn't do that," I told him. "I've been with them for months and they've grown used to me, haven't they? And Marsaya is kind to me!"

His glance was almost pitying. "Tuareg have words, 'It be wise to kiss hand thou dare not cut off.' "

This was scarcely comforting.

On the other hand, he continued, if I turned out to have good magic they would ask of me spells and amulets and charms and my presence would protect them. All was well now but he worried about me, he said, because if anything bad happened in the camp—if someone grew sick or died— they would know I caused it.

"How on earth could they blame *me?*" I cried.

He looked at me in astonishment. Although he began a garbled reply he was obviously surprised that I didn't understand why of *course* I would be blamed. From his tangled explanation I could only piece together the fact that I was tolerated but suspect. They were waiting.

He added dolefully, "And soon my peoples go."

"Go!" I cried in panic.

He nodded. "Go many places, Missy. Make spears, make saddles, make swords, go. To village next, far north—" He pointed. "Where there be *alwat* and *tamat* to feed goats."

My heart sank in dismay. "Oh, Bakuli!" Until this moment I felt I'd become relatively stable and was doing very well, not resigned but at least accepting the sameness of a life that once would have appalled me, still carrying anger at my fate but no longer hating the Tuareg for what Reason told me was Jacob's doing. But to lose Bakuli! This was too cruel and it hit me hard.

He nodded, saying, "Bakuli too big to cry, Bakuli's heart cries *for* him."

"When?" I stammered. "W-when do you go?"

He shrugged and sighed. "Work grow very small now." He gave me a quick unhappy glance. "Bakuli ask Master if thou come, too, Missy, but he very angry and beat me. Thou be useless, he said, but still eat food and there be not enough."

For this there were no words of Marcus Aurelius to comfort me, for I had never met the man, but Bakuli I had met and he was real and he was my friend. I felt like dying. This was bad but there was worse to come. . . . The next week it rained, the first rain since the Year of the Lost Caravan, they said, and although rain was a miracle in the Sahara, the Tuareg were ill-prepared for it. Water streamed down from the mountain peaks in torrents, tents collapsed, cooking fires suffocated, food was scarce, there was no way to keep dry and everyone shivered with cold. When the rains ended there was a sudden wealth of green springing up from what had once been rock and sand, but it was now that Sebeki grew sick. Very sick. The little boy had been listless for days, puzzling both Fadessa and Marsaya, but two nights before the enaden were to leave—they were already packing—there came high fever, vomiting and chills. I wondered if a scorpion or viper had bitten Sebeki during the rains, or if it could be typhoid, but Bakuli shook his head, it was *tenedee,* malaria, he said. Not good, not good.

Old women huddled around the child, medicines were brewed on the fire, the ancient Marabout appeared in camp again bringing fresh amulets and charms to hang around Sebeki's neck. Remembering what Bakuli had told me I huddled in a corner of the tent and tried to make myself invisible.

Toward sunset of the next day the poor boy had a convulsion and I crept out to find Bakuli, hoping he might give me needed reassurance before he left for the north with the enaden, but he was nowhere to be found. When I asked at his tent I was given sour and angry glances.

"Bakuli?" said an old woman, and she burst into a tirade about him, and spat. Obviously he was late in returning with the goats from pasture and would be badly beaten for this. They were to leave during the night and I wouldn't even be able to say good-bye to him, which induced even more panic and misery.

I walked back to Marsaya's tent but it was so crowded with people I retreated. Since the sun was near to setting, I walked some distance from the camp, and finding a sandy patch in the lee of a boulder I scooped out a hollow for sleep. I had scarcely lain down when I heard a *sssst* from behind the rock.

It was Bakuli. "Missy, come," he called urgently.

I was so glad to hear his voice that I flew at once to the rear of the boulder where he crouched, but, "No speak, Missy," he whispered. "Come."

He grasped my hand and I joined him without question, having not the slightest idea of where he wished us to go or why he was going anywhere. He wanted to show me something, I thought, or to find a more distant place to say good-bye, but in any case it was a relief to remove myself from the tent where Sebeki was so ill, and certainly I had wanted desperately to see Bakuli before he went away.

And yet . . . "Bakuli," I said at last, "we go far from the camp and your people leave soon, and where are we going?"

The moon was just rising over the Atakor, the high volcanic plateau that dominated the Hoggar to the east of us, and I could see Bakuli dimly now, and see that we were entering a canyon whose silence and shadows made me shiver. A jackal screamed somewhere in the cliffs beside us, turning the silence even deeper when his cry died away.

"Bakuli!" I said again uneasily.

He dropped my hand to face me. "Missy," he said anxiously, "Sebeki wear death on his face, he go to die."

"Don't say that!" I told him sharply.

"Missy," he began again, "thou know it. Bakuli afraid, Bakuli not want you die, too. You say once escape—"

"Escape!" I blurted out.

"Yes, Missy. Once Bakuli say escape *NO*. Now Jesus-boy say yes." He added in an anguished voice, "My heart full of pain to say bye, Missy."

"But Bakuli—the desert," I gasped, for I knew more now of hungry dry seasons in the desert, of dried-up wells and thirst, marauding tribes and jackals. What could he mean, how could we ever escape, and to what?

He said gravely, "This desert be kinder from rain, Missy. My peoples go north in night—" He pointed to the moon slowly rising in the sky. "Thy peoples think you go north, too. Bakuli and thou go *south*."

"But water, Bakuli, we have no water. Or food, or—"

His teeth flashed white in his black face. "Ahhhhh," he nearly sang at me joyously, "Bakuli learn mountains now and think big thoughts, I hide guerbas—" He

held up two fingers. "Big rope, knife—salt
—dates, and Missy—a donkey!"

I was staggered by this news, I would
have sat down and cried if I gave in to
what I felt at that moment: he was offering
escape, had even planned escape like a
gift to please me. More, he was offering me
choice.

But a choice between two deaths, I realized soberly, for neither of us knew the
wells of the desert, and a compass, two
guerbas of water and a donkey would
come to nothing if we found no more water
in that vast and scorching wasteland. It
was true the Tuareg would not expect me
to flee south, but to go south was to move
deeper into the desert and I had already
seen the bones of camels and men on our
way to the Hoggar, dead of thirst and miscalculation.

That was one death. If I went back to
the Tuareg camp, what then? I knew that
as Sebeki had grown sicker there had been
murmurs about me and speculative
glances sent in my direction. They would
test me first, I reasoned. When all the
charms and medicines failed and they
were desperate for Sebeki's life they would

dare taboo and give me the boy to hold, watching closely to see what magic I possessed that would heal him. They would learn then that I had no magic at all to cure Sebeki and was as helpless as they, and suddenly everything would change, for if I had no good magic then the wooden fingers that had spared my life had to mean *bad* magic, and—as Bakuli had explained to me—it would be thought that I must be the cause of the boy's illness.

Revenge among the Tuareg, Bakuli had said, was a very terrible thing, and he had shuddered. I'd not asked what he meant. His shudder had told me more than I cared to know.

All this passed through my mind in only a minute. My thoughts completed, I grasped Bakuli's hand and squeezed it, for to die with a friend was kinder than to die among enemies. Perhaps also I was awed by his lovingness and caring. "You are a real Jesus-boy," was all I could think to say. "We go, Bakuli."

We climbed up and down and slipped and slid all during the long cold night. Sometimes, from a cliff, I would look down into a valley and see the fires of other Tuareg camps below us and then we would move on. The moon rose higher and whatever it touched it turned as white as if snow had fallen. I could see that we followed a narrow path in and around and past great rocks, but in general we appeared to be moving always downward to reach the encircling desert below.

It was nearly dawn when we descended to the last plateau and saw the silvery desert ahead, with needle-sharp rock spires rising out of the sand. Bakuli turned back among the boulders and I saw that he'd tethered the donkey in a cave, and with it the guerbas and the small sack of food. I did not ask how many secret trips he'd made to provide for us; I was torn between gratitude and foreboding.

"Go now, Missy," he said firmly. "Before sun big."

Before anyone looked for us, too, he might have added. Tired as I was I nodded, and once the bulging waterskins were loaded on the donkey we set out walking across the gravelly sands to meet whatever fate the gods cared to measure out to us.

Since we had walked and climbed all

night to escape to the far reaches of the Hoggar we were not in the best shape to approach what lay ahead. The rocky foothills had dropped away to a treeless plain, utterly flat except for hills of gravel that rose sharply out of the reg, as if a broom had swept the earth bare and deposited debris and dust in huge tidy piles. Now we veered from west to southwest, walking still in the shadow of the Hoggar, for the sun's rise was hidden in the east behind its citadel walls. In this pale light the air was fresh and cool and we walked at a good pace beside the donkey, Bakuli and I grinning at each other from time to time at this taste of freedom and almost capable of forgetting that we were entering what the Arabs called the *Bahr belà mà,* or "sea without water," and what the Tuareg called the "Country of Dread."

Soon enough we knew it, though, for the sun cleared the peaks of the Hoggar and found us, two minute figures trudging hour by hour across the desert with a donkey plodding along behind us. The heat of this day was nearly overpowering, sucking everything dry, and the sun so scorching to the earth that it burned and blistered my feet and radiated heat back into our faces. We rested at midday, but even to find a rock large enough to shade us brought no coolness, and we had to drink sparingly of our water just when we yearned for it most. It was now that I rued my unexercised life in the Tuareg camp, for while I had plaited mats and only fitfully wandered, Bakuli had been carrying water, learning to bend iron and herding goats; his muscles were strong. With envy I watched him stride ahead in his ragged shirt, the square of cloth below it pulled up into a knot around his waist, his knees mere bony knobs in his sticklike legs, his bare feet blistering but his head high and well-wrapped in a faded blue cloth. My own clothes were scarcely better, my barracan torn and bleached, the *nails* on my feet flapping loose in need of mending; it was embarrassing to stumble along behind Bakuli and not stride as he did. We seldom spoke; our throats were thick with dust and sand, and after enduring the heat of the day it was necessary to brace ourselves for the cold of the night, when I shared my barracan with Bakuli and we shivered together until sleep arrived, with only the donkey contented for he would find stubbles of grass on which to feed. On one of these nights the moon shining in my eyes woke me from a dream to find the desert all shadow and silver. In my dream I had been seated on a merry-go-round horse at Laski's carnival but something had gone horribly wrong and the merry-go-round was spinning faster and faster until I grew dizzy and frightened, and then—but when I opened my eyes I couldn't remember how it ended except that it left its mark on me and I thought, *We could pass half a mile from a well and never know it, we're surely going to die of thirst.*

I'd not realized that I spoke the words aloud until Bakuli said hoarsely, "Missy, I have prayed to the good Yesu and I am Jesus-boy. No fear."

It was difficult to share in such confidence when my blisters had broken and my feet were a bloody mess. We rose, untied the donkey and walked more miles, the moon illuminating every stone and stick of grass, the sky dazzling with bright pinpoints of stars. When the moon sank to the horizon we stopped to rest again, but each fitful sleep brought new dreams: of

Grams, Mum, Umar, Jacob, and once, waking, I was certain I saw a shadow move and vanish. I remembered what Bakuli had said about spirits; I was in Africa now, not Boston, and I wondered if it had been a jackal or a djinn.

We had walked for three days and two nights, and had nearly exhausted our water, when we met with an old caravan trail. I had grown careless about checking the compass and found that we'd wandered a little to the east, and there it was: a line of clear-cut furrows stretching out ahead of us, a broad path so worn by use the stones had long ago been ground into the earth to strip it bare where caravans had passed.

"Maybe water soon," Bakuli said, studying it.

"Maybe," I said wearily.

We followed the trail until midafternoon when we lost it in a dried-up riverbed, a sandy oued lined with needle-sharp green bushes. Bakuli pointed to them. "Water make grow, and—look, Missy."

I looked and saw holes dug in the sandy bed from which bubbles of muddy water oozed. This was startling because such holes had to have been dug by people, and at this precise moment I heard drums begin to beat off to the east of us, at a distance, as if warning of our presence.

"Drums, Bakuli!" I gasped. "Hide!"

We crept along the bank of the oued and peered through the foliage: miles away we thought we could see the shape of several huts, but in the shimmering light this could have been a mirage. There was nothing miragelike about the tom-toms, however; they interrupted the silence of the desert like thunder, sending out unclear but ominous messages.

"Think they've seen us?" I whispered.

Bakuli didn't answer but joined me in looking for shelter. Behind us, beyond the opposite bank of the riverbed, the stony earth rose slowly but steadily toward a long hill that culminated in a great mass of boulders. I pointed, and Bakuli nodded. "Yes, Missy. *Fast,* Missy." Removing his head scarf he tied it around the donkey's jaw to silence him. Leading the way he climbed out of the riverbed, pulling the donkey up the bank while I pushed the poor creature from behind. We then began a circling of the great hill, a long climb that rendered us frighteningly conspicuous should anyone be watching. Passing a series of neatly piled rock mounds Bakuli said, "Graves," and he stopped to stare at them, and shivered.

"They're dead," I told him shortly. "People who beat drums are alive."

We passed three more rock mounds and I saw Bakuli cross himself; these graves appeared to circle the entire hill, like a necklace surrounding the great pile at the summit, and since they clearly made Bakuli uneasy I suggested we leave the donkey tethered to a rock and climb up to the crest to make camp for the night. I used the word "camp" with irony, for there were no camels to couch and unload, and no companions, only the two of us with no food and no fuel for a fire should we even dare one with the drums still pounding off to the west of us. In this haste to hide we left the donkey below and picked our way over boulders to the top of the great hill. We had just reached its crest when I looked to the south and groaned. "Oh God —look," I said helplessly.

A dust storm, huge, was building up in the southwest and heading toward us like a brown tidal wave, ready to overpower and take whatever it could into its greedy maw.

Bakuli stared in terror. "Make cave," he gasped. *"Must,* Missy—that one big gibleh."

The rocks were heavy; we worked desperately, not daring to look at the approaching brown wall of sand and dust. We prodded boulders loose, rolled them aside and tore at the next level of stones until we met with a cavity below the surface that eased our work, but there was no stopping Bakuli until he had cleared a hollow deep enough and wide enough for the two of us to enter.

"In!" he cried fiercely, and I crawled down into darkness. The storm hit us while Bakuli was still hauling into place the slab that would be tilted over us once he joined me. When he dropped down beside me clouds of dust and sand came with him, but we had secured a shelter against the storm. Tightly wrapped in my barracan, with Bakuli huddled beside me, there was nothing to do now but listen to the monster wind trying to reach us, thwarted by the rocks in which we'd taken refuge but exacting its revenge by showering us with dust through every crevice.

When the wind had changed from a shriek to a steady roar I thought it time to express my opinion. "This is a crazy place to hide, Bakuli, there could be snakes here. Or scorpions."

"Big, *BIG* storm," he said, shivering. "Bakuli never see one like mountain walking."

"But there could be *scorpions*," I pointed out.

"Y-y-yes, Missy," he said humbly.

There seemed no point in emphasizing how ill-advised this seemed to me now that we were here; we had probably seen the last of the donkey and with it our goat-skin waterbags, and a few scorpions were minor in comparison. I was wrong, there was more to come, for after a long silence Bakuli spoke again.

"Missy," he said uneasily, "there be spirits here."

"Nonsense," I told him sternly, "that's your imagination again, because of the graves down the hill, but they're far away, Bakuli. Go to sleep."

"Yes, Missy," he said in a scared little

voice, but it seemed a long time before I felt him sag against me in sleep, his head on my shoulder. The wind had lessened but no light seeped through the crevices; I judged it to be past sunset now, and night. I wondered if there were stars in the sky . . . wondered if the donkey had survived the storm . . . wondered if I should wake Bakuli to begin walking again, but I was too tired to stir.

And now, abruptly, it was I who sensed we were not alone.

ten

ありません

T here were two of us huddled together in this small space into which no one else could fit and yet there was someone else with us, I knew this with a certainty beyond all rationalization: *we were not alone.*

What atavistic sense had come into play I couldn't guess, for I saw nothing and heard nothing and yet I knew. It was as if a sense organ long atrophied, unknown to me and deadened by civilization had sur-faced from the deeps to feel what could only be called a Presence.

Beside me Bakuli had stiffened, awake. "Missy," he whispered in terror.

"Yes," I said.

We sat trembling; something cool as a wisp of fog, soft as silk, brushed past me and was gone, and slowly the sense of Presence faded. I drew a deep breath and grasped Bakuli's hand and held it tight.

I said shakily, "At least it wasn't a scorpion."

"Yes, Missy," he whispered. "You too?"

"Yes." There seemed nothing else to say and now that it was gone I went over and over it, determined to explain it away, to name it fantasy, hunger, hallucination— but why then, as I denied it, were Bakuli and I both trembling still? My rational mind rebelled at believing, yet my senses could not reject what I'd felt. I told myself to go to sleep, that I could ill afford a night spent flirting with madness, I needed *sleep.* "That knits the ravel'd sleeve of care," I told myself, forgetting the rest of my Shakespearean quote. "That knits the ravel'd sleeve of . . ." The wind had quieted outside and I was calming with it. "That knits the ravel'd . . ."

I fell asleep but the Presence was not done with me yet, for I dreamed a strange dream. Great clouds of pale mist rolled toward me, endlessly, in waves, until out of the mists there came toward me a tall, thin figure, almost Egyptian in appearance and wearing a simple garment and a headdress of ostrich feathers. This figure—surely a woman despite her height—smiled and spoke to me, but without uttering a sound, the words transmitted and translated to me in some uncanny telepathic manner.

"I sleep below you, Stranger from the North," she said. "Do not be afraid—I too was once a stranger from the North and felt the beating of your heart in my grave below. . . ."

The specter stretched out her hand to me; it held a stone that I saw more clearly than her face, it was flat and oddly shaped with a hole near its center. It resembled, I had to confess, one of the misshapen muffin or gingerbread men that Mum had struggled to bake at Christmas. I reached out to touch the hand but the figure was slowly dissolving back into the mists. I cried out, "But who are you? Who are you? Who—"

Bakuli was shaking me. "Missy, Missy," he whispered. "You make noise— ssh, we be heard."

I could see his face, it was morning. It had been a powerful dream and I felt dazed and disoriented, the weight of the rocks surrounding us were stifling and the space we'd occupied a tomb. "Let's get out," I said with a shiver. "Please, let's *go.* We can still get out, can't we?"

With both arms Bakuli sought to heave aside the slab he'd tilted over us but it wouldn't move. In a panic I knelt beside him to help, and when at last it was lifted aside and I saw blue sky again, I felt like kneeling to give thanks to Bakuli's God. With a last glance at the hollow in which we'd spent our stormy night I was about to follow Bakuli into the sunshine when I stopped. Behind me in the place where I had lain all night I saw a flat carved stone made white by a ray of sun, with something green shining dully in its center.

It seemed that I was not to forget my dream after all, for I recognized the stone by its odd, distorted muffin-man shape.

"Hurry, Missy," Bakuli said, his head

silhouetted against the sky, one hand extended to help my exit.

Well, I thought, trying to make light of this, *there are more things in heaven and earth than were dreamt of in* MY *philosophy.* . . . I leaned down and picked up the carved rock shape, reminding myself that she had been gentle, even kind, and in some strange way had known me, calling me Stranger from the North; the stone fitted neatly into the palm of my hand and I climbed up and out into the sun, sneezing and coughing at the dust. The heat of morning hit me hard, and so did reality, which was unchanged and harsh, for we still had no food and little water. I saw Bakuli looking at what I held in my hand, and I showed it to him. "I lay on this all night."

He peered more closely and shook his head. "No like, Missy." He touched it and made a face. "This maybe *bwanga,* maybe *bubi.* A charm, maybe evil, maybe prayed to, maybe full of spirits. No like."

At least he recognized it as something unusual and apart. Looked at in the light I could see that it was no mere rock but had been shaped by a tool; a topknot had been carved on its crude head and there were small protuberances that had to have been chiseled into its funny distorted body by a human hand. The surprise was the lump of dark green crystal embedded in the stone near the center of the figure, giving it a rather exotic navel. "Well," I said, "I'll keep it for a while. As a souvenir."

"Souvenir?"

This was hard to translate. "A charm," I finally said. "At least until I learn if it *is* a charm. I like it." I tucked it into the pocket of my barracan and brought out the compass, sighing as the full weight of our lostness fell on me. The Hoggar Mountains still towered behind us, three days away but still oppressively *there,* to remind me we dared not turn north, at least not yet. Beyond the oued, to the west, had come the ominous drums just before the storm, and neither south nor east promised anything but desert. And I was hungry.

"Missy!" whispered Bakuli, looking suddenly alarmed.

I thought for a moment that he was fearing spirits again, and felt a flash of exasperation but then I heard it, too: a faint murmuring below us, the rise and fall of a human voice. We picked our way over the rocks to gaze down from the hill at the western side of its base. A man was kneeling there in a patch of sand, his back to us. Abruptly he dropped forward to press his forehead into the sand, then straightened and after a second of repose prostrated himself again. The *tashah-hud*, I thought, *he is saying his prayers to Allah,* and then my gaze wandered and I saw that he had found our donkey and tied it to a rock close to him.

"He prays," Bakuli whispered.

"Yes, but he has our donkey. And our waterskins."

"*Yangu.* But he prays, Missy."

We looked at each other, weighing the risks, and then Bakuli grasped my hand. "Come, Missy."

I knew that he meant there was no choice. Looking me over sternly he said, "You be boy, Missy. Cover head tight."

We began our climb down the rocks but I found it strange that the man heard us at once, as soon as we began our first steps down the hill, for we were still at a distance from him and we walked carefully. As we approached him he stood up to face us, a man with a face as black as Bakuli's, not veiled, his head neatly wrapped in a soiled white turban. He wore ragged trousers and was barefoot. As we drew even closer I saw that his face bore a pattern of knife-cut tribal scars.

"He be Hausa," whispered Bakuli.

"How know?" I whispered back.

"Tribe marks." To the man he called in Tamahak, *"Mahulid,"* and then, *"Sannu kadai."* And to me, "Many peoples speak Hausa, I know a little much."

The man did not *look* dangerous; his face was round, with a somewhat beaked nose, but what I thought curious was that his intense gaze was fixed upon a point beyond us.

"Wane ne?" he said quietly, his glance remaining focused over our shoulders, and then I saw that both his eyes were filmed over with white and I realized that he was blind.

"Bakuli," I said, "he's—"

"Yes, Missy, he no see. *Salem alaik,"* he said politely, and told him that it was our donkey he'd found.

I decided it was time I entered into this meeting, and in my clumsy Arabic I told

him there were two of us, Bakuli and
Missy.

He seemed to understand; he nodded
and beckoned us closer, and when we
walked up to him he stretched out both
hands, seeking to touch Bakuli; I had to
smile as he found nothing until he dropped
a hand to Bakuli's nine-year-old height. He
smiled then, his teeth a brilliant white
against his dark skin. Very gently his fingers ran over Bakuli's face and his smile
deepened. He turned to me, his fingers
tracing the shape of my face, then touching nose and mouth and pausing at my
eyes. I remembered how acute his hearing
had been to sense us from so far away and
I hoped he wasn't equally as acute in discerning that I was female and an infidel.

His name, he said, was Musa and he
was a Bàhaushe, or Hausa. He spoke a
little French, some Arabic and understood
some Tamahak, all of which we were hard
pressed to discover and which took time. I
assumed that he must live nearby, perhaps
in the village where we'd heard drums—he
was blind, after all—but I was literally staggered to hear that he'd been traveling
many days and was on his way from In

Salah in the North to his home in the South. . . .

"Alone and blind? How can this be?" I asked in astonishment.

Bakuli was looking at the man with great respect. He said, "My smitt peoples have spoken of such men, Missy. There be such, yes, they have desert-eyes."

My thoughts circled this, returned to consider it while slowly possibilities acquired shape. "We go south too, Bakuli," I said. "We have only a thirsty donkey, no food and two almost-empty goatskin bags." I reached into the pocket of my barracan and drew out the silver Hand of Fatima that Mohammed had given me. "Ask him if for this he would buy food for us where we heard the drums beating, and if he will let us go south with him."

Bakuli's face brightened at the sight of silver. He spoke rapidly to Musa in Tamahak, with probably some Hausa thrown in, for I understood only the word *mouna,* or tribute. The silver was placed in the palm of Musa's hand, he weighed it, put it between his teeth and bit it hard, then smiled.

"i," he said. *"Wallahi, i."*

"I think," Bakuli said, frowning over this, "that in Hausa *i* means yes."

"*Oui?*" I asked, wanting to be sure. "*Naam?*"

Musa nodded vigorously and pocketed the Hand of Fatima. Walking over to the donkey he felt the two guerbas, nearly empty, and made sign language for us to remain where we were, he would fill them in the sluggish muddy water of the oued. "*Dawa,*" he said, and bringing out two pieces of bread he placed them in Bakuli's hand and led away our donkey, abandoning us to whatever faith in him we could manage. We tore into the bread hungrily, but he was gone a worrisome long time. The sun rose higher in the sky, the shadows grew smaller and the heat more searing. But he came back. While he was gone he appeared to have made friends with our donkey for he was talking to it as he approached us from the other side of the hill, and when we softly called out to him he patted the donkey, nodding and smiling. "*Bon,*" he said. "*Jākī bon.*" The two goatskins bulged with water, and the donkey, however *bon,* now carried a bale of fodder on his back as well. Musa proudly showed us the Hand of Fatima so that I understood he had paid with money of his own, for besides the leather bag that held his own possessions he had brought back a sack of dates for us and some tea and millet that he gave to Bakuli.

With a mixture of Hausa, Arabic and Tamahak he told us we must leave quickly now. The oasis was named Abalessa, (I would remember this) and the people there were Haratin, and very poor; he had felt their interest in the donkey and heard their whispers when he produced his coins. We must go fast, he said, and so we set out at noonday, the cruelest time of all, hoping this hour of the day would discourage our being followed and robbed. It would be four days to the nearest well—if it had not gone dry, he said—and we must beware of bandits. Neither of these warnings were inspiriting. Nevertheless, when I thought of what the Hand of Fatima had bought us, I felt that if Mohammed could know I was still alive he would be truly glad that his gift was restoring hope and life to me for a little longer, although how a blind guide would preserve us I couldn't imagine. But then I still had much to learn.

We had not traveled far when we met with a dreadful reminder of life's fragility in the desert; from a distance I saw vultures circling in the sky and was about to speak of this when Musa stopped us. He knelt, placed his ear to the ground, then rose and gestured us on through the scrub. As we drew nearer I saw the ground alive with vultures, ugly black creatures that flapped their wings and screamed their anger at us and flew away to circle overhead and wait, giving space for us to see what they fed on. It was not a pretty sight. We were looking at six corpses not long dead, for the men were still half-clothed. What astonished me was to see that two of the men lying dead in the sand wore remnants of uniforms.

"French, Missy," Bakuli said, and pointing to the other four, "they be Chaamba."

French! I had not remembered that when we crossed the Tassili n' Ajjer we had moved out of Turkish country and into French territory. In spite of the horror with which I gazed at the scene, my first thought was *French . . . dear God if only I can find a live one I may see home again.*

Musa bent over to search the bodies and I turned away at this, sickened, for not even the witnessing of an earlier massacre could inure me to the sight of what vultures did to the bare faces of these men, tearing the eyes from their sockets and the flesh from their bones. When Musa had finished, having found nothing left of value, he dropped to the ground and with his fingers examined the camel prints, sorted over the spent cartridge shells and picked up the dung and sniffed it. When he rose I was amazed at how much he had learned from what looked only a confusion of tracks. The French and their Chaamba guides had come up from the south, he said, and among their camels were two that belonged to the Tuareg; he could tell from the grass in their dung where they had last fed, and by whom they were owned. Here at this place fifteen Tuareg had overtaken them, demanding back their camels; there had been talk for a few minutes but the Tuareg did not like the Chaamba and the Chaamba did not like the Tuareg, and this was how it had ended. *"Iyaka ya kare,"* he said: the end. It is finished.

We went on, leaving the dead to the

vultures and leaving me to marvel at what an astonishing man this Musa was. He carried a long stick, for instance, but rarely used it and he certainly had no need of a compass. There would be moments when he would stop, stand very still and listen to the wind, feeling the course of it on his face, and then he would drop to the ground and smell the sand or gravel, after which he would change our direction ever so slightly and later, checking my compass, I would find that unerringly he kept us heading southeast. This in itself saved our lives, as I was to learn later, for if Bakuli and I had continued to the southwest we would have entered the Tanezrouft, one of the most fearsome stretches of the Sahara where no water hole existed for almost 200 miles.

Nor did Musa appear to need much water or food. He carried a guerba laced to the stick across his shoulders, as well as a leather bucket from which he produced kola nuts and a green-colored millet called *gero* that needed no cooking and could be mixed with a very small amount of water to quench both thirst and hunger. He carried many charms strung on a leather thong around his neck, and a rope, and five Maria Theresa thalers, or dollars. He did not speak much at first, as if the silence of the desert had entered him, but he led us without eyes to the well he called In Attel that was no more than a pinpoint in that vast wasteland. We hid near the well for a day, while a large caravan watered their camels there, and it was while we camped and waited that he began to tell his tales: of the caravan he'd guided to In Salah, from which he was returning; of hunting gazelle and *gwanki*—antelope—before the sun had stolen his eyes, of licking dew early in the morning from the coarse grass *afazo* or *tashrah* when his guerba was empty. He said the finding of the wells was in the hands of Allah but he had been taught by his father, and even without sight he knew the desert like the back of his hand. His greatest fear was that a well might have dried up since he last visited it—and of course there were the djinns, he added, one could hear them calling on many a night.

After the stop at In Attel we headed due south until the rocks and stones began to thin, and ahead of us loomed a flat, sandy plain. We made camp late that night and when I wrapped myself in my barracan and lay down to sleep the five stars of the Southern Cross shone with polished brilliance, looking almost near enough to reach out and touch. They had become a great comfort to me but someday, I vowed, I would travel toward the Northern Cross, which the Tuareg called Elkelzif, and I would go *home.*

At some distance from us I heard Musa stir uneasily in his sleep; he suddenly gave a sharp cry and thrashed about for a moment before he turned silent: *Sahara dreams,* I thought, closing my eyes, and slept the sleep of exhaustion.

In the morning Musa lay in the sand cold and still. We stood over him shocked by the look of anguish on his face. Bakuli whispered, "He be dead, Missy, O Yesu, he be dead."

"But how?" I cried. "He mustn't be dead, Bakuli, what can have happened to—"

I stopped because Bakuli had taken a step back in horror, pointing. "Look," he gasped, and then I saw it too: the long lazy curve of an S in the sand next to Musa, the one danger that in his blindness Musa couldn't see. Keeping my distance, I reached for his outflung arm and dragged him from the hollow in which he'd slept and now it was my turn to recoil: Musa had made his bed on a nest of vipers. The shapes of half a dozen of them lay coiled just below the surface of the sand, stirring and wriggling now as they sensed our presence.

"Oh God," I whispered, remembering his one sharp cry in the night. He must have been deeply asleep when the first viper stung him, its poison not quite enough to kill, perhaps, but as he struggled toward consciousness the others had surfaced to bury their fangs in his flesh and to do their terrible work. He'd not had a chance. Just that one cry before the flood of venom halted his life.

And we had lost our guide.

To bury him was impossible, for we lacked both tools and stamina, and so we returned him to the hollow that he'd scooped out for sleep and in which he'd met his death. To wish him a good journey Bakuli said in Hausa, *"Sanu da tafiya,"* and then, gravely, *"iyaka ya kare"*—the end; it is finished.

Following this we had nothing to do but take stock of our own future, which had suddenly become even more precarious. We had Musa's *gero,* his Maria Theresa thalers and the silver Hand of Fatima, but none of these held any value at all in the desert when we had water for only two days at the most. No flags or cairns marked the wells of the Sahara, they were often only holes dug in the sand, and the knowledge of where they might exist had died with Musa.

Wearily we slung the guerbas over the donkey's back and set out to the south again toward the sandy plain ahead, wondering just how long we might outlive poor Musa.

Book 2

Book 2

eleven

~

There is a pale sun shining in London today, and Deborah has interrupted my writing of these pages with one of her whirl-
wind visits of inspection. She arrives every
few days to be sure that Bertram and
Minna are not taking advantage of me, that
mantels have been dusted, the furniture
polished, my diet obeyed and my health
still reasonably sound.

"Minna hasn't dusted your books
lately," she says, running her fingers over
them.

"Minna and Bertram are growing old,"

I tell her, "and a little dust never hurt anyone."

When she sees the bouquet of roses
on my desk her lips, as usual, tighten in
exasperation. Since the greenhouse in the
garden was closed four years ago I order
flowers from a florist, but she is remembering that until our gardener died it was he
who brought roses to me each morning, a
ritual that I still mourn and have insisted
upon continuing. Deborah always accused
me of being too familiar with John, con-
stantly reminding me that it was not good
form to be friendly with a gardener, and a
one-eyed gardener at that, with a patch
over his eye, but what she was really saying all those years was that she resented
John, and when I chided her for her snob-
bery I was really saying, *Beware, don't
trespass. . . .* I find Deborah an interesting combination of environment and heredity, and proof of how perverse genes
can be, for I meet in her all of Mum's ambi-
tiousness in a more sophisticated form,
and this is heredity, but from Linton, whom
she believes to be her father, she has acquired a certain coldness and all of his fas-
tidiousness, and this is the effect of envi-

ronment, let scientists make of this what they may. When Deborah was still very young, for instance, I knew that she would never marry purely for love—Linton had taught her too well the values of a title, money and position—and I was right, I think, for certainly her marriage proved a chilly and ill-fated match.

I feel a deep compassion for my daughter: her son died young and she was nearly forty when Sara was miraculously born—lovely, ardent Sara—except that Deborah has seemed determined ever since to not release her, seeing in her all the color and laughter she's missed. But if I feel compassion for my daughter it's kinship I feel with my granddaughter Sara. She has much of me and of Deborah's father in her, so that it never surprised me that she loved the stories our gardener told her by the hour when she was a child. She would have delighted in Grams, too; it is even possible that she would have felt at home in Laski's Carnival.

I collect such ironies now, it's the only form of humor that pleases me. I find it ironic, for instance, that my travels began with Jacob, who had studied many languages, whereas I, who knew only one language, would eventually make myself understood in half a dozen. Should I call this his legacy to me? How many times I used to speculate on what my life would have been if I'd never met him, only to find myself leaning heavily on tiresome *what-if's,* such as what if I'd never been sent to Boston, or had not been so young when I met him; what if he'd never proposed marriage, or had already been married or, failing these, what if he'd chosen another country, another desert or had never spent an evening in Algiers talking with a French White Father from Ghadames. The strings that bind us to our fates go too far back in time to untangle, and what I am left with in the end is a mosaic with each of its pieces cemented unalterably together, incapable of separation or removal.

But the brightest of the tiles in the mosaic is Jared, whom I will love to the end of my life, and there is Amina and the strange circumstances that taught me Mind Magic . . . and always there is Bakuli.

.   .   .

We came very near to losing our lives, Bakuli and I, but the worst of times came after Musa died. Two days following his death we had to abandon the donkey, and rather than leave him alive for the vultures, Bakuli, tight-lipped, slit his throat, and from drinking his blood we gained another night of travel. By sunset of the next day, however, we had finished our last drop of water and although we walked all night across the moonlit sand we met with no water hole—the gods were not smiling—and after the moon set the sun rose to gild the sky and then to torture us. There was no shade, not so much as a shrub or stone in this sandy waste, and the hot dust clogged our nostrils, eyes and lips. Once, long ago in Tripoli, Mohammed had described how people die of thirst, how the body, demanding water, begins to steal it from tissue and fat, the blood slowly thickening until it can no longer cool the body, and as it congeals the temperature soars and it all ends in delirium and death. He had failed to mention the stomach cramps, or the raw parched throat and the tongue so swollen that speech becomes impossible. Our strength dwindled quickly; when Bakuli stumbled and fell I would help him up, we would stagger a short distance and then it would be I who stumbled and fell, and Bakuli who helped me to my feet. It was noon when we gave up and lay down to die, no longer caring except that one last flicker of feeling moved me to reach out and cover Bakuli's eyes, remembering the vultures.

Our savior in no way resembled a heavenly angel, he was an Arab merchant traveling alone with a string of pack-donkeys piled high with trading goods, and he smelled of goat. Opening sand-encrusted eyes I saw a dark bearded face close to mine and realized that a hand was pressing the nape of my neck and lifting my head to give me water. It was a mirage, I knew this, but obediently I parted my lips, which he brushed with a few drops of water and then, holding me firm, placed a cup to my lips. I choked as water met my swollen tongue, gagged and gasped and swallowed painfully. Not a mirage, then, I had died and this was heaven. I lay back, dazed, and watched him move to Bakuli and give water to him, too. Glancing beyond him I saw the same unchanging sands, the sky still bleached white, and hope stirred: it was possible that I was not dead, it was possible that in this huge desert so empty of living human beings we had been miraculously seen by another living human being.

A donkey brayed, and then another: my glance swerved until I saw their beautiful, funny heads and I loved each one of them and smiled a little in spite of the pain of cracked and swollen lips. When the man returned to give more water I struggled to sit up but he gave me only a little. "La," he said sternly, withdrawing the cup, and returned to Bakuli. I loved this man as well as his donkeys but at that moment, seeing Bakuli lift his head, I most of all loved Bakuli; even then, only half-conscious, I knew I was being taught something new and important by this odd little Jesus-boy, but I was too weak to think what it might be.

Once we could stand—we could not speak yet—the man carried each of us to a donkey, and with ropes tied us to the bales of trading goods so that we'd not fall. He was a knowing man: before setting out he gave us each a wet rag to suck on, and twice stopped to give us more water. I was feverish and ill and noticed little until sun-set-time when we crossed a broad dry riverbed and I glanced up to see that the sky that had nearly killed us at noon was ablaze now with tender shades of gold, cream and plum. At dusk we passed an acacia tree, and beside it a thatched hut with posts of wood carved with intricate figures. Beyond this, before darkness dropped like a curtain, I could see the brushwood fences of a settlement rising out of the earth. It was to this cluster of huts that our good Arab was delivering us, calling over his shoulder to say that here lived a woman named Amina who would make us well again.

We rode through a gap in the high brushwood fence and into a cleared space of beaten-down earth where a fire burned in the darkness like a lamp, with dim shad-ows surrounding it. Our entrance was ac-companied by a roar of thunder and the sky suddenly blazed with lightning that illu-minated dark faces turned toward us in surprise. Even Laski's Carnival couldn't have arranged a more dramatic entrance, and to top it off the sky opened up and we were deluged with rain. Blessed rain! There were joyous shouts of *"Ruwa! Ruwa!"* We had brought with us a storm, it seemed, but I had no idea what this meant for them or for us because upon being lifted down from the donkey I fell to the ground in a deep faint, to wander in and out of consciousness for the next few days.

Yet I was aware . . .

There was a woman who fussed over me like Grams except that her face was black, with a thin taut mouth and watchful bright eyes. Her voice was sharp when she forced bitter liquids down my throat, but it was she who was always there; others came to look at me and once—but this was surely a dream?—I heard the flutter of wings and a chicken squawk in outrage, and opening my eyes I swear I saw her slit a chicken's throat while five women crouched in a circle, pointing, talking and glancing toward me. Once I heard drums beating and I was frightened, thinking myself back among the Tuareg; on another occasion, waking, the hut was illuminated by great flashes of lightning, followed by thunder, or did I confuse this with the sound of drums? When it was dark there was a lantern and the smell of peanut oil and shadows that leaped up and down the thatch overhead; by day the smells were of a strange incense, hot earth, spice and dung, and always there was the beehive murmur of voices outside. I drifted in and out of sleep, utterly depleted, feeling a hundred years old and tired beyond words. I had no idea where I was but I felt safe, which struck me as funny in my lucid moments because I could have fallen into the hands of cannibals for all I knew. It was my spirit that was tired, I told myself, and this word struck me as funny, too, because I remembered how Bakuli had talked of spirits in trees and rocks, and hadn't I imagined a spirit when we'd spent the night in that hill of rocks near Abalessa? Bakuli had been with me then, and Bakuli had been in the desert with me, too, but where was he now?

I opened my eyes the next morning to find him standing over me, and being still very weak, I came near to sobbing with relief at sight of him. When last seen, his face had been a mottled gray, and shrunken, but now he looked restored, his cheeks round again, his smile radiant. "Missy," he said. "Oh, Missy, you be well, please."

I nodded, smiling. "Yes—better now. Oh Bakuli!"

"Amina make good medicine," he said, and went away.

The next time I woke the shadows were long, and the little sparrow of a woman was seated in the center of the hut mixing something in a calabash with a long wooden spoon. "Amina?" I whispered.

She turned, all smiles. *"Sanu! Sanu!"* she cried in delight.

Wild with hope I asked, "Do you—by chance—speak any Arabic? Any English?"

"Sanu da gajia," she responded, her eyes bright. *"Sanu, sanu,"* and pouring water from a clay jug she brought it to me saying, *"Ruwa, bako."*

Obviously she did not speak Arabic or English and this reminded me that I must have been sick for days and that it was time to end my convalescence and discover what lay outside, and find Bakuli who might explain where we were. Hastening my resolution even more was the realization that, perversely, and much to my surprise, I was missing the stars and great space of the desert, for lying on my back and looking upward my eyes bumped hard against a low ceiling of thatch. This so irritated and angered me that I wanted to tear aside the roof to see the sky.

The next morning, being alone, I rose and limped to the door and looked out to see more thatched walls encircling me. *These people do not like space,* I thought, for Amina's hut was one of many inside a crowded compound. I saw five goats, I saw a bare-breasted woman pounding grain on a stone, I counted four children chasing the goats and nine thatched-roofed huts, the center one the largest. My eyes moved to the sky, the great encompassing sky that for a year or more had pleased, awed, nurtured, guided, tranquilized and nearly killed me, and it was at this moment that I understood how the silence and space of the desert enters the soul, never to be exorcised.

Standing there thinking of this I saw Bakuli enter the compound and walk toward me, his face surprised and glad to see me standing. "You be up, Missy!" he exclaimed, and to the woman pounding grain he said quite grandly, *"Sanu du rana."*

With the crossness of a convalescent I said, "Bakuli, you're showing off, what language now?"

He grinned. "Hausa, Missy."

"And you're wearing a new shirt?"

"Musa's silver Maria Theresa dollar. You not be angry?"

"No. Poor Musa," I said. He, too, had been Hausa and now I determined to find out where we were, and with whom, and I asked.

Piecing together what Bakuli told me I learned that we were in a small Hausa-speaking village, called a *gari,* that had taken root in a belt of green at the fringe of the desert. It was thorn country laced with dried-up oueds that filled with water in the rainy season, and except in prolonged droughts there was underground water to be tapped for wells, so that the village goats and sheep not only had ample pasturage but I would see later that beyond the thatch walls there were fields of ripening guinea corn.

"And we bring rain," he said proudly. "They say so, Missy." He held up two fingers. "Rain this many days while thou sleep. They name it *fari* here when it be rain season and rain stop—*hai!* too soon. There be harvest soon, Missy, and"—he gave me a sly mischievous look—"we bring it."

"You know we didn't," I told him sternly.

He shrugged. "It rain, Missy. Thunder god speak and rain fall, we come."

"True." I didn't feel strong enough to argue. "Where have they put you, Bakuli?"

"Put me?"

"Where do you sleep at night?"

"With men, Missy; women no."

I was surprised. "You mean only women live in this compound where I am?"

He shook his head impatiently. "No no, Missy." Pointing to the large hut in the center he said, "Amina be wife to man who sleep there. She be first wife, new wife sleep there this day." He pointed to the smaller huts. "Sons sleep—" Again he pointed, this time to the right and left.

"Two wives," I murmured. "Well, well . . . Bakuli, she calls me *bako,* why?"

"It mean 'stranger.' " Having so

proudly explained our circumstances to me, he was silent now, gazing with a frown at a circle of pots nearby on a bed of ash. "Missy," he said at last.

"Yes?"

He sighed. "There be trouble here, Missy. This village chief be named Kadiri—very good man but his son Shehu sick many days now. Amina make good medicine, she heal many people but not Shehu. The witch doctor—"

"Witch doctor! *Witch doctor?*" I gasped.

"Yes, Missy, he be one to guard against witches, he throw cowrie shells to say when to plant corn, he make poison test learning truth in peoples. He say Shehu be possessed by spirit and he tell Shehu's father sacrifices to make, but Shehu still sick."

I said dryly, "I'm very sorry."

"Yes, Missy, but—" All of his bravado gone, he looked at me with a troubled face. "We bring rain, Missy, chief Kadiri say we have power to heal Shehu."

I said suspiciously, "What do you mean 'we'? *I* didn't bring rain."

He said stubbornly, "We come, Missy, it rain. And you know ettama."

I ignored the word *ettama*. "Tell the chief I have no power, Bakuli, I'm sick, I can't even walk yet. Is the son sick with fever? What's wrong with him, anyway?"

Bakuli confided that Shehu threw pots and broke them, he made noise, threw food to the earth and tore off his clothes. They had built a reed hut with a fence and gate to isolate him, but although they burned incense for him and gave him medicine he still roared and shouted.

"Good heavens, a madman?" I sputtered. "Bakuli, you've got to be *firm.* Tell this witch doctor—"

"His name be Isa."

"Well, tell this Isa that if the rains came as we reached this village they should be glad and ask no more—enough is enough. We've done our best and we're tired."

Bakuli said slowly, "I do not think this witch doctor *like* us bringing rain, it be village chief who want magic tomorrow."

"No, Bakuli!" I protested.

He ignored my anger. "Amina tell them you be woman and not Arab, your

skin so dark. I tell them you be Bāturē—
that be Hausa name for foreign peoples.
This witch doctor laugh at thee but village
chief say just see how Bāturē make war
and bring new gods, you must have *strong*
medicine."

"The chief is wrong," I told him coldly.

He gave me a reproachful glance and
walked away affronted. Turning once he
said stiffly, "I try to tell you softly, Missy—
chief say he send for thee in morning."

Appalled, I stared at the gate through
which he'd disappeared. Witch doctors,
madmen— *Oh, Jacob,* I thought, and crept
back into the dim hut to think what to do
about this unhappy decree.

It was Shakespeare who finally dissi-
pated my convalescent inertia and anxieties, and I must admit that I never expected to meet him again in a hot thatched
hut in the Sahara. It was one of those
Shakespearean passages that a very
young Caressa had memorized as she
thrilled at being sixteen and ready for *life*
and thought she could find recipes for living it in books. . . . Yet here again was
that mosaic, for I might so easily have become a juggler, a magician or a headless

woman in Laski's Carnival but I had met with books instead. The words I remembered from Shakespeare urged me to "screw my courage to the sticking point," and in one of the *King Henry*s there was something about "What fates impose man must abide and not resist both wind and tide." I decided that if my lack of *ettama* was going to be exposed I might as well get it over with and face the consequences because I couldn't hide myself forever in Amina's hut: it was boring, it was hot, and there was no sky. I now determined to confront what the fates imposed with a style that fitted a Caressa who had grown up in a carnival.

Amina slept that night, but not I. In the morning we ate corn mush with a hot spice sauce, and for me there was goat's milk. Reaching for Amina's calabash I drummed on it and by way of sign language told her I would need a drum. Nodding, she left the hut to reappear carrying one of carved wood and leather with skins stretched taut across each end of it, and soon after that a scared-looking Bakuli appeared in the doorway to announce that the chief was here, Missy, and I stood up nervously.

Kadiri was not as frightening as expected and under different circumstances I might even have thought he looked kind. He was marvelously dressed in a long cotton tunic embroidered with bright colors and his head was wrapped in a turban made out of so many yards of cloth that it continued around his neck like a muffler and fell gracefully to his waist. I bowed and he spoke warmly to Amina; I gave instructions to Bakuli who told the chief that he, Bakuli, must walk in front of me beating a drum. This was produced and we set out.

As soon as we walked through the gate of Amina's compound it became obvious that every hut in the village had been emptied to watch. A few daring women came near enough to touch me or peer into my face before they fell back, murmuring and giggling. "Where is this Shehu?" I asked Bakuli, and he pointed to a fence of thatch at the far edge of the village.

"Beat the drum," I told him.

Space was cleared for us and Bakuli moved ahead of me, noisily announcing our arrival. I walked with the chief, trying to look mysterious and dedicated. As we neared the end of the path and the hut of the sick man I could hear loud noises from behind his wall. At the gate a man stood waiting for us, and out of the corner of his mouth, between drum beats, Bakuli said, "That be witch doctor Isa."

Isa was dressed entirely in white: an immaculate white robe and white head-scarf, and the effect was dazzling against his shining ebony-black face. He looked pleasant enough, but as he stepped back from the entrance to Shehu's compound his glance at me was mocking. *Beware of this man,* I told myself.

With Bakuli thumping his drum the two of us entered what I would have called a yard, in which a grass hut had been built in one corner. Shehu sat in the doorway surrounded by decaying food and shards of broken pottery; we had interrupted his bashing of a huge clay water jug and his arm was still poised over it; he brought his arm down slowly, glowering at us. For a moment I thought he was naked, but as he rose to his feet I was relieved to see that he wore a loincloth. He was a short, stocky young man with an angry and suspicious face. Picking up the remnant of another clay pot he threw it at me; it broke into even smaller pieces at my feet.

I told Bakuli that he could stop beating the drum. I figured that whatever I tried to do had to be done with a flourish, because I had almost nothing to offer, and so, ignoring Shehu, I walked to the center of the yard and slowly sank to my knees. Lifting both arms to the sky I began to intone the only chant I knew, one that Indian Joe had taught me years ago after he'd met a real Indian and memorized it. I cried out, *"Hi lo eenie meenie ki ki umpchi wa pe wa wa,"* and then I threw back my head and began to hum M's like a bumblebee. Expanding on this, I chanted, "Minnymouseymoleymastermilky moo-moo mothymucky," and reaching a crescendo pitch, shouted, "Murkymoonymushymissy moonshine-*massaCHUsetts. . . ."*

Shehu had stopped throwing things and was looking at me as if I was crazy, which gave us something in common. Slowly rising to my feet I chanted, "Peter Piper picked a peck of pickled peppers a peck of pickled peppers Peter Piper picked. . . ." Approaching Shehu I did a few hops, skips and jumps—I had his attention now—and holding out a scrap of red cloth I waved it in the air, tucked it up the left sleeve of my barracan and after a few more dance steps drew it out of my right sleeve.

I was losing him, this didn't impress him in the slightest. I shoved both hands into the pockets of my barracan and went on mumbling, and then I shouted, "Shehu!" and when he looked at me again, thoroughly bored, I brought both hands out of my pockets with Mr. Jappy on one finger and the clown on the other, and I pushed them into his face.

He jumped in astonishment and then, peering at them, he burst out laughing.

I heard a stir of surprise from the audience behind me at the gate. I thought: *Well, Grams always said laughter's just like a laxative the way it clears the system.*

It was a giddy childish triumph for me, shocking this man out of his great despair. Later, when I knew more of his language, I found Shehu one of the most intelligent men I'd ever met, which must surely have taken him down the only path he could think of to express his frustration and his rage. If he had been truly mad, of course, I would have failed. In the meantime, thoroughly exhausted, I was returned to Amina's hut to rest on my laurels.

Unfortunately the mores of the village were so intricate and so exacting that I was not to enjoy my triumph for long.

It was the drums that night that sent me into a panic. Long ago, or so it seemed to me now, I had listened to the sound of drums echoing through the canyons of the Hoggar Mountains—that dark haunted fortress of the Tuareg—and hearing them I had often shivered. Bakuli said they were talking drums, but where I came from people didn't talk with drums, they sent messages Western Union, or by mail, or they rang a doorbell. The sound of drums represented everything mysterious and alien to me and resonated with vague and atavistic terrors. Nor had my fears been reduced at all by the sound of them when we neared the hill of rocks at Abalessa, implying that our presence was watched by unseen eyes.

I did not react well to drums, no, and Amina wasn't in the hut to reassure me. She was frequently gone; Bakuli explained that when she was absent it was her turn to cook for her husband and share his bed, and when she came back the new wife had taken her place. Alone and still recovering from fever and exhaustion I went berserk.

I fled the compound.

I ran, not even surprised that it was possible, knowing only that I had to get away from the relentless beat of the drums. I raced out of the village into the darkness, heedless of where I went, and the pale new moon was of little help to me for I stumbled again and again until I met with something seen once before, even though my recollection of it was dim: it was a hut standing under an acacia tree at a distance from the village, its thatch roof supported by posts carved with intricate designs. I felt my way inside, patting the earth to be sure there were neither snakes nor humans here, and reaching the farthest corner I sat down and hugged my knees. The noise of the drums was muted here and presently, calmer, I fell asleep.

It was not dawn that woke me but the light of a torch that found me where I lay. I opened my eyes and Amina was standing in the doorway looking down at me, shocked, while behind her a crowd of faces peered over her shoulder. I rose to my feet and Amina made room for me to come out, which I did, blinking at the light of the torches and at finding so many people outside, all of them staring at me accusingly.

Voices spoke: some were hard and some were shrill but all were hostile. I had no idea what was wrong and when several of the men moved toward me threateningly I wondered if they planned to kill me, except that Amina placed herself in front of me and spoke words to them I couldn't understand.

It was then that Bakuli stepped out of the crowd and held out his hand to me.

"Missy, come," he said.

"Bakuli, what have I done?" I whispered.

He said quietly, "This be sacred place, Missy, like Jesus-church. Village spirits live here."

Grasping my hand he led me through the crowd of villagers who fell back to let us pass, but not without comment. The principal word that I heard from their lips seemed to be *wawa,* hurled at me either in reproach or anger.

What, I asked Bakuli, did *wawa* mean.

"It mean 'fool,' " he said, and that was that.

I had been lonely before but not like this; I had been lonely in the days after the massacre but there had been a terrible anger to support me—at Umar, at Jacob, at life itself—and out of that I had fashioned a hope of escape that sustained me, and then I had met Bakuli and my loneliness had diminished. Now I felt I had lost him for he lived under a different roof and had recovered from the desert much faster than I, he was learning more Hausa words and the names of the people and he fitted in, whereas I was a bako and condemned to Amina's hut to nurse a stubborn fever that came and went. Even worse, I had shocked and embarrassed Bakuli by desecrating a sacred shrine and it seemed obvious that he also thought me a fool.

It was the next morning that I woke to discover that I couldn't move my left arm; overnight it had become lifeless, no better than a stick of wood. I lay on the mat gritting my teeth while I tried to feel it, lift it, move it, but my arm refused to obey; I tried until I was reduced to tears, and only then did I call to Amina.

She was outside feeding her chickens and came to me at once. *"Sanu, sanu, Amina,"* I cried, "but look—my arm!" Sitting up I slipped my right hand under my left arm and lifted it. "It's died, Amina," I sobbed. "It's paralyzed."

She took me in her arms and held me —she really was like Grams—and when I'd quieted she sat back and examined my arm, tested it by lifting it, and watched it drop to dangle uselessly when she let it go.

"Wàhalā," she exclaimed. *"Sihiri!"* Her lips pursed as she stared at my arm and then at last, "Bakuli," she said and went out.

When she returned it was with Bakuli and the chief, Kadiri. Behind them came Shehu, but it did not just then lighten my spirits to see him no longer filthy but wearing a clean white robe. He smiled shyly at me, but more important Bakuli was all worry and fear for me, I could read this on his face and see how morbid my imagination had been.

"Oh, Missy, Amina say it be black magic," he said. "She call it *sihiri*."

I laughed hysterically at hearing this, although my laugh ended in a sob, but no attention was paid to me for they all began talking at once. After a few minutes Shehu stopped talking and walked to the doorway of the hut. I saw him kneel down to examine the earth, and suddenly he called out to the others, pointing.

I went with them, carrying my dead arm, to see what had been found. On the path to the hut there were furrows and wrinkles in the sandy clay, as if recently the earth had been disturbed. Amina brought Shehu a hoe and bid me sharply to go back into the hut. She looked alarmed and worried. *"Sihiri,"* she kept saying, and gave orders.

Bakuli translated for me. "Thou must not look," he said, reverting to his old way of speaking, which I found very comforting just now. With Amina barring the door I could only guess them to be digging in the earth until I heard exclamations and Amina turned away, looking sick. Whatever had been buried was lifted out, placed in a cloth and handed to the chief, Kadiri, who went away with it. Hastily Bakuli followed, depriving me of making any sense of it all, and since this left me with Amina, with whom I couldn't communicate, I had no idea what dreadful object had been removed. I watched her walk around the hut and select herbs hanging from the ceiling. Frowning, she peered into clay jars and brought out strange twigs and leaves and ominous-looking powders; these she spread on a mat in front of her and sat down and looked at them.

I looked at them, too, baffled.

When she began a toneless chant my eyes moved to her face, half of it in shadow, half illuminated by the sunlight that fell across one cheekbone, the tip of her nose and then ran down her arm to fix itself brightly on the objects in front of her. She was all black and gold sitting there, her red head kerchief turned orange by the sun. When her chanting stopped she placed the mix in a bowl and added water, stirred until it was a paste and applied it to my lifeless arm.

I thought, *I'll go mad if I stay in this place. I've got to leave, there has to be a way.* In my mind's eye I tried to recall the

maps of Africa that I'd looked at so carelessly in Boston when Jacob had shown
them to me. There was the desert—I didn't
want to think of the desert—but when I'd
known Mohammed he had explained why
so few caravans came to Tripoli now and
he had spoken of colonies established in
the south by the French and the British below the Sahara. . . . Perhaps heading
south had not been such folly after all, in
spite of its being so empty of people and
so full of death. If I could only find one of
those colonies!

Thoughts of this occupied me for
most of the day until near dusk I borrowed
a wooden spoon from Amina and began to
trace lines on the earthen floor in an attempt to reconstruct a map of the continent. It was not until I had firmly grasped
the spoon that I realized I was holding it
with my dead hand. I cried out to Amina
and lifted my arm to show her that it had
come to life again, but Amina only smiled
politely and nodded without any surprise
at all.

There was no mystery to Bakuli about
an arm that had become wooden for those
many hours. We sat under a tree outside

Amina's compound and nearly quarreled over this until I learned to hold my tongue, not wanting to alienate him as well. It was very plain to him that one of the witches in the *gari*—

"*One* of them?" I gasped.

"Yes, Missy." One of them, he went on, must have become very angry at my entering the sacred shrine, so angry that he or she wanted to harm me, and had buried—he wouldn't say what—on the path where I would walk. He shook his head over this disapprovingly, because, he said in a troubled voice, this could have harmed Amina as well. I would have protested such indifference to my own fate except that he gave every evidence of being worried about me, too.

I pointed out in a mild voice that besides removing whatever had been buried, Amina had made good medicine for my arm.

He looked at me pityingly. It was not what had been buried, he said, or what herbs had been used, it was the words spoken over them, the incantations, that gave power. "Hausa word for power be *iko,"* he added. "Some person have much *iko* here. Amina speak to medicine?"

I nodded.

"There—thou see? She call spirits to heal."

This was too much. By now I had adjusted to the strange occurrences at the hill of rocks near Abalessa; it had become plain to me that I'd been hungry, tired and frightened, which made me easy prey to nightmarish imaginings, and since then I'd learned of Sahara dreams and fevers of the mind, but this . . . ! I said peevishly, "Bakuli, all this talk of spirits—show me one, just one that I can *see.*"

"Missy, what place thou come from?" He shook his head in despair over me. "Thou cut down a tree and it cry. There be rocks to sit on full of sadness and rocks to sit on full of blessings. They not know this in place you come from?"

"No," I snapped, and might have been drawn into argument again if Shehu had not suddenly appeared to interrupt us.

"Bako," he said shyly to me, and hesitated. His white cotton robe was dustier than it had been yesterday but his eyes were calm, and I was glad to see him because I had apparently offended everyone else in the village. Glancing furtively around him he sat down beside me and drew from under his robe a sharp knife— this alarmed me, but having placed this on his lap he brought out a small block of wood that had been trimmed and chiseled into the rough shape of my finger puppet. Although it was a very bumpy wooden egg shape there was already the beginning of a hole in it in which to insert a finger.

I looked at him in surprise, not expecting this.

He spoke and Bakuli, translating, said, "He asks to see thy magic finger."

It was the blond Isabelle that I drew from my pocket and held out to him. I watched as he gently grasped it with two long slender fingers, and there was no laughter this time at seeing it, nor was he interested at all in the yellow string curls and black lashes on the girl-face. He gave all of his attention to the smoothness of the surface and to examining the slant and depth of the hole that had been drilled, studying the size and craft of it like a serious scholar.

Or like an artist.

Very gravely he returned it to me, nodding, and looking closely into my face he stood up, pointed behind us, smiled and said, *"Zō nân."*

"He wants us to go with him," said Bakuli.

The village was nearly deserted, for both men and women were in the fields beginning to harvest guinea corn today, and only a few of the very old remained. Shehu led us through his compound and into a hut, at the back of which hung a screen of matting that he pulled aside to reveal a dark anteroom. Beckoning us inside he fumbled with a lantern, lighting it, and as the flame in it grew brighter I saw what the room held and I gasped.

It was filled with wonderful carved figures with strange primitive faces, two of them taller than Shehu. There was a totem-like pole leaning against one wall with serpents and faces carved on it; there were lovely small fun carvings of life in the village: a man beating a drum, a woman carrying water, a woman weaving, a child playing, all of these last carved or whittled with much humor. But the large figures were awesome.

"Oh, Shehu," I murmured.

Bakuli nodded, his eyes huge. *"Kai!"* he whispered.

Shehu beamed at us, a wonderful pleasure lighting up his face as he watched us.

And yet . . . "Bakuli," I said, "he *hides* these? Why are they kept here like a secret?"

He shrugged sadly. "Like Bakuli's village long ago, Missy, the man who carve wood in village must be son of man who carve wood and forefather be man who carve wood, and this man be Sallisu. And that be that."

"Waste," I sputtered angrily. "Absolute *waste.*"

Several days later when I was well enough to join Amina at work in the fields, I would see how hard Shehu worked there, too, this man who had to look and act like every other farmer in his village, obey the customs, obey his father, marry and sire children, put food in their bellies and appease his spirits while all the time there burned in him this great flame of creativeness that had to be hidden.

There was a hunger in him to learn as

well. "To fill his head," said Bakuli dryly, for Shehu was curious to know what language I spoke. To everyone except Bakuli I was *bako,* the stranger of a different color and habits, and even worse a mere woman and tolerated only because of Bakuli and my healing of Shehu. But to Shehu, for all these reasons, I was of vast interest. He was not afraid to speak with me in this village where women were regarded of little importance. Holding up a stone he would say, *"Dūtsē."*

Repeating this carefully I would nod and say, "Stone."

"Stoon?"

"Stone."

"Stone." He would touch the gnarled acacia tree and say, *"Itācē."*

I would imitate the throaty sound he made and say, "Tree."

"Tree." This one made him laugh.

And later, *"Tāshī."*

I would grin and stand up.

"Zaunā." I would sit.

"Nīnē," he'd say, and point to himself.

"Nīcē," I'd counter, pointing at myself. "It's *me.*"

"It's me," he would shout joyously.

I began thus to acquire more Hausa words. They were not Muslim here. When I could understand more of their language, Amina told me that long ago they had fled from the East to preserve their ancient beliefs, led by a wise oracle named Fagaci who had foreseen tribal wars, the coming of white men and the worship of an alien prophet. It was Fagaci's spirit that guarded their village now, and every year they made sacrifices to him. Tactfully I did not ask at what shrines they honored him; by now I'd learned there were other shrines, in particular an acacia tree that was very old and taller than any of the others that were scattered through the village, but the most sacred was the shrine that I'd inadvertently slept inside.

There would be more offerings and sacrifices once the harvesting was finished, Bakuli told me, and there would be dancing and *kadē-kadē*. "*Kadē* what?" I asked suspiciously.

"Beating of drums, Missy."

I would have to brace myself for that, but there was no drumming or dancing in the evenings yet, not after long hours of work in the sun. There was only Isa squatting under the acacia tree with his divining board, and someone asking questions of it while Isa tossed cowrie shells across the board in a complicated procedure that would produce an answer. To Isa I was invisible, however; he would not acknowledge my presence, as if he knew me to be a fraud when I healed Shehu.

This was my life, then, as well as the work in the fields and the harvest that was being gathered before the season of the harmattan began, which here they called the *hūntūrū,* and what I assumed was known in Tripoli as the gibleh, and certainly it should have been a fine harvest this year. With the exception of the short dry spell they called *fari,* which had ended with our arrival, the rains had fallen at almost precisely the right times for germination and growth, but tragedy struck when only half of the fields had been harvested.

The locusts came.

They arrived from the south, darkening the sky until it was like twilight; they descended on those fields that were still golden with ripe guinea corn and they devoured them row by row. The villagers mounted an attack. Drums were beaten, sticks and clubs thrashed away, but all that was left by night were great heaps of dead locusts that crunched under the feet. All during that night by the light of torches the dead grasshoppers were collected in sacks to dry, because with half of the harvest gone this, too, was food to keep away the enemy of hunger.

There was no celebration and there was no *kadē-kadē.* What had once seemed a happy village became a somber one now, but what I did not understand just then was the necessity for the village to uncover the cause of this catastrophe. As I would learn later, they believed in a Supreme Being whom they called the Giver of Life and Breath, but apparently their Supreme Being left most of the work to the hierarchy of spirits below it, and whatever technicalities were involved in their detective work—and Isa's divining board was kept busy—the loss of half their crops implied a punishment to the village. Something was very wrong. A spirit had been offended.

This led to the bako who had violated their sacred shrine by entering and sleep-

ing in it. Obviously the spirits of the shrine
had been angered by this.

"Who says so?" I demanded of
Bakuli.

"Isa."

"Isa doesn't like me," I told him. "He
didn't like my success with Shehu when
he'd failed. He doesn't like a woman and a
bako doing that."

"You sleep in shrine at harvesttime,"
Bakuli told me reproachfully, and I had to
remember that in spite of his being a
Jesus-boy, he'd been bred in a village just
as cluttered with witch doctors, spirits and
medicine men. All this was making him
very unhappy, I could see that.

"I think it's Isa who wants me punished," I said indignantly.

Bakuli shook his head. "He very fair,
Missy, at dawn he make sacrifice at shrine
and ask for dream to say what needed."

"Well," I said angrily, "he can make
up any dream he pleases, can't he?" But
underlying my anger was a growing fear of
helplessness as I realized that my life was
suddenly in the hands of a witch doctor, of
all people, and a hostile one at that; it was
not an agreeable feeling. Bakuli went away

looking worried and Amina avoided looking at me. I supposed, rightly, that we were all waiting for Isa to produce his dream.

By midmorning Isa's dream had been produced—rather quickly, I thought—and Amina began looking at me again, but with compassion. It needed Bakuli to explain the outcome to me: Isa had been advised in his dream to turn this matter over to the spirits of the shrine and to ask for a sign from them as to whether I should be punished or forgiven for the desecration of their sacred home. I was to be taken there and I was to stay at the shrine until—but here Bakuli became vague, mumbling something about a clay bowl and looking depressed. After this Amina further alarmed me by heaping charms in my lap and telling me in words and signs that she would bury more charms in the earth to protect me, but protect me from what was not clear.

So it was that when the sun was almost noon-high Kadiri, Isa and half the village came for me.

"Zō," Isa said, and Bakuli reminded me he meant "come," and Amina said, "Rânkà yà dadē," which Bakuli said was her wish that my life might be prolonged, which was not reassuring, and after this we all streamed in a procession out of the village and across the scrub to the distant solitary acacia tree and the shrine. Once there my uneasiness increased when I saw thin leather ropes brought out. It seemed that I was to be tethered like a goat to one of the posts of the hut, unable to stand or walk and apparently capable of creeping only as far as the hole they were digging several feet away from me, which was dug for what might be called bathroom privileges.

"Zaunā," said the chief gently.

I sat down and glared at the two men as they distributed the ropes around me, measuring the slack in them and tying knots. I was shown a clay bowl, not understanding why, and politely looked at it; a drab object with a thin crack on the outside that had not penetrated to the smoother clay inside. The bowl was then placed on the earth some eight or nine feet in front of me.

"Why there?" I asked. "What's that for?"

Bakuli, subdued and a little frightened,

translated Isa's words for me: it was through the bowl that the spirits of the shrine would speak.

"How?" I demanded. "You can't be serious!"

I swear I saw tears in Bakuli's eyes. If the spirits forgave me, he said, the crack in the bowl would open and the bowl would break into pieces. "If they forgive thee," he repeated.

I gasped, "But that's impossible, I'll be here forever!" Certainly if this was a test it was one I couldn't foresee ever passing; looking at Isa suspiciously I said, "How long must I be tied here, surely there's an end to this?"

Bakuli spoke haltingly to Isa who said, *"Biyu,"* and held up two fingers.

"Two days, Missy," Bakuli said.

"And nights? This was in his dream?" I asked bitterly. Seeing the look on the witch doctor's face I did not ask what would happen to me when the bowl remained intact, as it must; this question I swallowed since it not only had a bad taste but I refused to give Isa that much satisfaction. He was certainly looking very smug. Conceited, too, I thought, in his dazzling white robes that gave him the look of a black king. Kadiri, on the other hand, who was the chief of the *gari,* looked precisely what he was, a farmer with a worn kind face that had endured drought and abundance, hard and good times. Isa, I decided, had experienced only power. Or *iko,* as Bakuli named it.

As for me, I could see that I had made a powerful enemy. "And when it's dark," I pointed out coldly, "and there are snakes and jackals?"

Bakuli said uneasily, "He say spirits be with thee. Please, Missy," he begged, reading the thoughts on my face. "Bakuli pray hard to Jesus-God for thee."

"You will have to pray hard then, Bakuli," I told him, "for I know of no way to break a bowl I can't touch."

Bakuli said with dignity, "I pray hard to spirits of shrine too, Missy."

Placing a jug of water near me, they all walked back to the village, leaving me alone in this hot bleak landscape, ostracized and abandoned—and abandoned was how I felt, tied to a heathen post in the middle of Africa and all because I'd slept in their blasted shrine and desecrated it. For a little while I cultivated this anger but it had little nourishment when it did nothing to alter my situation, nor did I feel playful enough to bring a finger puppet from my ragged barracan to share my stormy thoughts.

"Break, darn you," I shouted to the clay bowl. "Break—*BREAK!*"

I tried throwing pebbles at the bowl and grew quite skillful but the bowl remained impervious to attack. I stared hard at it, ordering it to break. I sprawled out as far as my leash would allow and talked to the bowl, scolding it, shouting to it to break.

When this grew tiresome I made little hills out of the sand and then little houses. A spider walked across one of my houses and I watched it. "Hello," I told it, "did you know that in Hausa you're called *gizo-gizo?*" He was not impressed and disappeared under the acacia tree. I returned to staring at the bowl, trying hopelessly to make my stare so piercing it might affect it. In the hot and drowzy stillness I began to notice my breathing, and became curious as to how long I could hold my breath. I counted to five and thought this a macabre way to entertain myself, and so I began to recite aloud what I remembered from Marcus Aurelius, then Shakespeare and Omar Khayyám.

After this, by a glance at the sun, I saw that scarcely an hour had passed.

In midafternoon a boy I'd never seen before brought me a fresh jug of water, and food. He did not linger or speak; I slept a little, but when I woke nothing had changed, I was still captive and the earth glaringly hot. Just in case there really were spirits at the shrine I addressed them with authority and then plaintively, asking them to forgive me and break the bowl, but nothing happened. I began to study the carvings on the post behind me and then the lacy shadows cast by the acacia tree. I picked up stones and made designs with them, circles and squares and triangles; I noticed they were not alike in color, which surprised me because they'd all looked the same at first glance. I wondered if I preferred the dull green stones to the gray, or perhaps the brown, and then I saw a pale blue one and named that my favorite.

As the shadows lengthened, I finally brought out my clown puppet, and then

Mr. Jappy, knowing that I'd saved them for this hour when night was coming and I would be afraid, but even they couldn't ease the terrible sense of desolation that kept me company, and after a few words I put them away again. I watched an orange sun slide behind the village, leaving the sky a fiery scarlet, and I took one last look at the level ground between me and the village gate: at the patches of low scrub, the pair of stunted acacia trees and the worn path leading past me to disappear at the gate, but it was what might lie behind me that made me the more uneasy. Darkness fell quickly and there came a great stillness; I sat unhappily and waited for the moon to rise high enough to show me the danger that I felt was all around me. Somewhere off in the distance I heard the cry of a jackal. Behind me, behind the sacred shrine, a twig snapped and I tensed, and then came silence, but I felt watched now, and very cold.

The moon slowly cleared the acacia, desert-bright, so bright that I could see each pebble and even the crack in the bowl so tauntingly out of reach. The last glow of lanterns in the village was extinguished. In the rear of the hut I heard more rustling sounds, something was moving, but animal or human I couldn't tell. As the moon climbed higher my eyelids grew heavy; I curled up against the post and tried without success to stay awake. I woke with a start, trembling as I heard jackals quarreling behind the hut. The sound rose, lifting my panic; I covered my ears and waited for them to find me, the noise subsided into growls and off to my right a dark shape ran into the night and disappeared into the brush. I thought next I heard a laugh and wondered if I was going mad.

Around midnight I dozed off again but in my dreams horrible demon faces swam toward me and then receded. When I woke it was to hear frightening noises, snarls, movements all around me. It was an endless night, full of shadows, sounds, cries. When dawn came I was exhausted.

It was Bakuli who brought me goat's milk and found me shivering and crying. "Oh, Missy," he whispered.

"The jackals," I gasped. "Bakuli they were here; I can't imagine why I'm still alive."

He sat down on the ground facing me while I thirstily drank the milk. He looked puzzled. "Jackals, Missy? No jackals."

I said impatiently, "How could you know? They were all around me, I heard them, I even saw one as he ran away."

"Missy," he said quietly, "no jackals."

"Bakuli—"

He shook his head. "Missy, Bakuli watch all night over thee." He turned and pointed to the pair of stunted acacias halfway between us and the village gate. "I sit and watch thee all night, I see thee wake, I see thee sleep."

"You did that?" I marveled. "But surely you heard how they quarreled and fought near the shrine."

"Missy, I hear nothing. Nothing," he repeated.

"I didn't imagine it," I told him. "You must have fallen asleep."

"No, Missy, Amina give me medicine to keep eyes open. No sleep."

We had reached stalemate. I said limply, "Well, I'm terribly glad to see you, Bakuli, and thank you for watching."

"Amina bring food—and Isa come, see?" He turned to watch them walk toward us and his glance fell to the bowl. "Bowl not broken, Missy."

I shrugged. "I have no ettama for that, Bakuli, the bowl will not break and no spirits will break it. And," I added, "there were jackals here in the night."

He did not comment but he looked worried, thinking perhaps that I was halfway to madness. Isa reached us, and following a quick glance at the bowl he gave me a look in which I read triumph. Amina was kinder, she said, *"Sanu da dajia,"* meaning "greetings to my weariness"— and I was certainly weary after the terrors of the night. She had brought corn gruel, and once this was set down beside me Isa said, *"Zō."*

I watched them walk back to the village through the scrub and sand and nothing felt real to me anymore. When they disappeared I was engulfed by such feelings of loneliness and despair that I burst into tears. Crying hard I lay down on the warm earth and sobbed until it felt as if every emotion had been wrung out of me; I lay there, eye to eye with the stones I'd made into designs the day before; I touched the pale blue one—it was hot from the sun—

and picked it up to examine more closely, finding it as smooth as glass. I wondered if the winds had polished it or the sands, or both. Sitting up I leaned back against the post, calmer now, still holding the pale blue stone. Sunlight filtered through the acacia leaves, touching my left cheek, and I sighed. Utterly drained now of rebellion I gently gave myself up to whatever must happen; half a day and a long night had passed, and once this was repeated I would be untied but the bowl would not have broken.

I looked for the green stone, and then the brown one, seeing how differently they had been worn by time; some of them had lines and rough edges, others were smooth, like jewels, really. Earth gems, I thought. As the sun rose higher in the sky the spider returned, passing me by, and I laughed. *"Gizo-gizo,"* I called after him.

Soon, dropping the stones, I simply sat and looked at them, feeling the warming earth beneath me, the great space of blue sky over me, and as I sat there, letting go of all but the moment, something in my mind shifted, clicked, and like a switch turned off all thought. I found myself looking at the clay bowl and seeing it—really *seeing* it—with a feeling of unshakable serenity and sureness that was neither concentration nor meditation. A strange power was being released, I could feel it, and it was flowing effortlessly from me to a clay bowl that no longer had a name or a use but was a shape of great beauty, fashioned out of the earth and vibrant with earth colors. . . . My mind stood as still as the caught-breath silence before a storm: time no longer existed and for a succession of moments or hours this circular shape and I were linked together by a communication that softly deepened into communion—and then abruptly the storm broke. Like a tidal wave all my thoughts and anxieties swept back into my head again, the shape was only a drab bowl and I was literally earthbound. It was over.

But not quite: the bowl had broken open and lay in shards on the ground.

I stared at it, bewildered. No spirit had done this, I was sure of that, but neither could I say that I had done it—certainly not consciously—yet no hand had touched it, the earth had not shaken and I remained alone. The bowl was shattered but of much more importance to me just then was what had taken place inside of me. Something new and unknown had shown itself—but what?—and when I'd stopped struggling—was this important?—an inexplicable power had been tapped.

I sat very still and thoughtful, stirred by this, awed by it.

This, I thought, *is real* iko. *And it is in me. In all of us,* I thought, *not yet realized.*

Then I remembered the enaden's performance at the feast before we crossed the Tassili n' Ajjer, and how they'd held red-hot irons to their bodies without being burned or scarred, and I wondered if this was their secret. I wondered many things, I was flooded with startling new considerations. I thought of the mysterious events of the night and of how Isa's face had betrayed his hope that I would not survive this test from the spirits of the shrine, and I wondered if he knew better than I the power I'd just met with—this was a humbling thought—and had tried to use it on me. Looked at from this perspective—upside down, so to speak—certain events acquired a crazy logic. There had been those dreadful shadows and cries in the darkness when Bakuli had insisted no human or animal had been near me. I wondered if they could have come from Isa's mind, projected with just such a power into mine. I remembered what had happened to me at the hill of rocks near Abalessa—really there was no end to this now—and I knew that I could accept that too, it had been a beginning.

I had met with no spirits here but I had met with my self. And with *iko.*

When they came bringing food Amina saw this at once, and I think Isa did, too. He might say—as he did—that the spirits of the shrine had forgiven me and had spoken, shattering the bowl, but his eyes were thoughtful when they met mine and there was no mockery in them now.

As for me, I had been given a glimpse of what I would call Mind Magic for want of a better word, not aware yet, for I was young, that in obscure corners of the world there were others—saints, mystics, psychics, fakirs, healers, even charlatans—who already knew of this.

twelve

               ~

I had pleased Bakuli, whose eyes were shining with pride—*my family,* I thought, and smiled back at him, and then I was untied and free to leave the shrine, which I frankly did not care to see ever again. Scarcely capable of walking I was helped back to the compound by Amina and Bakuli, leaving behind a crowd of excited villagers staring at the broken bowl.

    I had pleased Amina, too. Once back in the hut she began a long and animated conversation with Bakuli, whose gift for languages both Amina and I depended on heavily. At the end of this Bakuli told me solemnly, "Amina say *'Bako yanā dā kibā'* —the stranger has strength. She make good medicine, Missy. She know charms, spells, medicine to heal. She say you have good *iko* so you be good to teach such. She want to teach thee."

This sounded a better exercise for my thoughts than the work in the fields and the water carrying that I'd been doing, and I agreed at once. I was curious, too, remembering how ill I'd been when I reached this village, and how Amina had quite possibly saved my life with her medicines and her care.

In this way I became attached to Amina as her apprentice and all during the season of the cold and windy *hūntūrū* she taught me her medicines, beginning first with the incantations spoken over each herb to give them power. These I learned by rote, but even knowing the little I did of Hausa I could make absolutely no sense of their meanings so that I came to believe what Bakuli had told me earlier, that the power attributed to them by Amina lay in their sound, and certainly the sounds covered a variety of octaves. Each incantation that I faithfully memorized began with an appeal to the collective spirits called the 'iskoki—this much was clear to me—but what followed would remain forever gibberish to my ear. In any case, between the incantations and the medicines, Amina cured Shehu's baby son of fever and a rash, and during the cold and dust of the hūntūrū even Isa was among those who came to Amina with bad coughs that she eased.

She taught me to work with leather, too, which was more important to her than I'd realized, for living in such barren thorn country she had to acquire many of her herbs by trade with others. It was community work to slaughter the goats and tan their hides, but a portion of the skins were Amina's to dress and decorate. Dressing the leather was as hard as hoeing in the fields: using the brains of the goat I would rub the skins hard and then rub them again and again with damp sand. Next, with knife and awl and a polishing stone Amina would begin her work of cutting, dyeing and fringing, making really handsome leather bracelets, sandals and belts that she would trade when an Arab merchant, such as the one who saved Bakuli and me, stopped outside the village with his camels or donkeys and his trading goods.

If I had expected great changes in me from my experience at the sacred shrine I was to be disappointed; I was both too young and impatient for the solitude that was obviously needed to court its recurrence, and soon enough I found it difficult to believe that it had happened at all. . . . The medicines became of more interest to me, although due to the gaps in my Hausa it was Bakuli who often had to translate for Amina when his own work was done.

One evening when Amina was showing and naming her various herbs to us, Bakuli took particular interest in a pouch of small red seeds, in fact I heard him draw in his breath sharply at sight of them.

"Where you get these?" he asked Amina, and then, fumbling for Hausa words, *"Yaya*—how? *Inā*—where?"

They came from far away, Amina told him, and she had bought them with her leather goods from a traveling merchant.

Bakuli nodded. "They be from *my* country," he said. "Zambezi country! They *ba no busungu*—poisonous, *ee?"* Since he'd slipped into Bemba for this, only I knew what he was saying, and while he went through a pantomime with Amina, clutching his throat and rolling his eyes, I picked out a few seeds and examined them.

Bakuli turned to me. "You swallow like that, no harm. You crush and—*Kai!* you die fast and nobody know how. *Nobody.*"

We both looked questioningly at Amina, who only shrugged and moved to open the next pouch. Bakuli and I exchanged glances; he grinned, nodding yes to my unspoken question, and moved in front of me to hide what I did next, for I helped myself to more of the red seeds and dropped a handful of them into the pocket of my barracan.

We had just acquired our first defense against harm, and during the next weeks I would add to our cache.

Now my worldly belongings consisted of two finger puppets—two now, for I had given Isabelle to Shehu as a gift—a silver Hand of Fatima, a new headscarf, the curious stone I'd taken from the hill of rocks near Abalessa, my compass, and a collection of hard red seeds. So much had I changed that it felt like wealth to me, for not so long ago I had possessed much less and had come near to losing even that. My head might be shorn of hair to preserve me from lice and my clothes be in tatters, I might be lean as a boy and dark as an Arab, unrecognizable to anyone in Boston or Tripoli, but I was still alive and so was Bakuli.

Wealth was strictly relative; I would remember this.

And so I grew more settled, for it was not an unhappy village in which to live. Despite its strange customs and trials, there was no underlying melancholy such as I'd sensed among the Tuareg. I might feel captive but it was not by them, having been delivered to the village half-dead. Amina would often sing as she worked—I liked this—and if she resented her husband taking a new young wife, I would frequently see her and Halma gossiping and laughing together.

There was this too: the next time the drums beat I did not flee. It was to be a *wasā*, Amina told me, and what this meant I didn't understand, but I knew that an Arab trader was camped outside the walls that night, and with him was a handsome young man who had been made much of by the villagers that afternoon. He was a Hausa from the South, and a Muslim, for I had seen him pray at sundown. The young unmarried girls had teased and flirted with him, being much impressed. Amina said he was also a *dan tauri* and this was the reason for the *wasā,* which would be something to see.

And see it I did.

It took place under the stars, which pleased me, and the firelight made a garden of color out of the bright head kerchiefs and shirts and tunics surrounding it. Only the performer, the young Hausa named Akulu, was bare-chested, and what came first was what Amina called Praise-Singing, which sounded like a poem to me as Akulu chanted it to the chief: *The drum drums health, The drum drums wealth, He takes his wife six hundred thousand cowries. . . . The drum drums health, the drum drums wealth, He takes his son six hundred thousand cowries. . . . The drum drums health, The drum drums wealth. . . .*

After this the drums began. Four of the

villagers had calabashes which they beat with their hands, and five of them had proper drums made of hide stretched taut across wood and beaten with sticks; these were of varied size so that their *kadē-kadē* spoke with different voices. The drummers began casually, almost idly until they found a rhythm, and as they developed it the villagers began clapping their hands to the beat. There came a shout and Shehu moved out of the circle, clapping his hands high over his head; Amina joined him, and then Halma and Bakuli and Kadiri and Isa, and soon everyone was dancing to the music, clapping, moving, laughing, swaying. Except for me, but I sat quietly and watched, seeing the most ecstatic of them all to be the strange Hausa who twirled and leaped with something like real joy.

This Hausa who was a *dan tauri.*

An hour later when the drumming and the dancing stopped I would learn what *dan tauri* was and I would again be puzzled and moved, for this man Akulu knew the same secrets as the enaden. What a performer he was! He sat first on the earth, cross-legged. Drawing out a knife he grasped a stick and with a flick of his wrist he sliced the stick in two, showing us how sharp the knife was, and then—stripped to the waist as he was—he drew the knife across his bare chest and *it left no cut behind it.* This was only his introduction, however. He next stood up and Isa handed him a long knife that he himself had sharpened. Akulu accepted it with a smile and a bow, and this time he drew the knife very slowly across his body, and deeply enough to leave a visible cut behind it, and even I could see *there was no bleeding.* What's more, even as we watched—what a shout went up at this!—the cut we had seen healed itself and disappeared, leaving no sign.

This left me gasping, for here was no carnival trick; once again I had witnessed Mind Magic and it was real.

"Inā?" I demanded of Amina later, asking how Akulu could have done this.

To Amina the answer was very simple: a magic charm had made Akulu invulnerable.

"What charm? *Mē* charm?" I asked.

Amina did not know what charm, she said, it was a charm that only the *'yan taurī* knew.

This truly excited me for I knew it could be no charm. The man had not gone into a trance, of this I was certain; the music and dancing might have contributed but there had to be more. I sensed a kinship here with what I'd experienced at the sacred spirit shrine, a use of exceptional energies that few people knew existed, a power buried deep and waiting to be disinterred. By what convolutions of thought and command this had been done I couldn't guess, but Akulu, I decided, must somehow have told his body that it would not bleed and that no knife could harm it, and his body had *listened*. . . . But how had he spoken to his body, I wondered, or was it perhaps not his body at all that had heard him?

This occupied my mind for several days and then, being youthful and careless, I put it aside to think about another day.

And so the weeks went by, the season of the *hūntūrū* ended, the dry months passed and the time of planting neared. The grain silos were almost empty now, food was scarce and the skies were watched for signs of rain. Sacrifices were made at the shrines, the blood of animals offered as libation, and clay pots made and presented to the spirits as gifts. Prayers were said and Isa's divining board was busy again. A wizened old man with a lined black face was carried out of his hut to sit each day under one of the acacia trees beyond the gate. Bakuli said he was the village rainmaker, not because he made rain but because for all of his life he'd studied the sky, the clouds, the winds, the sun and the moon; he knew which clouds would bring rain and where it would fall, and which clouds were barren. His name was Funtua and he was old, very old, Bakuli told me solemnly. I was curious and nearly every day managed to find a minute and go out to watch him. When I said, *"Sanu da aike,* Funtua," he would regard me with amusement and say gravely, *"Sanu du rana, bako."* I felt a great gentleness in him that soothed me, and once or twice I lingered, joining him and the boy who kept him company, and we would watch the sky together.

One day he grunted and lifted a hand to point northward, to the desert.

"Mēne nē?" I asked.

"Ruwa."

Far away to the northeast I saw the flat unbroken line of the horizon and just above it an equally unbroken line of silver that was slowly descending over it like a gauze curtain. A moment later the horizon was obscured.

"Ruwa," he said again, nodding.

The boy left, excited, shouting, and soon half the village was at Funtua's side waiting for his conclusions, but when he spoke there were groans.

"What did he say?" I asked Bakuli.

"He say *'ruwa yā yi gyārā,'* the rain does good—but not here."

"Surely it will come south?"

Bakuli shook his head. "He say it go—" He pointed to the east. "Not here."

Funtua was right, the rain did not move south to us and the watch was resumed.

It was the next afternoon when Bakuli caught up with me as I left the village to fill both of Amina's buckets at the well. Usually I went later, with the other women, but who can guess the workings of fate? Amina had been sleeping and cooking at her husband's house for two days and the buckets were empty, whereas Bakuli had just carried a newly made hoe to Isa's compound and saw me leaving the village by the side gate. Together we moved off diagonally across the hardened dry earth toward the wells near the riverbed. It had been a long time since we'd been alone and we chattered away like magpies. Bakuli showed me his hands—"Very good now, Missy, Bakuli make good smitt now" —and I told him the gossip about Isa's daughter refusing to marry the man chosen for her. Having captured a few minutes for ourselves, we left the buckets next to the well and jumped down into the dry riverbed, walked across it and climbed up its high opposite bank. Here we heard shouting, and looking back I saw it was the boy who sat with Funtua by the main gate: he was waving and calling to us. We waved back and resumed our walk until we reached the next dried-up riverbed, one of the many that seamed the area.

It was then that we heard it. "Thunder?" I said, puzzled and turning to Bakuli.

He stood very still, listening, and then, "No, Missy—*run!*"

I froze, not understanding. The sun

was shining, there were no clouds in the sky, I could see the village in the distance and our two water buckets waiting for us next to the well, yet the thunder continued. Bakuli had dropped down into the riverbed to run across it, but away from the village, which seemed stupid to me. Seeing me still rooted there he stopped and screamed at me, *"RUN!"* but only when he started back to get me did I come to life. Still not understanding I followed him down into the oued and in a panic he pulled me up the bank.

"See!" he gasped, and pointed behind me to the hills of sand and thornbush that had been hiding what was nearly upon us.

I turned and looked. A tidal wave of furious brown water was racing toward us, carrying with it everything that it met. It leveled the low hills of thornbush in an instant and on the crest of its wave before it broke I saw the body of a man, a drowned sheep and a tree.

I ran for my life. The rain that had fallen miles away in the mountains yesterday was reaching us after all; I had never seen a flash flood before and it was terrifying. I scrambled up the hill behind Bakuli but seconds later the roaring water had filled this riverbed, too, and was churning below us threatening the hill on which we stood. Far away I saw the water lapping at the gates of the village and this was alarming because Amina had explained to me how carefully the village was distanced from the oueds so that in all its history it had never been touched by floods—but it was being touched now.

I thought, *When the flood has finished with us at least the earth in the riverbeds will be fertile for planting.* Aloud I said, "The village will be safe, it has to be, it's stood there for years and years and years."

"Yes, Missy," Bakuli said uneasily and hurried me eastward toward a low rocky mesa that promised more security from the rampaging waters and just in time, too, for when we looked back the sand hill on which we'd stood had disappeared.

For several hours we waited in the shade of the mesa, watching the sun and a thirsty earth begin to drink up the water that had followed us. When the sun neared setting time we waded back across the plain to measure our prospects for returning. The floodwaters were retreating from the land but there was no possible way to cross, for the oueds were in full spate and boiling with debris. This was depressing, but when I lifted my eyes to look for the village I gasped in horror because it was gone; I couldn't believe it. Where it had stood I could see only a hill of sodden thatch and the acacia tree under which I had sat for two days and a night.

"Oh, Bakuli," I whispered, pointing.

He nodded, his young face grim.

"They would have run away," I insisted. "They would surely have seen the water spreading out and they would have left in time, wouldn't they, Bakuli?"

"Bakuli see no peoples, Missy. Where be sheep, goats, peoples?"

Amina, Shehu, Funtua, Halma, Isa, Kadiri . . . an agonizing sense of loss overwhelmed me and I sat down on the sodden earth and cried. If they had fled, as they must have, I told myself, they would be far away now, as hungry as we were and without shelter. They would have lost their spirit shrines, the seeds carefully preserved for planting, their silos for grain, above all their history and their huts. And we had lost *them.*

Then I realized a worse possibility and looking up at Bakuli I cried out, "Oh Bakuli, what if we'd not left the village together!"

His smile was singularly sweet. "Yes, Missy, Jesus-God look after Jesus-boy."

Darkness fell swiftly, mercifully blotting out the lone acacia tree standing over what had once been a village of happy people. When I dried my eyes and stood up, Bakuli touched me on the shoulder. "Look, Missy," he said, pointing south beyond the mesa where we'd sheltered earlier.

Far away in the darkness a light shone softly in the night. It had the look of a campfire, a caravan, perhaps, taken out of its way by the floods. "What do you think, Bakuli?" I asked.

"Where there be fire there be peoples, Missy."

I had been foolish even to ask, for we had no choice: there was no way to cross the flooded oueds and there was no village to return to. We set out in the darkness to find the light.

thirteen

On the night of the flood when we reached the distant campfire it was our poverty that spared us rejection or robbery. The men bedding down among their camels saw only two ragged boys, one small and black, the taller one presumably of mixed or Targui blood. There was no thought of turning us away or robbing us; they didn't notice the weight of the pockets I'd long ago sewn in my barracan, and this was fortunate for among my small treasures I carried the Hand of Fatima, and Bakuli, who had worn our remaining Maria

Theresa thalers in a pouch around his neck, had given them over to me for safe-keeping on the way. These men were Arabs heading south to Agadez, but they spoke Hausa and in this language Bakuli explained to them that I was a mute, incapable of speaking, and that we'd lost our way in the flood. They gave us a handful of sandy dates and when they broke camp several hours later we were allowed to walk behind their camels and share their food and water.

Four sunsets later, having eaten much dust on the way, we halted outside the walls of Agadez. Here it was made known to Bakuli that we had been given the hospitality of the desert, and peace go with us but they would feed us no more. It was here, too, that we learned that Agadez was a French military outpost, captained by one Frenchman and a troop of black soldiers called *tirailleurs.*

"So there be *ba mweni* here, Missy," Bakuli said, scowling. "Foreign peoples?"

I was stunned at hearing this. I had dreamed for months—*years*—of finding rescue, and here in this oasis in the middle of the desert there was actually a French soldier, we had heard the Arabs say so.

With studied indifference Bakuli said, "You go to foreign peoples, Missy?" He took great care to avoid looking at me, picking up a handful of pebbles and frowning over them while he waited for my reply.

He had a long wait because I was picturing myself meeting this French captain of the military. I imagined his skepticism, his doubts and then his shock as he understood at last that I was neither Arab nor Tuareg but actually an *American,* and what a thrilling moment that would be! And yet . . . and yet . . . There was something troubling to me about this picture taking shape in my mind, for I wondered: if I made myself known to this French captain in the hope of being sent home would he see to it that Bakuli was sent home too? I wondered if the fate of one black boy among so many would be of interest to a European. Nor could Bakuli say precisely where his home might be, having been torn from it at such an early age that he remembered only that it lay near a great river called the Zambezi.

It seemed there was no decision to make after all.

"Bakuli," I said, "what is the name in your language for brother?"

Puzzled he said, *"Ndume."*

I nodded. "I do not go to the *ba mweni,*" I told him in his vernacular, "for thou be my *ndume,* Bakuli. We stay together."

He glowed with pleasure, quickly concealing it by kicking at the sand with his bare foot. "Where then, Missy?"

I now abandoned all thought of going south to find the Niger River, for if Bakuli's home lay to the east, near another great river, then we must head east until we met people who had heard of the Zambezi. "We will go east," I said firmly. "The Arabs spoke of a caravan leaving soon, I heard them. Let's see what our silver can buy for us in this town, and ask about the caravan."

And so we entered Agadez, a town spread out across the slopes of a foothill of the distant Tarouadji Mountains. What captured the eye approaching it was the minaret that rose above its crumbling walls, with a tower that resembled a great brown cactus plant bristling with thorns, but as we drew nearer the thorns turned out to be wooden beams protruding like toothpicks from the tower that gracefully tapered to a blunt point on its way to the sky. Once inside the town walls we strolled through its outer dusty lanes looking at houses of dried mud, finding many of them no more than empty shells—we would shelter in one of them when night came—and from this I concluded that Agadez had known kinder days. As we made our way toward the town's center, however, we met with the marketplace, the heart of the town and obviously its soul, for it was as lively as a carnival. Here were crowds of native blacks in colorful cotton gandouras, groups of Tuareg looking haughty and splendid in their indigo robes and veils and Arabs dusty from travel and prepared to trade and bargain. After the austerity and silence of the desert it was glorious to see so many people and there was certainly a richness of color and noise: a constant chatter of voices, the smell of charcoal smoke and roasting meat, scents, perfumes and spices, heat, dung and dust. There were stalls selling needles and palm ropes, kola nuts, baskets, leather goods and bolts of bright cloth, daggers, knives, guerbas, but most of all there was food to buy, cooked deliciously over charcoal fires. Out came one of our thalers and we gorged ourselves on couscous and chunks of tender mutton swimming in gravy. We ate with such gusto that when we'd scooped out the bowl with slabs of bread there was not so much as a single pearl of couscous to be seen. Following this we bought a sack of dates, a handful of kola nuts and two loaves of flat round bread for the next day, all of which reduced our resources considerably.

Looking at our purchases Bakuli said, "These not take us east, Missy."

"No," I sighed, and agreed that it was time to learn when the caravan going east would leave, and how many days remained for us to beg or steal money for travel. Obviously I must pick some pockets here in Agadez, but it would be dangerous: the Tuareg wore their wealth in purses that hung around their necks and were tucked securely inside their robes; as for the Arabs I knew they must conceal their coins in pockets, as I did, but their clothes were many-layered and voluminous. We were in brigand country now, where thieves were anticipated, and any failure might cost me my life. Nevertheless it had to be done if we were to leave Agadez or we would soon become beggars and there looked to be enough of them already.

We left the marketplace and found our way to the camel market at the edge of town where we judged that news of the caravan would be the more reliable. "Am I still a mute, Bakuli?"

"Oh yes, Missy," he said earnestly. "You not talk Hausa good, you be foreigner to it, a *baubawawa.*"

I accepted this meekly for it was true enough, but it was certainly frustrating to be silent.

The camel market was a noisy place, full of Tuareg minutely examining camels who snarled and spit and in every manner protested their humps being squeezed and their teeth probed. We walked in among the traders, taking care to keep clear of the rebellious animals, and I soon noticed one man in particular who stood out from the others. For one thing he was not a Targui— we hoped to avoid the Tuareg—but an

Arab who looked quite grand. He wore a clean white burnous and a cultivated look enhanced by a black beard neatly trimmed to a point. Two black men stood beside him, Sudanese servants by the look of them. When Bakuli hesitated I pushed him forward, and approaching this man he asked with a timid smile when the great caravan for the east would be leaving.

The man turned his full glance on Bakuli, studying him with penetrating eyes set into a thin stern face. In Arabic he said curtly the caravan would leave at the full of the moon, and he watched the two of us as we walked away.

We would need money very quickly, I was thinking, for we had walked the night before under a nearly full moon that had drenched the desert with light. We had four Maria Theresa dollars left, the equal of forty thousand cowries, but a good donkey cost nearly thirty thousand cowries and we would probably need two of them to carry guerbas and food for the trip, neither of which we possessed at the moment either. Aimlessly we wandered back to the marketplace, Bakuli no longer smiling while I wondered at our prospects and found them depressing.

As we reached the edge of the market I heard a man call out in Hausa, *"Gātanan, gātanan, ta je, ta komo!"*

How many times I'd heard these words in Amina's village! We had found a storyteller calling out, "A story, a story, let it go, let it come."

Except that no one had come. He sat on the ground cross-legged, a small black man wrapped in voluminous shabby robes. We stopped to look at him and to listen as he tried again, calling, *"Wanan tātsūnīar dugan daji che, da shi da Namijin-Mijin-maza,"* and again, *"Gātanan, gātanan!"*

"Namijin-Mijin-maza," I repeated. "Bakuli, that's the story of A-Man-Among-Men, isn't it? The one where you explained all the hard words? It's a *good* story, why doesn't anyone stop to listen?"

Bakuli shrugged. "Peoples with full pockets have empty heads, not want talk. He beggarman, I think."

I considered this, stirred by the thought that we too would be beggars soon if we couldn't summon some resources, and here at last was a resource if I applied a little showmanship from a long-ago different world. We needed money and the Storyteller needed money, he had a good story to tell and I had not grown up in a carnival for nothing. I wondered how much skill had been lost during my sojourn among the Hausa and decided that nothing ventured nothing gained, and in any case it should be safer to join him than to attempt robbing a Targui. "Bakuli," I said, "give me three of our silver dollars."

"Missy—"

"And your head kerchief," I added, for Amina had given one to me and one to Bakuli, and they matched. Withdrawing to a deserted corner, I tossed a silver dollar into the air, then a second and then a third, keeping them in motion with such success that it seemed I'd not lost the knack of juggling, and this pleased me very much until one of the dollars crashed to the earth. Nevertheless Bakuli's wide-eyed astonishment had reassured me. "I need something bigger, I need three round stones," I told him. "While I search, you go and bargain with the Storyteller. Ask him if he'll share half of what's given him if we bring many people to hear his story."

The Storyteller's name was Damau, and if he was skeptical at such a boast he must have felt that he had nothing to lose, having nothing anyway. Thus it came about that we put on a show after the muezzin's afternoon call to prayer, and after much practice of old skills on my part. With great enthusiasm Bakuli played the role of carny barker, shouting and beating a piece of discarded tin with a stick. After a few people had gathered out of curiosity I stood up next to the Storyteller and began to juggle my three stones, keeping them smoothly in motion and sending them higher and higher; soon a bigger crowd stopped to watch in amazement, never having seen juggling before. Following this I held up one silver dollar, caused it to disappear, and extracted it with a flourish from the Storyteller's ear—there were gasps of awe at this—and then I palmed my red headscarf in the left sleeve of my barracan and drew out Bakuli's matching headscarf from the right sleeve. With a full audience watching now I bowed and pointed to Damau, and the Storyteller rose with dignity to call out, *"Gātanan, gātanan, ta je, ta kōmō!"*

This time the crowd called back the ritual, *"Ta je, ta komo!* Let it go, let it come."

And he was good, this Damau, he had a melodious voice that rose and fell and paused dramatically. One by one his listeners squatted down in a circle around us and then settled on the earth without stirring as they grew immersed in the tale—and it is a long one—of how the braggert who called himself A-Man-Among-Men meets the Giant of the Forest. After many humbling experiences the man's wife sums up its moral at the end, saying, "Whatever you do, make little of it, for whether you excel in strength, or in power, or in riches, it is all the same—someone is better than you!"

I liked that ending. When I'd first heard the story, understanding only two words out of five, with Bakuli explaining those I'd missed, it was the only taste of philosophy that had come my way since Marcus Aurelius, and it had satisfied a hunger in me. The story pleased me now, too. At its conclusion the three of us bowed as we might have done at Laski's Carnival, and as the crowds wandered away my eyes feasted on Damau's calabash overflowing now with cowrie shells. When we came to divide its contents we found not only cowries but slivers of sugar, shavings of salt, a bronze French centime, two copper 5-para coins and some trading beads. We were not rich but we would have food for another day.

And it was a beginning. Damau grasped our hands, his eyes bright now, and nodding vigorously he repeated over and over his wish that Allah might give us good health, that Allah would give us life and protection, and would we come back tomorrow?

Solemnly we agreed to return.

The passing hours of the day had been punctuated by the muezzin's calls to prayer, the el Duhr at noon, the Asr in midafternoon, at sunset the el Mogh'reb. Night overtook an apricot sky, softly blurring shapes until the darkness turned those walking home into phantoms. Lanterns flickered like fireflies in the narrow lanes until a pale nearly full moon rose, and gradually the village stilled.

Bakuli and I had foraged among the ruins for a hut with a roof, and we had found one by dusk. It was surrounded by rubble, half of one wall had collapsed but there was a roof to hide us. Here we cleared away chunks of fallen banco, made pillows out of the sand that had drifted inside, and after the last *Allah Akhbar* of the el Aschïa we lay down to sleep.

It was now that we heard someone stealthily approaching our snug hiding-place, his footsteps inadvertently turning over fallen stones. Bakuli warningly reached out to touch my arm; I sat up and fumbled in the dark for a weapon, a stick or a stone, but found nothing so that we could only make ourselves small and silent and wait. Abruptly the silhouette of a man stood outlined in the doorway, black against the lighter night sky.

He said, *"Salaam aleikum,"* and then, *"Bemba wāled?"*

Bemba boy . . . By the sound of the voice I knew it was not Damau but somewhere it had been heard before. Confused and frightened we huddled together, still silent. The man stooped under the doorframe to enter and once inside he set down a lantern. In the first flicker of light I saw long slender fingers adjusting the flame and recognized the face: we were being visited by the tall bearded Arab from the camel market, except that he had exchanged his white burnous for a dark and shabby one such as his servants had worn. This in itself was strange but so was his presence here.

"Bemba wāled," he repeated, nodding to us.

"Naam?" said Bakuli in a small voice.

Shadows leaped up the half-walls around us, the man squatted near the lantern appraising us, and in turn I stared at him, seeing eyes that burned with an intensity brighter than the flame in his lantern. *An uncomfortable man,* I thought, and as he moved slightly I caught a glimpse of striped silk under the worn burnous. A rich one, too, I decided, but I wondered how on earth he'd found us—it went hard for me to be a mute in Agadez—and as if Bakuli heard my unspoken question he asked him this.

The man gestured impatiently. "My

servants followed you all day." He looked from Bakuli to me. *"Inta!* You!" he said.

"Missy hear, Missy no speak," Bakuli told him in Hausa and pointed to my lips, shrugging.

"All the better then," said the man.

He was not one to linger over words as Arabs usually do, caressing them and tasting their flavor, or perhaps, considering what later occurred, his life no longer had space for the formalities. His words were needle-sharp and brief: we wished to go east with the caravan leaving in two days? If we would carry a message and deliver it for him in Bilma he would see to it that we had two camels and a donkey, and food and water for travel.

Here was a miracle indeed. I glanced at Bakuli and saw that his mouth had dropped open in astonishment at this. He stammered, "Thou mean—you speak of the caravan leaving at the full of moon?"

The man nodded. *"Naam,"* and in Hausa demanded, *"i or a'a*—yes or no?"

Bakuli gave me a sidelong glance and smiled. *"i,"* he said.

"It is a bargain then." Reaching inside his burnous he brought out a slip of parchment and rolled it into a thin tube. "I will not speak with you again," he said sternly, "nor will you speak to me. We have never met. Two sunsets from now, after the el Mogh'reb, my servant will bring all that you need—camels and donkey, fodder, guerbas and food—and take you to the hills where the caravan gathers."

He held out the scrap of paper. "Hide it well and see that in Bilma it is given to Abu Abd el Wahat."

"Abu Abd el Wahat," repeated Bakuli. "From what person, *Sidi?*"

He said carelessly, "Muraiche." As if to atone for his harsh manner he handed Bakuli several coins—I heard them clink and my heart lifted at the sound—and with courtesy he added, *"Bismallah—in the name of god . . . Emshi besselema."* He then extinguished his lantern and left us.

It was in this strange manner that we met Muraiche, except that I would wonder many times if this was his true name. I had no knowledge then of what was happening in other parts of Africa, I knew nothing of the intrigues, assassinations, treaties and betrayals, battles, rivalries and ultimatums among the French, Turks, Italians, British and Belgians as each of them raced to swallow up as much of the continent as possible. I didn't know that in Tripoli the Turks had been struggling to extend their power into the Sahara, or had been sending secret expeditions into the Sudan, or that Italy was plotting to invade Tripoli. After all, I had been traveling for a very long time in the only part of Africa that nobody wanted—the desert.

Long after Muraiche left us, Bakuli and I talked in whispers about our mysterious visitor and the miracle of his singling us out, and yet we wondered, over and over again, why us? When it grew light I unrolled the tiny slip of paper to see what it contained but the message was written in Arabic with all of its incomprehensible curls and flourishes. I brought out Mr. Jappy and inserted it into the hole drilled for my finger; it fitted neatly there, well hidden.

As to who Muraiche might be, Bakuli dared ask only one person and that was Damau, who said that at the camel market he was called a brave man but a reckless one because he had arrived from the west three sunrises ago, riding through dangerous country with little baggage and only his two servants, and at such a pace that six of his camels had died of exhaustion upon reaching Agadez. It was rumored that he might be a Senussi, but since neither Bakuli nor I knew what a Senussi was this didn't enlighten us, and Bakuli dared not ask too many questions lest Muraiche hear of them.

Whoever Muraiche was, he was a man who kept his word, for two nights later, after the el Mogh'reb at sundown, his servant came for us as promised, leading two loaded camels and a donkey. We were guided out of Agadez and up into the hills where hundreds of campfires burned in the night, waiting for departure at dawn.

But in the morning the mystery of Muraiche was only compounded, for when the first rays of sun reached the hills and the muezzin's cry sent hundreds of men to their knees, who should we see among our neighbors but Muraiche and his two servants. It seemed that he too was traveling in the caravan to the place called Bilma. *A rich madman,* I thought, much like Jacob in his way, or so I believed until the third dawn of the march destroyed such innocence.

It was a wondrous sight to see the caravan begin its march eastward that morning, the camels fanning out across the plains to come together later, at night, for safety. The name of its elected leader was Saad el Riffi, or so Bakuli told me after flitting eagerly among our neighbors to glean information, and under his protection were dozens of small caravans from all over the Sahara, carrying cloth, rugs, hides, leather goods, kola nuts, grain and jewelry to sell in the east or trade for precious salt from the mines of Bilma. There were hundreds of camels, as well as donkeys, sheep and goats, and the humans accompanying them were an exotic sight: veiled Kel Aïr Tuareg with magnificent pale camels, Bedouin in checkered headdresses, black Sudanese in tarboosh and white gandouras, Arabs well-wrapped in hooded cloaks of goat or camel's hair—to which had been added one small Bemba boy and a reluctant mute from a far country disguised as a boy.

The triumph of our departure was somewhat tempered, however, by what I began overhearing about this desert we were to cross. Its name was the Tenere, which had been meaningless to me when I learned of it in Agadez but now I was among men who had crossed it before and I did not like what I heard of it: the Tenere had killed many men, they said, and was far crueler than the Sahara for there were no wells at all in its eastern half . . . the nearest oasis was over 300 miles away and Bilma lay another three or four days march beyond it . . . there were dunes in the Tenere that stood four and five times higher than the minaret in Agadez, and when the wind blew one could hear the djinns calling, and the cries of dead men who had gone mad from thirst or sand-storms. All these words I regarded with caution, aware that men enjoyed their tall tales, but later when we had left behind the sharp silhouette of the Azzuager and had seen the last of the trees and rocks I was to share the dread with which these men approached the Tenere.

As for Muraiche, I noted that he trav-eled with only sixteen baggage camels, he rode a donkey and wore a shabby bur-nous, giving no sign of wealth at all. We walked not far from him, our two camels and the donkey roped together in single line behind us, and although he never so much as glanced at us I acquired the habit of looking for him each day and each time we halted. He was, after all, our benefactor, our sponsor, and it was his food that we ate. Which is how I happened to see what took place just before moon-set on that third day, never daring to speak of it even to Bakuli but keeping it secret out of fear.

It had been a bitterly cold night and I woke up shivering and full of regrets about heading east without learning first the nature of this desert. Already I was feeling a lassitude new to me; I was also tired of being a mute and never speaking, and tired of taking care to answer the calls of nature alone lest someone know I was not a boy, and so I lifted my head that night, but wearily, to look at the sleeping camp. The moon was still bright, the only shadows being those cast by the walls of piled-up saddles and bales of fodder that circled us for protection. In this light the sleeping men were so blanketed they looked like bundles of old clothes rolled up and left in the sand. Beyond the wall the camels moved restlessly, their shapes blurred in a creeping ground mist. I glanced toward the place where Muraiche had lain down, having marked his black-and-white striped blanket in the firelight before it died.

Out among the camels something moved and my glance shifted. A shadow emerged and I saw a man climb over the saddles and quietly make his way past the sleeping forms. I thought it the caravan's watchman; he paused beside Muraiche's striped blanket and leaned over it, his burnous falling around him in folds. He was there only a minute but as he straightened he looked in my direction, his face clear in the moonlight, and we exchanged interested glances across the sleeping men. Then he was gone, vanishing over the wall and among the camels again. It seemed of no consequence to me, my eyes closed and I slept until the cameleers stirred, when a fire was lit, coffee brewed and Muraiche did not rise to shake off his blanket. Instead there came a sobbing cry from one of his Sudanese servants and then a wail from the other; a man bid them be quiet, walked over to strike them silent, stiffened and called out, "Andak! Andak! The shaykh has been killed!"

I was incredulous and hurried to look, but Muraiche was truly dead, he lay still as a rock in his striped blanket and already his skin had taken on the blue pallor that creeps over the flesh once it no longer breathes. What had killed him was there too: a dagger that protruded obscenely from his chest. The men made way for El Riffi, who came to examine the dead man; there were uneasy murmurings of "Masch' Allah!" and "Bismallah!" The caravan leader ordered a grave to be dug and began to question the two Sudanese.

"Wallāhi," interrupted a man, pointing. "Look! That Sudanese wears the brand of Allah—only a Senussi brands his slaves!"

"Malesh, but he has not been robbed?"

"What brings a Senussi to the West, so far from Kufra or the Sudan?"

"To spy?"

"Revenge—niqmah—is more likely. Someone has displeased them."

"Or betrayed them," muttered another man.

"The Senussi are fierce, it is truth, but all in the name of Allah."

"Pious, yes. They live by The Book."

The man next to me shrugged. "But they would have us drink no palm-wine and it is said they cut off the hand of any man who touches tobacco. They are fanatics."

"But they hate the French, there's that in their favor."

"Yes and still trade in slaves—one must admire them for that when the Christian infidels forbid it."

"Bismallah, they kill infidels too," a man said dryly, "but we will be late starting today, I think."

I turned away, troubled not only by Muraiche's death but by the words these men had spoken, for I had understood too much and too suddenly. I saw now the reasons for Muraiche's appearance in Agadez with exhausted camels and no guards, I understood his stealth, his secrecy and his choice of Bakuli and me to carry his message; he must have guessed that he was traveling with Death behind him. I felt pity for him because I too had known fear and the taste of it, but if the Senussi killed infidels then I must certainly be careful never to relax my guard lest I meet one again without knowing it.

We left Muraiche behind that morning in his lonely grave, consigned to the vast silence of the desert, to its sun and its stars, and to his all-merciful, all-compassionate God—and who knew which of us would be next, for this was harsh country. Day after day we plodded along in silence except for the soft swish of padded camels' feet or the occasional groan of a camel too exhausted to go on. We were like ghosts wrapped in shrouds, white with dust, our minds rendered equally as vacant. Behind us the camels were strung out in an endless line, their shapes melting and reforming like watery mirages in the heat-glitter, while ahead lay an unattainable horizon bleached white by a murderous sun. Our donkey had collapsed and died four days after the last well. There was the cruelty again of scorched eyelids and blistering hands and feet, and always the obsessive dream of water, clean or brackish it scarcely mattered so long as it was liquid to wet a parched throat and thin the dust: one lived for it, doling it out at sunset and dawn and watching the once-fat guerbas shrink in size.

This was the Tenere, lifeless, waterless, merciless, its only trail signs the bones of camels and men who had died here.

There was no thought of riding now, men walked to preserve the camels. Sometimes, stumbling along over the glazed sands I would remember that one among us in the caravan was Muraiche's murderer and when we halted, which was not often, I would think to study the shapes of the men, wondering if this one or that one had the look of him; I would wonder, too, how clearly he'd seen me and I kept my face well-wrapped to prevent recognition. Perhaps he did too. Mostly I counted the days, taking care at each sunset to be accurate and teaching Bakuli the numbers to help me remember.

We had been two weeks and three days on the march when it was said that— *Inch'Allah*—we would see the walls of Fachi the next day. Bakuli, licking his blistered lips, said hoarsely, "Water, Missy!"

I could only nod weakly. Sometime after passing the Tree of Tenere—that solitary beautiful tree growing like a miracle out of the sands—a fever had overtaken me that brought a wild thirst and an aching head. Now I was having stomach cramps, too, which seemed very unfair, because I'd drunk foul water many times since Tripoli but only now was it choosing to exact a toll. I lived in fear of becoming delirious and of being left behind in the desert but almost as alarming was the knowledge that after watering the camels and resting briefly at Fachi—if I made it there—we must travel three or four more days to reach Bilma.

On the following day I would dimly remember a shape appearing on what had been for days an empty horizon, and most glorious of all it was a shape that cast a shadow across the sands, a lovely cool blue shadow. I remember shouts from the cameleers, and as we drew nearer I saw what a fortress this town of Fachi looked in spite of the fringe of green palm leaves above its walls.

After this there was only a darkness in which I could hear Bakuli crying in a panic,

"Missy! Missy!" and later a man questioning him in Arabic. I was vaguely aware of being picked up and carried, and then of other voices speaking, arguing. Meaningless words penetrated my nightmares . . . *Salaam aleikum . . . i, Sidi . . . harara* . . . but Laski's Carnival was on fire and I couldn't speak, I was struggling to escape the flames and finding myself held down by Sharkey Bill. "No," I shouted. "No!"

Suddenly there was water. *"Ruwa,"* a woman's voice said and a man repeated in Arabic, *"Mayya,"* and then I heard the blessed voice of Bakuli saying, *"Shā,* Missy. Drink."

I opened my eyes. I was lying on the floor in a small, dark fetid room lit by a lantern, and Bakuli was holding a cup of water for me to drink. It was beautiful clean water such as I'd not tasted in what felt a century, and I drank it down. The second cup Bakuli poured over my forehead, cooling it. In the shadows behind him I saw a tiny, strange-looking black woman, with hair tied in long beaded strings, and beyond her a man whom I couldn't see distinctly except that he wore a burnous. I heard the sound of coins that he pressed into the hand of the woman and he seemed to be giving her instructions, I heard the word *shabb,* meaning young man, and the woman tittered. *"Shabb?"* Vastly amused she repeated, *"Shabb?"* and burst into a peal of laughter. *"Ita Bàhaushiyā ce!"*

The secret was out: I was not a boy but a Hausa woman.

"Masch' Allah!" exclaimed the man, stung by her words.

He moved closer, bending low to peer at me; I looked at him and he looked at me, a long glance such as we had exchanged in the moonlight not so many nights ago when he'd risen after bending over Muraiche and killing him. I knew his face well, just as he'd known mine, but I'd made it easy for him to find me. As I slipped into unconsciousness again, angrily and against my will, I wondered if he would kill me now or wait, and whether in my nightmares—there would be fresh ones, I knew—I would feel the coldness of his dagger against my flesh.

fourteen

As I wandered through the turbulent dreams of fever I would hear voices occasionally, but I recognized only two, that of Bakuli and of the man who had killed Muraiche. Once there was another voice, a new one that kept saying *"Gedash?"* and "Bismallah, *gedash?"* I thought I heard Bakuli say in a stricken voice, *"O Yesu,"* and he didn't sound as if he was praying. I was aware of being poked and prodded once, too, but then the loud voices receded, and when I opened my eyes Bakuli sat on the floor beside my straw mat, his eyes troubled.

I was still alive and this surprised me. "Bakuli!" I exclaimed, and smiled.

I remembered that we were in Fachi, but I couldn't understand the airless and cavelike room in which I lay, or the strange texture of the wall when I touched it. "It be *gishiri,* Missy," Bakuli said when I asked.

"But—*gishiri* means 'salt,' " I protested. "You can't mean *salt?*"

Bakuli nodded. "All Fachi made of salt, Missy, just like mud bricks. Walls, houses yes."

The next time I woke he was still there. My stomach had quieted and I was weak, but my head was clear at last. "The caravan," I said.

"It be gone, Missy. To Bilma."

"Will there be another caravan soon?" I asked anxiously. "There's that message of Muraiche's to deliver."

"There be no big ones, Missy, but caravans yes."

"How long have I been here like this?"

He smiled. "One sunset, two days. Not long."

"And that man," I persisted. "There was a man here, Bakuli?"

His eyes dropped. "Yes, Missy."

"Has he gone, too?"

When he nodded I felt a deep sense of relief. I'd not told Bakuli of what I'd seen in the moonlight that night; perhaps my fears had only been symptoms of my fever, because if he was gone— Frowning, I said, "He was kind, then? It was he who carried me here?"

Bakuli glanced away, not answering, but actually I needed no reply because if the man had gone that was enough for me, I was out of harm's way. Soon the woman with beaded hair bustled in with bowls of mush for us—what Amina had called tuwō, made of grains—and I sat up and ate with appetite. Following this she produced goat's milk and after this fresh dates. The man must have paid her well, I thought, for I had not expected charity here. I decided that my collapse must have had its roots in foul water and the heat, not typhoid or malaria as I'd feared, because after drinking from the wells of Fachi and lying in a dark room I was ready to get up.

"Show me Fachi," I said to Bakuli. "I have to grow strong again, I need to walk."

Bakuli went from the room into another to speak to the woman with beaded hair; he returned, nodding. We could go, he said, but her little boy must go with us to show us the way back. I would see why, he said, when I saw Fachi, and helping me to my feet I took my first steps. My weakness nearly overpowered me but I steadied myself, hoping Bakuli wouldn't notice and thinking fresh air would surely revive me, as well as the sun, however fierce.

The child's name was Elfali and I guessed him to be five or six years old, but he had the face of an old man. We walked from this dark airless room into another one and then squeezed through a narrow passage to a small door built of palm trunks. When the boy opened this it was not to sunshine but to a street so narrow that no sun could possibly find it; this curved into another that twisted like a snake past other windowless houses with doors like barricades. "Is there no sun?" I complained.

Bakuli spoke to Elfali, and leading us down another passage we arrived at stairs, and as we mounted them I saw sky and sunshine above, and with each step felt the weight of darkness grow lighter. We emerged on a flat rooftop curbed by a shoulder-high wall, but there were holes carved in the wall to look through and a section facing west had eroded and fallen away. We moved to this space and from here we could look down on Fachi's palm trees and gardens, while beyond lay a cream-colored desert under a blazing white sun. I turned to see what lay behind us: set into a level just below the rooftop were long serried lines of huge clay jars. I said, "What on earth! Look, Bakuli."

He nodded. "This be fortress, Missy. Once many Tuareg raids. Arab, too. Everybody come, everybody take."

"So they live in darkness but they're safe," I said, and wondered if to be this safe was to always live in darkness, a strange thought for one who had known so little of either. But whether I understood it then or not, the desert had greatly changed me, I had lived in it now for a very long time and in the desert there was no safety. But there was light.

I gave up counting the jars, they would

have food stored in them for a siege, I supposed, and returned to the scene below me. I saw a man walk to a wooden door in the outer wall that circled the village, open the door, disappear for a moment and then reappear. I saw that he was carrying a sack on his back to a caravan that was camped outside, a small one, with no more than a dozen baggage camels and a few riding camels. "Look—a caravan, Bakuli!"

"Yes, Missy. For Bilma in morning."

I frowned, thinking it was good to know of that small hidden door. I would have moved closer to the edge of the roof to mark it better but I was suddenly overwhelmed with dizziness and sat down.

"Missy, *mēnē nē,* what is it?"

"I have no *iko,*" I told him, catching my breath. "All gone." For a moment I wondered if I was going to faint as both sky and Bakuli whirled dizzyingly, but it passed, leaving me light-headed.

"Thou *huta*—rest," Bakuli said firmly, and spoke to the boy who led us back down the stairs. My body might be weak but my head was clearing, and I carefully counted the turnings that we took through the serpentine passages, attempting to memorize them for the future in case of necessity: to the left, then right—right again —left, right . . . Once back in the room I took a piece of charcoal out of the brazier and wrote down what I remembered of the route on the wall.

There was more *tuwō* waiting for me, and a cup of milk. "What is this, Bakuli?" I asked. "This is more food than—Bakuli, speak," I said, seeing his troubled face. "Something is wrong, *kō?*"

He nodded and said miserably, "I speak. While thou sleep, Missy, we be sold."

"That's ridiculous," I gasped. "That's crazy—it's *bushilu.* What do you mean, 'sold'?"

"Thou be *bawa* now—slave, Missy."

I stared at him incredulously. He said the man who had taken pity on my illness, or so Bakuli had thought, this man who had carried me to this room and paid the Beri-Beri woman to feed and give medicine, he was no *ābōkī*—no friend. Not at all.

"There be *bauri*—bitterness in Bakuli," he said. "This man be devil, a jackal."

"But he's gone," I faltered. "You said he'd gone, Bakuli, how could he do such evil?"

"While thou sleep," he repeated, "he sell thee and me to a *bako,* I think an Arab. He say, *'Gedash?'* and then in Hausa, *'nawa'*—how much?—and other man speak Hausa and say make offer. Oh Missy, thou be sleeping."

"Oh how dare he," I cried in a fury.

Bakuli said miserably, "It happen, Missy. Bad, bad."

The man had not stuck a dagger in me while I slept, nor suffocated me with his headscarf, he had been cleverer than this, he had *sold* me? I couldn't believe it but I saw the cunning behind it; he had murdered a man of importance, a shaykh and a rich Senussi, and I had seen his face in the moonlight. Oh how adroitly he had arranged that I never bear witness to his act, and as I saw this I felt a chill as cold as death. My first thought was, *We must escape quickly—get away at once,* but I was too weak to go anywhere, the climb to the rooftop had left me trembling and drained and I remembered that I had come near to fainting there.

Bakuli put a finger to his lips, bidding me be silent and just in time, for the tiny woman with beaded hair entered the room, and with her came two men. One was rough-looking, his burnous shabby, his eyes shrewd, and Bakuli, nodding toward him, whispered, "He be man who buy us, Missy." The man who followed him into the room wore a silk turban and gandoura, and there were gold rings on his fingers.

"*Salaam aleikum,*" said the rich one politely, and to the other in Hausa, "This is the *yārinyā*—the girl?"

"*Naam,* Sidi."

He gestured to me to stand up, which I did, shakily and against my will, and in anger. Indifferent to my anger he forced open my mouth and examined my teeth and then pinched each of my breasts. I could scarcely claim undue modesty at this, having lived among bare-breasted Hausa women, but I was furious at such impertinence. He unwrapped my head-scarf to see my hair, which had grown to a length of an inch or two, having not been shaved recently. Looking into my face and studying it he nodded. "*Naam,*" he said. "*Gedash?*"

I was incredulous; there was to be a second transaction and we were to be sold again?

"The boy too?" asked the other man.

He shrugged. "He's young, he has good teeth, why not? The girl is thin as a plucked chicken but fattened up she'll bring a good price in Murzuk." A faint smile stirred his lips. "I may even send her to Constantinople if she fattens up enough, the Sultan should find her pleasing as a gift for his harem." To me he said, *"Dogum yeriniz nedir?"*

This had the sound of Turkish heard at the Consulate in Tripoli; he thought me Turkish, perhaps.

When I was silent he said in Arabic, *"Inta mineyu*—where do you come from?"

Meeting only a blank face he said in a Hausa worse than my own, *"Kai, wānē nē?"*

When I did not respond he shrugged, spoke to his companion, bid the woman feed me well, and they left.

I sat down on the straw mat, glancing only once at Bakuli's sad face. Fragile as I was at that moment, I knew what had to be done, and quickly. I said, "Help me to the roof again, Bakuli. This time just you and me—I marked the turnings as you saw me do. See if the woman's gone."

"Why, Missy? Thou need *huta*—rest!"

"Just see," I told him.

He returned, nodding. "No peoples."

"Help me," I begged, and leaning heavily on him I whispered to myself: *Left, right, right again, then left, right . . .* He unbarred the door, giving me a furtive anxious glance and slowly, clumsily we made our way down the narrow winding passage, withdrawing into deeper shadows when we heard footsteps.

We found the stairs and I nearly wept with relief that we'd not lost the way. We reached the rooftop and I pointed to the break in the wall through which we'd looked at the desert. "Bakuli," I said, "you must go."

He looked at me in horror. "Missy, *no!*"

"You can jump—it's not that far," I told him, "and you saw the door in the wall below. If it was unlocked half an hour ago it will still be unlocked, and there's the caravan beyond it, ready to leave for Bilma."

"Missy, not without *you!*" he cried.

"You must," I said. "I'm still too weak, too sick, but *you* can go. Look," I told him, drawing Mr. Jappy from the pocket of my barracan. "Take Muraiche's message to Bilma, the man you deliver it to may help you, the message is inside, as you know. They say the Zambezi is south—go there even if you have to beg or sell dung to find your river. Take this, too." I brought out the Hand of Fatima and reached for his hand, placing it firmly in his palm. "Do this for me, Bakuli. Go before it's too late."

"But you be slave, Missy," he sobbed, the tears running down his cheeks.

I said, "I have the red poison seeds, Bakuli."

He recoiled in shock. "Missy, *NO!*"

"To give to the man who bought me," I lied. "There will be time for me to escape later and—you heard him, Bakuli, I will be fed. Do this for me—for me, your sister, your *mukalamba.*"

"Oh Missy," he whispered.

"Before it's too late, *GO,*" I pleaded. "You remember the name of the man in Bilma?"

He nodded miserably. "Abu Abd el

Wahat. Missy, Bakuli not even know thy true name."

"Caressa Bowman," I told him.

"Ressa Boman," he repeated.

"And yours?"

"Bakuli Mumbulaka."

"My *ndumē*," I said, smiling, but afraid now that I might faint before I saw him safe. "Jump now—*jump*, Bakuli."

He jumped. Leaning over the parapet I saw him stumble to his feet and run to the wooden door. Mercifully it opened for him, I watched him pass through it and the door close behind him. It was a terrible moment for me; his escape was the only gift I could give to him but the loss wrenched at my heart.

They found me there moments later, only half-conscious, and carried me back to the dark little room.

Book 3

fifteen

The stranger who came to my door some weeks ago here in London has written a letter formally requesting an interview. He identifies himself as an anthropologist, a very grand one, with many initials after his name to prove his erudition. He writes that he has been in London giving a series of lectures but must leave in a few days and he hopes that I am no longer "indisposed" so that he may call on me. He explains that until a year ago—and it has taken him this long to trace me, he adds—he spent eighteen months in a village in northeastern

Zambia studying the customs, language and religion of the Bemba. The chief of the village, the *mfumu,* told him many marvelous stories, he writes, but strangest of all was a story, very strange indeed, about a white girl, Ressa Boman, with whom he traveled many years ago in the Sahara and how they stayed one night on a hill of rocks near Abalessa, a hill surrounded by tombs and full of ghosts, and here his companion found a carved stone figure with green glass in it. The anthropologist describes how the name Abalessa tugged at his memory until eventually he recalled it being the site of Queen Tin Hinan's tomb, discovered in 1925. Writing to friends he secured news clippings and photos of the excavation and these he showed to the Bemba chief, who said yes, this was the place, and "full of spirits."

So Bakuli still lives and is the chief of his village, but "Oh, Bakuli," I tell him silently, "thou *mukwakwa,* thou talebearer, thou has spoken too much." I will remain indisposed to this man, for I've no interest in becoming a footnote in a book, but I'm grateful to him for his news of Bakuli, it's wonderful indeed to know that he reached home safely at last and that his God gave him many more chapters to live. I see him dispensing wisdom to his people and I wonder if he still smiles that radiant white smile and if he has many sons. He must be a happy man, for to find one's place in the world is no small thing, and it is because of him—because Bakuli and I were both of us slaves once, bought and sold like so much merchandise—that I contribute all that I can now to the Anti-Slavery Society here in London (they will never know why, of course) and receive reports that wring the heart, for there are still slaves living nightmare lives in Asia, the Middle East and in Africa . . . babies sold at birth, children sold into prostitution or as apprentices to labor night and day, literally chained to their work.

There but for the Grace of God . . .

In my desk I have the same newspaper clippings this anthropologist writes to me about, yellow with age now, of course, but I bring them out to look at again. My eyes go at once to a photo inset of the great rock mound they excavated near the oasis of Abalessa, and how astonishing it is to see that hill again, to remember how

the drums beat so ominously in the distance that even now, decades later, I am
not immune to the panic they brought.
Throughout the report of the tomb's discovery—and it occupied much of the front
page of the *Times*—there is a sense of
astonishment that what had once been a
Tuareg legend and myth was proving to be
true.

Here too are photographs of the jewels found in the tomb of Queen Tin Hinan,
but enlarged and given prominence is a
photograph of the object that most excited
the archaeologists, and startled me as
well: a carved stone figure no different
from my muffin man, except that it has
womanly protuberances where mine suggested a male figure and there is no green
stone in the hole carved out near its center.

They have named it the Venus Libya,
and the reporter describes it as "almost
unique in archaeological research. The
mystery," he writes, "is how this statuette
came to be in a tomb that is ancient, but
many thousand years more recent than the
Venus Libya, which is guessed to be Stone
Age. Perhaps," he speculates, "it was a

sacred object handed down for countless generations. . . . It is probably as old a piece of art as exists in the world; it resembles the Venus of Lausanne in southern France, which is attributed to Paleolithic times; it is also much like the Venus of Willendorf in Germany, which is dated not far from Neanderthal. . . . It may date as far back as 100,000 years before Christ."

But there is also a fourth Venus, I tell him silently; it has lain here on my desk for many years: Deborah played with it as a child and so did Sara after she was born and when she came to visit.

The *Times* report concludes: "Queen Tin Hinan was obviously buried with much honor, for her skeleton, when found, had been placed on a leather couch and with her was interred a wealth of jewelry: massive gold bracelets, necklaces of bronze, ivory, garnet and glass, carnelian and turquoise, and the remains of her crumbling garments are fringed with leather painted red and yellow. . . ."

Yes, I think, nodding, *I saw that fringe and this is true, it was red and yellow.*

Jared was more interested in the muffin man, thinking the limestone figure so primitive it might be prehistoric, and in this he was right. As for the green stone he thought it of little value, a tourmaline or green garnet—and in this he was wrong. He was sure that it didn't belong to the figure, and knocking it sharply against a rock—I gasped at such recklessness—he proved it when the green stone dropped out and fell to the earth. "See?" he said. "Someone placed it there—playfully, I imagine—because it fitted perfectly and was lovely."

If only we'd known it was an emerald! Instead I remember saying that even tourmalines must have barter value, and could buy us food—we were very hungry that day—but he shook his head, saying no.

"Why?"

"Because we could be even hungrier next week," he said with a flash of that smile that breaks my heart to remember still. "And because for so long as you have *something,* my sweet, you walk tall. When you've nothing at all it shows, and the jackals gather."

"And what do you keep?" I asked.

"You," he said.

"You'd never sell or barter me, then?" I teased.

He gave me a long deep glance. "Don't flirt, Caressa, you know very well that no matter what happens—if ever the desert separates us—I'll find you somehow, wherever you are."

"Nothing will separate us."

But Jared was a man who saw things; he'd lived among Africans long enough to know their spirit worlds and to respect what Bakuli called *ba wa ngulu,* the soothsayers. He was familiar with a magic I couldn't know; he'd acquired a sixth sense.

Sometimes I wonder how many people have been truly loved, which is not given many to know because what is called love is so often barter and trade. I would guess that Grams loved me in her way but I'm not sure about Mum, who thought it was love that pushed me out into a world she really wanted for herself and that I was ill-prepared for. What I do know is that it was Bakuli who taught me the patience and the generosity that love truly is, and from him I learned it was possible for me to love, too, and for this I have been forever beholden to him.

All this I understood as never before when I opened my eyes again in that airless room in Fachi and knew that Bakuli was gone. If the human spirit is like candle flame then mine had too often dimmed, but in Bakuli it burned bright and constant, sustained by faith in a God I could neither understand nor feel, being still affronted by the tricks fate had played on me. Now life was playing new tricks. What I felt at this moment was black despair—but no, this was wrong because the color black has vitality, the night is black and has stars and a moon, and mysterious and important events can happen in darkness. Despair, I decided, was gray: endless, bottomless, without night or day, time, sun or stars. Bakuli was gone and I had been sold, but I couldn't grasp what it meant to be sold. A person bought food and clothes—but human beings? I was myself, a body, face, two arms, two legs, a mind and a heart—all mine and surely not to be purchased like a loaf of bread, yet this had happened; I did not like the sound of Constantinople or harems or of Murzuk either.

As I recovered my strength some of the fatalism of the desert I'd lived in for so long began to assert itself. Among the Tuareg it was said that unless a man was killed he lived forever; there was Marcus Aurelius, too, who had written "whatever may happen to you, it was prepared for you from all eternity," and of course there was Mum's counsel on rolling with the punches. *Mektoub,* the Arabs say—it is written—and *Inch'Allah,* if God wills it, and so, knowing I had to regain strength quickly for whatever lay ahead I applied myself diligently to this, and in the five days before leaving Fachi I climbed the stairs often to the roof to sit in the sun, glad to be removed from the dank and oppressive labyrinths below me and to breathe desert air.

The name of the man who had bought me was Achmet el Kazza and he turned out to be more of a merchant than a slavetrader. Much as any European traveler would pick up gifts to carry home to his friends he seemed to have made his purchases with apparent casualness, and he had added to his caravan thirty Hausa who caught his eye on the way; this struck me as more callous than if he made his living at buying and selling human beings. His caravan was of good size, with nearly two hundred baggage camels, but he had come to Fachi to negotiate with the Kel Aïr Tuareg for fifty of their cream-colored camels to sell in the north. His caravan had started out in the south, near Lake Chad, and the freighted camels carried ivory, kola nuts, cloth, hides and salt as well as food, water, fodder, sheep and goats—and thirty-one of us not there by choice.

Among el Kazza's collection of slaves there was one young woman who apparently had possibilities for Constantinople too, because while the other slaves walked she and I were given donkeys to ride, and goat's milk to drink. Her name was Ramatu and she was a Fulani, her skin a pale tawny brown and her features almost European except for a tribal scar at each corner of her mouth. She wore huge silver circles in her ears and beaded necklaces, and had small pointed breasts, quite bare during the day, her only covering a bright cloth tied around her waist and extending to her knees. I thought her stunning, but although she spoke Hausa she was proud and not given to talk. The men were Hausa and looked strong, which was no doubt why el Kazza had selected them; they had already walked a great distance and there were many more days of travel ahead, although later I would learn that five had died on the way to Fachi and had been left behind for the vultures, which sickened me to hear.

Thus we left Fachi one day after the el Subr prayer had been said at sunrise. At midday we stopped for the el Duhr, in midafternoon for the el Asr, at sunset for the el Mogh'reb and each night for the el Aschïa. Until now I'd not met with such devoutness among the desert Arabs, who might pray once or twice a day on the march, but this caravan was accompanied by a muezzin who marked the hours and at each stop pointed the men to the East, and Mecca, with great preciseness. I was not unmoved by this. We would be plodding across the plains under a blue enamel sky when suddenly there would ring out the melodious cry of *"Hya alla Salat! Haya all fallah!"* A hundred men would dismount from their camels and begin their ablutions, ardently washing themselves with sand after which they would prostrate themselves in prayer, their words rising and falling in a muted chorus that ended, always, with a great and joyous cry of *"Allah Akhbar! Allah Akhbar! Allah Akhbar!"* until the sound of it echoed among the dunes and must surely have penetrated even the low-lying cliffs in the east.

We stopped only briefly at Bilma, camping outside of its walls while the camels were watered and the guerbas filled, and then we turned north to head toward an oasis they called Seguedine, a five-day march from Bilma, *Inch'Allah.* Soon we were exchanging desert sand for the gravelly plains of a reg. There was no hope of escape, for a man was appointed to keep an eye on us, and in any case where could one go? Some very inhospitable cliffs were surfacing to the east of us and to the west there lay only a wasteland of dull red gravel.

I had begun to notice one of the Hausa men who walked near me, he was stumbling often and had several times come near to falling toward the night of each endless march. If I had recovered physically now from the crossing of the Tenere my emotions remained fragile and it

pained me to watch the man; I found myself suffering with and for him. I guessed
that he had fever, and one day in guiding
my donkey closer I saw that this was so; I
asked his name but he only looked at me
with distant bloodshot eyes so that I knew
all of his concentration to be fixed upon
the next step to be taken, and on survival.
Once I gave him water, which startled him
out of his reverie and he became aware,
but briefly. There came a day when his
eyes were glazed and each step torture for
him and I could endure this no longer; I slid
from my donkey and told him, *"Dauk!* Take
it! *Huta*—rest."

He looked frightened, his eyes still un-
focused, vision blurred, but he mounted
the donkey and I walked beside him. For
several hours he rode until the overseer
saw this and pulled him off the donkey, angrily gesturing me to mount it again.

Ramatu gave me a reproachful look. I
made trouble, she said—*Wahalā!* Did I
want to live or *mutu*—die, she asked.

"Kayya, but you are hard," I told her.

She only shrugged. "With *tsauri* I will
live, they say I will have silks and many
jewels."

When the caravan stopped that night in the moonlight to feed the camels and rest and make a fire I saw the Hausa man fall to the ground and lie motionless, gasping for breath.

Going to him I said, *"Ina gajiya?*—how is the tiredness?"

He did not answer and I saw that he was dying. I touched his cheek and he opened his eyes, purged of fever now, and smiled at me. He said in a clear joyous voice, *"Za ni gidā."*

He had said, "I am going home."

His eyes widened, his breath came hard and stopped; he was dead. There would be no more fever, no more struggle; instinctively my fingers sought the hard red seeds in the pocket of my barracan and then, reassured by their presence, I leaned over and closed his eyes for him.

There is a dangerous way of removing oneself from reality, and this I began to practice now, cutting myself off from all feeling. I could look without seeing: at tufts of grass beginning to soften the hard edges of the reg, the appearance of a tree —an acacia I decided without caring—at rocks that rose sharply out of the gravel like monuments, some of them huge, and once a rock that I thought at first to be a very tall man wrapped in a cloak. There began to be a tilt upward in the earth, we were climbing toward a rocky plateau and leaving behind the gravel plains, and with this there came a merciful change to cooler air. This almost brought me back to life, but not quite, for I still remained . . . I could not say the word "slave." In my previous world slavery had been outlawed years and years ago and now I cursed people in Boston and London for being so complacent as to believe it was no longer alive in these faraway places. Such thoughts were dangerous because I could afford neither rage nor fear nor sorrow nor awareness of any sort, I could only finger the red poison seeds in the pocket of my barracan and numb myself to what lay ahead.

By evening of the sixth day we were discovered by a dozen small black boys who romped along beside us as we made our way into Seguedine. It was a larger settlement than I had expected, but if it was shabby and poor it had water, and while el Kazza greeted the elders of the village the camel drivers headed for the well where they would spend all night watering so many camels. I stared at two young women carrying jugs of water on their heads; their smiles startled me, as well as the large silver rings each wore in one nostril, but Ramatu and I were immediately hurried off to a mud hut, denied even the sky and the stars for this night.

The flimsy door closed and we sat, each of us scratching flea bites, a smelly oil lamp throwing out a feeble circle of light between us. "I don't like it here," I said angrily, "why can't we sleep outside?"

"He hides us," Ramatu said. "Did you not see there is another caravan here?"

"Who are they?" I asked.

She only shrugged, having neither conversation nor curiosity; she was much given to shrugs, which I found tiresome. Soon the door was set aside and a boy brought us bread and a bowl of lentils with shreds of lamb in it. We ate with our fingers, scooping up juice with slabs of bread, and then lay down on the palm mats to sleep. This did not come easily for there were continuing noises from the village, the sound of a peculiar raspy instrument being played, shouts of men, a laugh or two and a rise and fall of talk in Arabic and Hausa; el Kazza was obviously making merry at a campfire after six days of the desert. I had nearly fallen asleep when the door was suddenly removed and el Kazza walked into the hut with another man.

"*Tāshī*—stand up!" he ordered, and in Arabic I heard the word *gameel,* or beautiful. Then I understood as I rose that he was boasting, showing us off to a friend, that too many kola nuts had overstimulated him or that perhaps, despite his devoutness, he had been sampling palm wine. I heard the words Sultan and Constantinople, and walking over to Ramatu he patted her breasts and smiled at his companion: he was showing his merchandise.

His friend said in Arabic that we were beautiful indeed but it was a long way to Murzuk, and longer still to Constantinople and would he consider selling one of us now?

El Kazza roared with laughter; he was truly a changed man this night. He said that was out of the question but weren't we beauties?

His friend moved to Ramatu and

looked into her face, and then with a glance at me he said, "That one looks a Targuia. I can offer gold, *Sidi.*"

Oh God, I thought drearily, and gave him a look of hate. El Kazza's friend was muffled against the cold in burnous and draped headscarf but his eyes had a strange sheen, he looked younger than el Kazza and yet his eyebrows were white.

"La, la," el Kazza said, laughing. "Whatever she is, she too is for the harem."

"Much gold," said his friend.

"*Nawā*—how much?" asked el Kazza curiously, looking him up and down as if he'd not expected his companion to have such wealth, and now I realized the man was not of this caravan but a *bako* who had been sharing the campfire with el Kazza.

I did not speak: why should I speak when I was not a human being to these two, merely chattel to be bargained over— but I could hate them both.

The *bako* was offering two gold pieces.

"You call that 'much gold'?"

"Two gold pieces," repeated the man.

"For which *yārinyā?*" asked el Kazza, resorting to Hausa.

The man shrugged and pointed to me.

El Kazza hissed through his teeth. "Bismallah, you offer little. La!"

"Three pieces of gold then."

El Kazza shook his head. "Five."

"Three," repeated the *bako.*

"La—forget it."

The man shrugged and turned away, saying words in Arabic I couldn't understand.

El Kazza watched him a moment and then spoke. "Show me the gold."

The man turned his back to us, burrowing through layer after layer of clothes. When he faced el Kazza again he held up a single coin that glittered in the lamplight and I saw el Kazza's eyes widen at the size of it.

"Four," said el Kazza. "Four of them."

The stranger shrugged and then, *"Naam,"* he said.

I had just been sold for four gold pieces, and to still another man. I thought wearily that at the very least this spared me the slave market in Murzuk or a harem in Constantinople but what manner of man this was I didn't know, and as my spirits plunged I fingered again the handful of poison seeds in my pocket.

"*Zō,*" he said to me in Hausa, and I went with him out of the hut into the night. We circled a dying fire and he led me some distance away from the well where el Kazza's caravan had camped. In the thin light of a gauzy moon I noticed that unlike el Kazza's men, who slept on the earth, this man had set up a tent of hides laced to four poles, like the Tuareg, but high enough to stand in and with flaps for closing. He led me inside and lit a lantern that gave so dim a light that I still couldn't see him clearly.

"Take off your clothes," he said.

I stared at him, speechless and outraged.

"Take them off," he said curtly in Hausa.

Frightened I slipped out of my clothes. He walked over to me and touched my breasts, cupping them, and then he ran his hands lightly down my body. I closed my eyes and gritted my teeth; when I briefly opened them he too had discarded his clothes and bid me lie down.

I lay down. He was no Jacob. My God he was no Jacob, I was played on like an instrument, reaching sensations never dreamed of; I lay spellbound until a wildness rose in me and I met passion with passion, the flames rising higher and higher between us until—ending, I fell limp and utterly astonished. We lay for a moment interlocked, but I did not look at him or even consider him, I was centered on the discovery of an entire universe unknown to me. *Poor Jacob,* I thought, and rolling over and away from this man I said, "Good heavens!"

He jerked away from me as if bitten by a scorpion. "That's English!"

I was so bemused it needed a minute for me to realize that when he'd said "That's English," it was English that he'd spoken.

"Who are you?" he demanded. "You're no Targuia—you said in English, 'Good heavens.' "

I sat up and stared at him and suddenly all the weeks of fear, anger and bitterness exploded and I cried out furiously, "What does it matter to you who I am? You bought me for four gold pieces and now you've *raped* me and you'd have done it whether I was Tuareg, Hausa, Fulani or Arab, so why should it make any difference who I am, and I hope you speak enough English to understand that I think you a vulture—an *ungulu*—a monster and a bastard."

Without hesitation he said in a hard even voice, "I speak and understand English and I paid four gold pieces for you for reasons I don't care to mention just now, and I took you fast to put my brand on you because if you were a Tuargia you'd think ill of me if I didn't, and be out of here by morning. Who are you?"

"A slave," I said bitterly.

"Oh?" In the dim light I thought the corners of his mouth tightened in a faint smile. He said dryly, "I wonder which of us is the more surprised and which the slave now. *Who are you?*"

I was silent, suspicious and worn out.

He rose, pulled his burnous around him and rummaged in a leather bag. "I've some brandy, you'd better have some." He handed me a canteen with a canvas cover and I cautiously drank from it. Hand-

ing it back I said defiantly, "And who are
you? You're not an Arab, you can't be."

"It seems we're both imposters." He
shrugged. "I've been hunting in Abyssinia,
trying to make a fortune in ivory, but things
grew too hot for a white man so I decided
to do some traveling and see more of the
continent. I'm a Scotsman."

"What do you mean 'hot'?" He was
stuffing a blanket into a sack now, I
couldn't guess why and didn't really care
to know, but it was of some interest to me
to learn whether I'd been bought by a man
wanted for murder.

"The Emperor's dying," he said.
"King Menelik. Some say he's already
dead, some say he had a stroke and is
half-dead, but when a ruler in these parts
loses power—and he's been a damn fine
ruler, I liked him—it's every man for himself. Robber bands everywhere, tribes
fighting tribes. Pure anarchy."

Not a murderer, then. "Why are you
taking down the tent?" I asked, watching
him remove the hides from their poles and
roll them into a bundle.

"Because we're leaving now. I've a
suspicion el Kazza may have plans to steal

you back once he's counted his four gold pieces a few times and rued his sale."

"You mean—oh God," I said and hastily drew on my tattered clothes and rolled up the mat on which we'd lain. For just a second I remembered what had happened on that mat and I blushed, but this was no time for thought; when he carried the tent poles out to the camels I followed closely behind him, pausing only to glance back once—out of fear—to el Kazza's shadowy camp, and for comfort to the stars overhead. Four camels were prodded to their feet, two of them loaded with guerbas bulging with Seguedine water, and the third with baggage. When I helped him tie down the bales of fodder, he gave me a quick glance and said, "You've lived with the Tuareg." It was not a question and I didn't answer. A great deal had happened to me in the past few hours and it was impossible to sort out my thoughts and my feelings.

He said, "We'll walk the first miles."

"Where are we going?"

"To Zouar—east. El Kazza heads north." He tied the camels' headstall to tail and led them single file in and around the rocks with me following. The mountain air cooled my flushed cheeks and the stars were luminous in a black velvet sky. This was hammada now, littered with stones and boulders and sharp pebbles and he walked the camels slowly, carefully choosing the way. I had no idea what time of night it was but we walked for a long time before the sky in the east began to pale. In this cold predawn twilight he chose a high rock behind which to camp, tall enough for shade at noon and well-concealed from anyone who followed. From one of his sacks he drew out dried camel dung and built a small fire. Over this he set a battered tin pot into which he measured two cups of water and a handful of tea. I looked only at his hands, not wanting to see his face, uncertain of this new situation and of this man, wary, a little frightened still, yet curious. I knew that I'd been spared Murzuk and a slave market but I had also made startling discoveries about myself that threw me into confusion. Tired and hungry, I ate the fresh dates his hand presented to me and found that strong tea was even kinder than brandy for distraught nerves.

"You'd better sleep," he said, stamp-

ing out the fire, and I spread out my barracan, lay down and immediately fell into a
deep sleep. . . .

The heat and the brightness woke me.
Opening my eyes I saw my new captor sitting against a rock writing words on paper
with a pencil. I had seen neither pencil nor
paper for a very long time but my eyes
went to his face, which I'd seen only by the
light of a lantern and since then had
avoided; now I wanted to see what manner
of man had bought me for four gold pieces
and taken me to bed. It was a deeply
tanned face much weathered by the suns
of the desert, with a map of thin lines ra-
diating from the eyes and two horizontal
lines threading the forehead: a hard strong
face but with a pair of startling green eyes
under the bleached white brows. It was the
eyes that held me as he lifted his head to
look at me; they had the look of a very private person and of one who saw things,
and I had no idea what I meant by this except they made him different and puzzling.
Examining him by daylight, and with interest, I could not help but dislike the manner
of his "taking" me, as he'd put it, but I had
not been raised on the Elsie Dinsmore

books or the pious romances that had been devoured by the girls at Thistlethwaite School. In my situation I could count myself fortunate that I'd not been bedded by a Targui or by el Kazza or a Turkish sultan, and I thought it even more fortunate to learn that passion wasn't foreign to me and that with this man I'd had a perfect moment. Still, as we stared at each other and I remembered the events of the night, I felt my cheeks grow hot with blushes and quickly looked away.

"You too?" he said gently, reading my thoughts, and as he rose and came to me I knew that it was going to happen again, and the anticipation of it erupted in me like wildfire, so that I was trembling. Obviously I would never be a lady.

Hours later, lying together, we talked a little, two human beings unalterably tied to each other by the flesh and in search of what lay beyond it now.

"So you're American," he said. "News travels fast in Africa. I heard of that massacre south of Ghadames but no one knew there was a survivor. It was a long time ago."

"Yes," I said.

He shook his head. "You have to be the first white woman to reach this part of the country, and the first American. Were you with the Tuareg long?"

"Until I escaped."

"And have been trying to get home ever since, I suppose."

"*Yes,*" I said fervently, except there abruptly slid into my mind the thought, *Home to what, Caressa,* and this was not something that my homing instincts had remotely considered. "Yes," I said doubtfully.

"And then?"

I did not care to talk any more. *"Mu tafi?"* I asked, slipping into Hausa.

He nodded. "You're right, it's time to go but—" His smile was a surprise, completely changing his guarded face. "But you've not told me your name, am I to call you nothing but 'you'?"

"My name's Caressa," I told him. "Caressa Horvath Bowman."

"I'll call you Caressa," he said, "but I suspect you're really an *'aljan,* a djinn of the desert. Or an houri."

I ignored this. "And what do I call you?"

"Jared's my name. Jared MacKay."

I nodded. There seemed no point—
and I could certainly find none—in nursing
hostility any longer, in spite of the shocks
I'd sustained during the past few hours,
and I had to ruefully admit that I'd sustained them shockingly well for I felt alive
again in every pore of my body. When
we'd lain together in the sun he'd been
gentle, and afterward we had talked; a
woman appreciates talk. There would be
more of it but not yet, because the silence
of the desert was a part of each of us, but I
knew that something was being established, something important; it had the feel
of kinship and it was as free and as spa-
cious as the desert—*and as dangerous
too,* I thought, but I was content.

sixteen

H e had started backward, this Jared who had assumed I was a Targuia, and he made no apologies for his actions, but in a subtle manner he began to court me. This struck me as funny because it was so difficult to do, each of us engaged as we were each day in lugging guerbas, feeding, loading and reloading four camels, traveling ten or eleven hours only to unload the camels, feed them, build a fire, make a meal, chase after any camels that wandered away and finally collapse into sleep, only to begin again after several hours of rest.

"Where are we?" I asked on the third evening, which I thought intelligent of me, for it seemed time to know. "And where are you going?" He traveled well, this man, his camels carrying sheepskins, salt wrapped in hay, a loaf of sugar, wheat for unleavened bread, and coffee such as I'd not tasted since Tripoli. Besides this there were three rifles and the tent—but it had not been used again—the kit of medicine with its canteen of brandy, several sacks of fresh and dried dates, wooden utensils and a leather bucket with long ropes for lowering it into a well. There was even a leather sack of twigs and dried camel's dung for fires, a bag of trading beads and a book, and his guerbas were well-cured. I could only think of how little Bakuli and I had traveled with, and wish that he might be here to see such largesse.

It was night and he was nursing a fire and I huddled as close to it as I dared, warming my hands on a cup of coffee. The sun had retreated in a burst of color—a blaze of crimson striped with shades of purple and mauve, and the moon was frosting the sands with silver; we had descended into desert again and it was cold.

He said with a frown, "I think we're in French Equatorial Africa, which not so long ago was the French Congo."

"French, then."

He nodded. "Roughly speaking, yes— by one of those treaties they keep making, or so I heard when I was in Djanet but I doubt there are any French *here.*" He waved a hand at the empty landscape around us. "This would be called the Chad Military Territory, I think. As for tomorrow, we should reach Zouar, climbing all the way."

"And then?"

He sighed. "That's what I'm trying to puzzle out." He glanced up and smiled that quick magic smile that warmed his face and was already beginning to reach my heart. "Abyssinia's out for the moment, I was lucky to get away with my skin. The consul at Addis Abeba sent a messenger warning me, but still I made my getaway with a horde of natives in pursuit." He hesitated and then, "There's Egypt and the Eastern desert where I've a friend among the Bedouin . . . we could camp safely there for a while."

We . . . this word had an unexpectedly pleasing ring to it, for I had begun to appreciate all the dimensions of this man: I liked the way he talked, with an odd twist to his words that I guessed to be Scottish, and if he was sparing in speech what he did say had meat to it. He was also a man who worked hard, and he was competent. Of all this I had become increasingly aware and it helped steady the new emotions that he roused in me. "Where's Egypt?" I asked, draining my cup of coffee.

He left the fire to sit beside me. "A long way from us. Here, I'll show you." Drawing a pencil from his pocket he leaned over and sketched a map in the sand. "Egypt's up here in the corner, next to Tripolitania where you entered Africa. Just below Egypt is the Anglo-Egyptian Sudan, a huge country, and squeezed in next to it on the right—the farthest east you can go in Africa without running into the Red Sea —is Abyssinia, some of which is below Egypt, too, but only its tip."

"Abyssinia, where you hunted ivory. . . ."

"Yes." With his pencil he drew a straight line from Abyssinia across the Sudan. "And this is how I traveled, the shortest and most direct route—but avoiding El Fasher where a rather nasty Sultan named Ali Dinar cuts people's heads off—to eventually pass through Zouar and Sequedine on my way west."

"But why did you risk nasty sultans who cut people's heads off to come so far?" I asked.

He smiled. "Because I wanted to see the Tibesti Mountains and cross them, then head into the Sahara and up to the oasis of Djanet and see the Tassili n' Ajjer, which you visited by accident and not willingly." He hesitated. "Except that once in Djanet—once there I felt, no I *knew* I had to turn and come back. It's like that sometimes."

"Like what sometimes?"

"I feel things," he said with a shrug, but he didn't explain.

I said naïvely, "Do you write papers for a Geographical Society?"

For the first time he laughed, a roar of laughter that subsided into a chuckle. "No, my sweet, but I have it in the back of my mind—a secret I'll confess to you—that one day when I'm through adventuring I'd like to write a book or two about this land. It's been home to me for over a decade and it never stops fascinating me."

"A whole ten years?" I said in surprise.

"A whole ten years," he said. "I'm twice your age, I imagine. How old are you?"

"I don't know," I told him. "I was still sixteen, although nearly seventeen, when we left Tripoli but there's no time in the desert, is there? I don't know whether I'm nineteen or twenty now. Are you really twice my age?"

"Not quite, being thirty-one."

I said shyly, "I saw you writing words in your notebook, is that why?"

He nodded. "Much of Abyssinia I know well, but this is new to me, so yes, I write things down from time to time."

"And will put them in a book one day . . . you must read lots of them, too, then?"

He shrugged. "Not now, but I grew up bookish. My father taught school in a village not far from Edinburgh, a poor village and he was a poor man, but books we always had. My mother died first and my father when I was eighteen. They'd set aside money to send me to University but with them both gone I took stock of myself and my future and decided to set out for Africa instead, thinking to be another Bruce." Seeing my blank look he said, "James Bruce, a fellow Scotsman who went exploring in Africa back in the 1700s."

I said politely, "I've never heard of him, what did he explore?"

"Abyssinia, of course!" He rose and walked over to one of his saddlebags, and digging deep he extracted the small book I'd noticed when he unpacked; he handed it to me. It looked quite old, its page edges ragged, and I opened it carefully. On its title page I read:

TRAVELS
Between the Years 1768 & 1773
into
ABYSSINIA
To Discover the Source of The Nile

Being the substance of the Original Book
by

JAMES BRUCE, Esq.
Printed Glasgow 1818

"Shortened version," he said. "Very efficient for travel."

I opened the book to the middle and read, *Between the two rivers Geshen and Samba is a low unwholesome, though fertile, province called Wallaka and southward of that is Upper Shoa. This province was famous for the retreat it gave to the only remaining prince of the house of Solomon, who fled from the massacre of his brethren by Judith about the year 900.*

"It sounds a violent country," I told him, handing back the book.

"Oh it is, definitely. They have a saying in Abyssinia that all kings wade in blood to the throne."

"And because of Mr. Bruce you came to Africa and headed for Abyssinia!"

His eyes rested on me with humor. "Yes, but it wasn't that simple. I first spent a year in Alexandria learning Arabic and Swahili. That's where Saalih and I became friends—it's he whose family and roots are in Egypt's Eastern Desert, and later I spent a few weeks there hunting ibex with him and his brothers and father. Alexandria's also where I swallowed my penchant for avoiding Authority and became downright cozy with British officials, knowing I'd need their influence to get me into Abyssinia. Any more questions?"

I laughed. "Yes, did you make your fortune there?"

He nodded. "Enough. I couldn't risk traveling with it but it's well-hidden in Abyssinia."

Puzzled I said, "There? But if the country's—"

"It's safe in the bank all the natives use: the earth," he explained. "In my case I buried my gold under a cairn of rocks just before I crossed the border into the Sudan, before heading for Sennar and El Obeid—and having paid four gold sovereigns for a desert djinn I'm left now with only two gold rings and a sack of Maria Theresa thalers." His smile deepened the network of sun lines around his eyes, making his smile important because it was rare. "I like looking at you," he added. "Your Tuareg have a saying, 'A man and his woman friend are for the heart and the eyes, not just for the bed,' and yours is a face to feast the eyes on."

I put down my empty cup of coffee and smiled back at him. "When you look at me like that—"

"Yes," he said, and we lay down on the still-warm sand, wrapped together in a sheepskin, and made love under the moon and slept deeply with no sounds in the night except the stirring of the camels, and in the morning set out again for Zouar.

Zouar was set among towering pinnacles of rock, a mountain village of circular mud-and-stone houses slowly crumbling under the harsh sun. Almost at once Jared decided that we mustn't linger: a caravan was expected soon and this was to be avoided as well as any French patrols who might be in the neighborhood; Zouar, it seemed, was also a stopping place for caravans on the way to Murzuk, but these came from the southeast, from Borku and the Wadai. After we had worked hard filling the guerbas Jared said, "Stay and look meek while I have more words with the elder and learn what news the caravans have brought." He smiled faintly. "You're an Arab now, and while it's true I've never met an Arab woman who wasn't as strong-willed as her man, the women play at meekness. Be meek." He extracted a small leather bag from the others, pocketed it and turned to go. "Guard the camels, another day I'll teach you to use a rifle."

From these words I understood, not happily, that a man traveling with well-loaded camels, a woman and no guards, could be of great interest even here. I should not have been startled by this, having known the Tuareg, but these people were Tibbu, or Teda, and looked friendly. Yes, Jared said, but once they'd been famous raiders, and clever enough to raid even the Tuareg, and so I sat quietly, surrounded by curious grinning children and tried to look both meek and intimidating, but I was relieved when Jared returned. He was carrying a pile of goat hides and he looked troubled.

"There's news," he said. "Italy has invaded Tripoli—there's fighting there."

"*Tripoli?*" I gasped, remembering its sun-drenched calm, and remembering Mohammed, too, and the Hand of Fatima that had gone south with Bakuli.

"Even worse, it's spilled over into the deserts," he said. "The desert tribes—led by the Senussi—have rallied to support the Tripoli natives. It seems they despise the Italians more than the Turks in Tripoli, because the Italians are infidels while the Turks are at least fellow Muslims. All hell's broken loose."

"Does it mean trouble for us too?"

"It certainly limits us," he said dryly, "because there's only one direction we can go now—east." The logical way out of the mountains, he explained, was the known caravan route heading south out of Zouar, down through Borku and across to the Sudan, but this would lead us through Senussi territory, and if by chance it was discovered we weren't Arabs we could be killed. He had ruled this out, but now there was no hope of veering north at some point to cut across the desert to Egypt.

He said grimly, "We'll have to go the way I came, at least until we're out of the mountains. I had a guide for the trip so I know the route, but it's brutal." We would head up into Bardaï, he said, which lay in a valley high in the Tibesti—there would be water there—and after that drop down into the foothills to Yebbi Bou and risk there being a decent trail east across the plains to Egypt's Western Desert. *"Inch'Allah,"* he added with the twist of a smile and handed me one of the leather hides. "I traded for these, the Teda call this a *farto.* It'll be cold, very cold in the mountains and we'll have to race both winter and the winds." As I grasped the bundle he added wryly, "And then there will be desert and heat."

I found the *farto* to be a leather tunic made out of skins sewn together in a primitive manner with a hole for the head and each arm. It certainly looked unappealing, and I suspected lice, but I conceded that it would be warmer than my ragged barracan.

"Let's go," said Jared, and we began wrestling the camels to their feet and loading them again, and within the hour we had left the village.

After Zouar we followed tracks upward through a wilderness of rocks, heading into the high—really high—Tibesti Mountains. If it was hard for us, it was harder on the camels, just as crossing the

Tassili n' Ajjer had been. We led them up and down steep trails, through forests of stone lined by high cliffs and then down into a gorge and up again. Pausing on one cliff we saw a marvelous sight below us: the crater of a volcano filled with a pale jade-green substance, and after this we descended through narrow gorges to a dried-up oued, or wadi, and once in the canyon's bottom we made camp because there were thornbushes on which the camels could graze. . . .

That afternoon Jared explained the workings of a rifle to me, taking it apart and putting it together again, showing me how to clean and load it, how to hold it and how to aim it. "That's lesson number one," he told me. "We can't afford many bullets for practice, so that'll be for another day. Now take it apart again."

I grew bloody sick of taking it apart and putting it together again, at least until I'd mastered it, and then I felt a glow of pride. "You'll do," he said, and built a fire before the sun set in a sky the color of plum and damask, and that night we finished the sour goat's milk bought from the Teda in Zouar.

"Tell me about the Senussi," I said, washing my hands in the sand.

His brows lifted. "You've met them?"

"One," I told him, and spoke of Muraiche, murdered in the night by the man who later sold me.

Jared nodded. "He *could* have been on an errand of revenge, for it's unusual to find a Senussi in that part of the country, but they travel everywhere, their mission being to spread the faith. In the Fezzan desert the Bedouin are ardent followers. But they can't abide Christians or foreigners."

"Us," I said, nodding.

"And of course," he added almost casually, "they still involve themselves in the slave trade."

My head jerked up to stare at him. "It's true then?"

He nodded. "Senussi himself—Mohammed ben Ali es Senussi—has his headquarters in Kufra, in the far west of the Fezzan. With the blessings of the sultan of Wadai, far to the south, slaves are still brought from Lake Chad and the Sudan up through the Wadai and to Kufra and then to the coast. In the Koran, you see, the

words were spoken by Allah through Mohammed to the desert people, and there's
nothing in The Book forbidding slavery."

"I'm a slave," I reminded him sourly.

"You know you're not," he said, but
seeing how seriously I spoke, and how sad
I looked at this moment, he reached into
his pocket for his pencil and held it over
my head. "Thou, Caressa Horvath Bowman, are now a freed woman, no longer a
bāwā." Very softly he added, "And if
you're determined to go to America I'll help
you get there but I warn you, Caressa, I'll
do my best to make you never want to
go."

"Oh," I said stupidly, and then, being
a woman I must add, "Never?"

"Never," he said in a harsh voice,
"because you know damn well we belong
together."

That was when he spoke of how he
had turned back from Djanet to retrace his
steps to Seguedine. "It happens sometimes, it's something I was born with, perhaps because my mother was Irish and the
Irish are known often to have a third eye."

"Third eye?" I repeated, puzzled.

"An awareness of the future, of what's to happen."

"Oh, the sixth sense," I said. "Do you mean you have it?"

"I don't enjoy talking about it," he said, scowling, "but ever since I was a child I could sense when something was going to happen. My mother's death, my father's . . . warnings, you might say. At Djanet I felt pulled back almost physically —against my will, a strange feeling—aware that I had to return to Sequedine, that I'd left someone there who was important to me. It's hard to explain," he said uneasily, "and even harder for others to understand, but I'm trying. I reached Sequedine and there was nobody and nothing, and I swore at myself heartily, and then an hour later el Kazza's caravan began straggling in, and when I saw you I knew—I simply knew." He added ruefully, "But I had to spend three long and damnably boring hours with el Kazza before he'd let me see the girl he called a Targuia."

So that was how it had been, I thought, and feeling curiously humbled by his words I ceased to be maidenly and admitted truth to myself. Turning to him I said softly, "You told me you know damn well that we belong together, so you must know damn well that I've no interest in leaving you. Ever."

"Such language," was all he said; he was looking straight ahead, watching the camels graze, but I saw a corner of his mouth turn up in a pleased smile.

Gonoa, Bardaï. . . . in Bardaï there were palm trees and I remember we were offered a hut made of reeds for the night, but, "I'll miss the stars," I told Jared and he understood. That was when he said, "The Tuareg have a poem—I forget all but one line that says, 'I sleep where night overtakes me . . . my house will not crumble.' "

The words pleased me and I repeated them to myself: *"I sleep where night overtakes me. . . .* You like poetry too, then."

He nodded. "There's another that might interest you, written by an Arab seven hundred years ago, and with an approach to Islam rather different from the Senussi sect. The poet's one of Islam's finest, an Egyptian named Omar ibn-al-Farid;

unfortunately I remember only a few verses, but,

" 'If a pious man prostrates himself before the stone in a heathen temple,
Then—for him who understands—there is little cause for fanaticism.

For perhaps he apprehends in verity the Almighty Allah
Behind the stone he worships.

From Allah the warnings have reached those for whom they were destined,
And by the grace of Allah mercy is granted in all religions.'*

"In all religions," he repeated.

"It doesn't rhyme but I like it," I said. "Was Omar Khayyám an Arab?"

"He was Persian and a Sufi, as ibn-al-Farid was, and Sufiism is the glory of Islam. Why?"

"Because I know a little of his poetry, especially about not letting slip a perfect hour which I despaired of ever knowing until I met you. I thank you for that, Jared."

* Nicholson's translation.

"You're welcome, Caressa Bowman." His lips were caked with dust but he managed a smile. "I know those words—a little melancholy for my taste but on the other hand—" He leaned over and kissed me and his lips were rough as sandpaper but his hands were gentle; there are other languages than words.

After Bardaï it blurred. Sand and rock, rock and sand, frigid nights and scorching days. I learned to shoot and one day shot a gazelle, which broke my heart to do, but we needed meat, and after this Jared gave me the rifle as mine, and I wore it slung across my back like a man. We traveled at night to avoid the heat and spare the camels and slowly I learned more of the stars because Jared could name them: Orion, and the Pleiades, Sirius and the Pole Star the Arabs knew by the name of al-Jadi. I remember the kindness of the nomads at Yebbi Souma, but their well had gone dry and we struggled on to Yebbi Bou, where the water was full of sand and foul-tasting. Here Jared bargained for two extra guerbas to carry more of the sour water because ahead of us, we were told, lay seven days of travel across a waterless hammada. At each oasis he had gathered information about the route east, it being unfamiliar to him, and from this we learned that if we set our course by the stars and headed east-northeast, there would be a well at Bir Sara. On this crossing we would lose one of the camels, the beautiful cream-colored one; we would drain its stomach of liquid for drink, and eat what meat of it we could swallow, and when we reached the little sun-scorched oasis of Bir Sara at the end of seven days and nights there were five more days of travel beyond it to reach the oasis of 'Uwainat. There was no longer need of a compass, though, for now we could see the Jebel 'Uwainat etched on the horizon, towering thousands of feet above the oasis.

During the terrible heat of the day with only the hides of the tent above us to give scant shade, I would often entertain Jared with tales of Sharkey Bill, of the Sword Swallower or of Grams, and he would tell of adventures in the bush even though we had to spit out dust to talk and our voices were hoarse with it.

"A pickpocket?" he said in astonishment. "You?"

"Yes," I told him.

He looked skeptical. "Ever get caught?"

"Once," I told him.

"What happened?"

"He married me."

His roar of laughter sent dust flying and ended in a spasm of coughing, but in such manner did we make war against heat, dust, fleas and thirst.

When at last we stumbled into 'Uwainat we had traveled over 600 miles, forcing ourselves to push ahead 30 miles every night. I guessed myself to be as gaunt as the camels that we'd seen grow thinner each day, and my skin was as dry as leather. We had felt the savagery of a dust storm, endured mirages of trees and lakes, had lost water from a leaking guerba and seldom slept, we were hungry and flea-bitten, but we'd survived.

And not far to the north lay the border of Egypt, the Western Desert, "and then Assuan and the blessed Nile," said Jared, "but we'll spend our silver dollars in 'Uwainat now and hire a guide, for we've taxed the gods enough."

seventeen

———～———

We had no choice but to enter 'Uwainat, but we did so with some anxiety because we no longer knew what country we were in; frontiers were only vaguely defined in the desert, nomads knew no boundaries at all and maps could be treacherous. Soon after leaving Yebbi Bou Jared had begun to suspect, after checking both compass and stars, that we might be traveling through a remote corner of Tripolitania's desert and this was confirmed when we halted at Bir Sara for water: we were indeed in Tripolitania. Worse, we learned that a trail out of that oasis led directly north to Kufra, the stronghold of the Senussi, and was only five days by camel from Bir Sara. It seemed that our shortcut to Egypt had been drawing us like moths toward the very flame we'd set out to avoid.

"Damn," said Jared. "I expected 'Uwainat to be in the Sudan—and perhaps it is—but we'd better not ask, just get out of it as fast as possible."

Whatever the allegiance of the Muslims in 'Uwainat we had underestimated the hospitality of the desert. If the village chief was a Senussi looking for infidels under every stone he gave no indication of it. Hearing that a caravan of two people and three camels had emerged from the empty plains to the west he presented himself at once, saw to it that we had food and water and promised Jared advice about a guide. We set up our tent at a distance from the other caravans and I remained hidden in the tent and heavily veiled, which proved no hardship for me since I was content to rest, cook our food, sleep and wait. It was assumed that Jared would rouse no suspicions; he was bearded now, dark as a gypsy, and he spoke the colloquial Arabic of Alexandria so that it was quite in character that he inquire about a guide to the Nile, although considering what happened later, who knows? On the following day he succeeded in trading our three exhausted camels for three fresh ones and bought a fourth with Maria Theresa thalers, and on our second evening a guide was produced for us.

His name was Onkeir and he was a cheerful wizened little man with a white beard and a seamed face like old polished dark leather.

"*Naam,* Sidi," he said after the formal greetings had been completed, and he proceeded to tell Jared for how many years he had guided caravans up through Darfur to the Nile and into northern Egypt. He knew a little Italian, he said, a little English and a little Turkish. It was true that he limped from an old camel bite, but if he was old he welcomed the opportunity to be useful again, for his wife had died recently, two of his sons had taken his place as caravan guides and his eldest sold carpets in the Asyut suks while his daughter lived in the oasis of El Hagar, near Baris.

I brought him tea heavily laced with sugar and retired again to the shadows while he and Jared bargained amiably over his price until both were satisfied. He was a good man. Once engaged as our guide he insisted on checking every item Jared had accumulated for the next weeks, and "O Prophet! O Apostle!" he exclaimed, pointing out a frayed strap in need of mending. He added another guerba and after sampling one of the dates Jared had bought in a sack he made a face. "O Prophet! O Apostle! *Dry,*" and off he went to the suks to bargain for sweet yellow dates from the Tibesti that he called "Egnechi," and a few red and sugary "Merno" dates.

Three nights later we left the oasis, not entirely rested but still uneasy lest some careless word or gesture betray us for what we were and not too certain of the outcome should this happen. We set out with Onkeir in the lead and we couldn't help but smile at his jauntiness and obvious pleasure at being on the move. The moon sailed high above us in the west, crisp as a slice of melon; it shadowed the spiked bushes and the air was sweet. Toward dawn I unveiled my face and Onkeir smiled at me and told Jared that I had the eyes of a gazelle.

"Yes," Jared said in English, deliberately.

"*Malesh!*" exclaimed Onkeir, scrutinizing him closely, but he said nothing more except that after this he would occasionally, without comment, inject a word or two of English in his talk.

He was a good *khabbir,* guiding us always east by the stars—I would check this on my compass—toward the well at Bir Misaha, after which he said there was a good well at Bir Dibis and another at El Shab, and the Sidi wished to go to Assuan on the Nile? A matter of fifteen or sixteen days, he said, full of dust and heat but with only a few days' travel between the wells—*Inch'Allah,* of course.

But it was now, ironically, after all that we'd gone through, that we met with trouble.

We had been traveling at a relaxed pace and resting when it pleased us. On this fourth night in the desert Jared and Onkeir were in the lead, walking, while I followed mounted on one of the camels.

The stars were like crystals scattered across the sky and the only sounds were the creak of straw in the saddle on which I sat, and the soft swish of our camels' ridiculously large and padding feet. We had not been long on the trail, having stopped for Onkeir to say his evening prayers, and the well of Bir Misaha lay not many hours ahead of us. The only flaw to the perfection of the moment was that Onkeir had begun to glance frequently over his shoulder at what lay behind us. His uneasiness was becoming palpable.

Jared had noticed, too. "What is it?" he asked at last.

"Sidi," Onkeir said, "the skin of my back grows cold, and this night is not cold."

"What is the skin of your back telling you, Onkeir?"

"It says *khatar*—danger—behind us."

Jared brought his camel to a halt with a softly spoken "Khr. . . . Who's tracking us, Onkeir, men or jackals?"

Onkeir only shook his head, studying the moonlit terrain ahead of us. He pointed: at some distance away there rose a scallop of low dunes and stones, the only hope of shelter to be seen, but shelter against what I didn't know, not yet. I dug my feet into the camel I was riding and with Onkeir and Jared leading the others we pushed our way quickly toward this pathetically small rise in the plateau. Hastily we couched the camels and unloaded them, piling saddles and packs on the dune to make a wall, and after hobbling the animals Jared loaded both our rifles and handed mine back to me.

Onkeir saw them first, his old eyes sharper than ours: four small dark figures in the distance. "Horses!" he whispered. "Bismallah, they ride horses!"

I had not seen horses for a long time, and as the distance narrowed I could that each horse carried a man; they traveled with no baggage, which was strange.

"Min da, Onkeir—friend or foe?" asked Jared. "What do you think?"

"I say they track us, Sidi. See how they stop now to study signs. Soon they will see where we left the trail. . . . Sidi, I think them bandits."

"Bismallah," Jared said fervently.

"Yahudi," murmured Onkeir; he spat into the sand and then drew out a long

khanjar, well-sharpened and gleaming in the moonlight.

Now the four men had noted our departure from the trail, I could see this, for they turned and began riding toward us. All four of them wore black, even their headscarfs were black, drawn across their faces to mask them, and I could see the rifles they cradled in their laps.

"The Four Horsemen of the Apocalypse," muttered Jared, and lifted his rifle.

Some yards away from the dune the men halted to face us, drawing tightly on their reins to discipline the skittish horses. We crouched low but they knew we were here; our camel prints were written in the sand. Once formed in a line, side by side, they whipped their animals and with loud cries rushed us, firing their rifles into the sky to frighten both us and our camels. It was now that I lifted my rifle and learned what it was like to fire at another human being; I took aim and pulled the trigger as they leaped over the dunes so near to our heads that I felt the heat of their horses. Something wet dropped on my arm, black in the moonlight. *That's blood,* I thought, *one of them's been hit.* As the fourth horse passed over us I saw Onkeir stand up, lift an arm and slash at its belly with his dagger but the horse only staggered and went on.

Once behind us the men reined in their animals and turned to charge us again, no longer playful or teasing but grim. Rolling over with my back to the dune I took aim and fired and one of the men fell motionless on the earth. Now Jared was firing and one of the bandits clapped a hand to his arm but he remained on his horse and what happened next became a blur, for their leader rode furiously toward us and leaped from his horse to hurl himself at Jared, holding a dagger that shone silver in the moonlight.

"Jared!" I screamed, but the two other bandits were riding toward us now. Whispering a prayer that my aim be true I shot them both dead. One more bullet was fired, and so near to me that I dreaded turning my head lest I see Jared dead; I looked and saw that it was Onkeir who had saved us: he had seized Jared's rifle and shot the bandit overpowering him, and may Allah bless him for this forever.

Jared was not dead, no, but the man's

dagger had done vile work before Onkeir killed him.

The last bandit, wounded, was galloping away to the west. I crept to Jared, who gave me a small tight smile and closed his eyes, biting his lips in pain.

If Allah had sent this to humble and test us he had also, out of his infinite compassion, sent us Onkeir who was already tearing strips of cotton from his gandoura to staunch the bleeding in Jared's shoulder, chest and arm. I raced for the medicine kit, aware as I groped for it that one of the camels had been shot and was dying. I drew out the bottle of brandy and shouted to Onkeir, "Wait!" Taking care to save enough for Jared later I poured copious amounts over each wound that I could see, and then nodded to Onkeir, who applied bandages. As he worked at this he muttered words over and over that I couldn't understand until, leaning closer, I realized he was praying for Jared in the name of Allah, the All Merciful, the All Compassionate. Oh he was a good man, Onkeir. When he had finished binding Jared's wounds he went off to the camels, leaving me to give what comfort I could, although I doubt that

Jared was even aware of me. Outside I could see Onkeir slitting the throat of the dying camel so that, as a good Muslim, the meat might be eaten. When he returned he was carrying tent poles and skins and without a word he set up a tent over Jared to shade him when morning came.

I asked haltingly, "Will Sidi . . . tuwafiyya—be called to God?"

This, he said gravely, was in the hands of Allah but I must not despair.

I nodded. "There will be"—I touched my forehead, groping for words—"harara . . . temperature? Fever?"

"Naam," he said, but soon he would build a fire and cauterize the wounds.

I flinched at such a thought. Sitting beside Jared I sponged his hot face with precious water while Onkeir buried the three dead bandits in the sand and then built a fire. The cauterizing of the wounds with a red-hot iron was terrible to see. . . . Jared screamed, and the smell of burnt flesh was sickening. Dawn came and while the moon still hung pale in the western sky, the sun rose in the east, huge and round like an orange globe, but with this sunrise Jared's temperature mounted and I knew no human being could endure such fever for long and that I was going to lose him.

Onkeir saw this, too. We talked in our mixture of Arabic, English and Hausa; I thanked him for not deserting us and for all that he had done, but he shook his head at this. It was Allah's will that he remained, he said; he and the Sidi had made contract together, it was a matter of responsibility.

"But," he added gravely, "the Sidi is dying."

I said fiercely, "He mustn't."

"*Rahmut Ullahi Allaheim*—the peace of God be upon him," he said sadly.

I crept closer to Jared as if to shield him bodily from the death that had entered the tent to wait for him, and it was now, looking into his face to memorize it, that I noticed a line of blood, thin as a thread, running from his cheekbone to his jaw. Of all his wounds it was this that held my attention and I was puzzled, wondering why this was so, until I realized that it was very like the thread of a line I'd seen on a clay bowl placed in front of me at a sacred spirit shrine, and I wondered. . . . Did I dare? It was crazy to think of Shakespeare now but, "Our doubts are traitors," I remembered, "and make us lose the good we oft might win by fearing to attempt . . ."

I asked Onkeir to leave, saying that I wanted these last moments alone with Jared. He understood, and once he'd left I lowered the flaps of the tent for privacy. Amina had said that when neither incantations nor medicines were enough her people turned to the god they called the Giver of Breath and Life and they prayed.

I prayed now, silently.

Kneeling beside Jared I heard the flutter of a sigh from him—he was still alive at least—and I sat down next him with my legs crossed under me. After moments of quieting I thought, *Heal, Jared . . . heal . . . HEAL!* But then I realized this was all wrong because I'd used words, and *iko* had nothing to do with words, I had been impatient; I stopped words and struggled for an endless interval to put aside my doubts and my fears for Jared's life. "Be still," I told my turbulent mind, "let go, let go." Time passed—a long time—before a stillness came to me and Time stopped. My arms began to feel heavy and charged. Slowly, without my willing it, they insisted upon rising out of my lap to begin a curious circling movement: upward to describe an arc and then down and around and up again, all in this strange circular motion as if completely detached from my body. Though I knew no thought there was a sense of recognition—this was *iko* passing through me—and then slowly, gently, my arms ceased their motion and returned my hands to my lap. It was ended; I drew a deep breath but there was no tiredness: it had happened again—and for the last time, I knew this—and *. . . what will be, will be,* I thought.

Onkeir had said that Jared would die but Bismallah, he lived.

Book 4

eighteen

Since hearing of it I had not given any thought to Jared's buried fortune in Abyssinia, but once his fever broke I would hear a great deal about it, for during the next restless hours he tossed and mumbled over and over, "Got to go back, dig gold . . . get it *OUT.* Got to go back . . . *MUST . . .* get it *OUT.*"

When I considered this I could see his point. I daresay it was enough to haunt any man who had nearly died to remember how cleverly he'd buried his gold so that no one else would find it. I could only do my best to soothe him, but now that his terrible crisis had passed and he was going to live, Onkeir and I had to deal with fresh worries. Our present situation, for instance, was untenable: we were stranded on a vast plateau of gravel, pockmarked stone and shifting sand dunes, we had very little water left, and although Onkeir volunteered to ride to the well at Bir Misaha and fill our guerbas this would leave me vulnerable should the last surviving bandit return with friends to exact revenge. It was not a pleasing situation. By the second night Onkeir was even more uneasy, and when I asked what troubled him now he admitted to still another fear: the spirits of the three dead men buried nearby.

At this I nodded; enough was enough, we would go. Stamping out the campfire we packed up the tent and slung a sheepskin between two of the camels, and once this was secured with ropes Jared was lifted onto this primitive stretcher. He rallied enough to swear feebly at his helplessness, which drew a smile from Onkeir. "Sidi better," he said. *"Keif halaki, Sidi?"*

"Tayib, damn it," growled Jared.

Under a moonless sky we led the

camels to the well at Bir Misaha and rested for two days before we set out for the well at Bir Dibis. Once we were there, said Onkeir, we must decide what next to do because Bir Dibis lay on the Darb-el-Arba'in, the old Forty Days Road that came up from the Sudan, and there might be caravans. From Bir Dibis, he said, we could continue east to the Nile as planned, or—

"Or what?" I asked.

"Follow the Forty Days Road to the north."

"Why?" I said, puzzled.

To the north lay el-wah El Kharga, the Great South Oasis, he explained, and at its southern tip lived his daughter Saadiya, in a small oasis just below Baris. The Sidi might have planned to go to the Nile and to Assuan, but when he reached it, what then? The Sidi needed a place to heal and to grow strong, the Sidi needed a *beyt,* a home, and in the oasis of El Hagar there was a well with good water, many date palms—and his daughter.

Jared, overhearing this, said, "How far?"

Either was far, said Onkeir, but the trail

north—perhaps a day longer, perhaps not —was safer, a well-traveled route as the Sidi must know, having heard of it, surely, and it led to El Hagar, where he could rest.

I looked at Jared and smiled. "Well?"

He nodded. "There's sense in what he says. Let's go north."

We joined the first caravan that came out of the Sudan on the Forty Days Road— natron smugglers, confided Onkeir, whispering the words—and with them we traveled north over treacherously rough ground. As the Tuareg say, if a man is not killed in the desert he lives forever, and by the fourth day Jared had not only forgotten his buried gold—or so I thought—but sat astride one of our camels, although not yet strong enough to mount without help.

Once in a while as we drank tea by the campfire at night Onkeir would speak of the Great Oasis toward which we headed: it was big, very long, he said, and it lay well below the desert with half a dozen villages inside it. "If it lies below the desert you mean a depression?" said Jared, but Onkeir didn't know the word nor did I know what it meant. "They happen in the deserts but they're not usually inhabited," he explained.

I couldn't imagine what a depression was or even that an oasis could exist in this sterile, desolate country with its cone-shaped heaps of gravel, and slippery round stones, but one day I saw the outline of mountains ahead, and running parallel to them a high wall of earth or sand. "We are nearly there," said Onkeir.

When he had ridden ahead Jared turned to me. "They're all Berbers at Kharga and I don't speak or understand their language, so we'll be entirely in Onkeir's hands."

"We can trust him, surely?"

Jared said dryly, "He seems to regard me with a hell of a lot of awe since I 'rose from the dead' as he calls it. Yes, we can trust him. He'll tell them I'm a Turk from Alexandria, but heaven only knows who he thinks you are, it's best you say nothing and keep your face veiled."

"I'll soon forget how to talk," I told him gloomily.

"Ah, but you can talk to *me,*" he teased. "I'll now have exclusive rights."

When we reached the earth walls that

spilled into the stony desert we parted from the caravan of smugglers; apparently El Hagar was too small and insignificant for them and they would water their camels farther north, at Baris, and so it was that we three descended alone into this strange depression below the desert floor, almost literally dropping down into it as we slipped and slid into a different world to meet the little oasis of El Hagar.

It stood inside a wall of acacia built to hold back the encroaching sands, a dozen or more mud huts baking in the hot sun, shaded thinly by a green garden of noum palms while in the center stood its greatest attraction, a large artesian well from which water was coaxed into irrigation channels to feed the palms and the rice fields. It was dry, hot and untidy—not exactly a paradise, I thought, but after the harsh country through which we'd traveled its water and its trees looked beautiful.

And for Onkeir there was Saadiya.

I would notice later how the women of the village were seldom seen, and then only as faces in a window, but Onkeir's daughter Saadiya was of a different breed, her vitality still intact and her nature free. I would see her stand outside her mud-brick house, hands on her hips, while she harangued her children, her veil askew and her eyes alight with mischief. "O Prophet, O Apostle, she is like her *'umm,* her mother," Onkeir said proudly, and he would tell of how Saadiya had refused to marry the man that he and her mother had chosen for her in their village. She had wanted Ismael, the caravan guide who passed through their village often, and she had acted like an *enerregreg,* he said, using the Tuareg word for a camel who roars mournfully when separated; I could imagine this for myself because Saadiya held nothing back, neither anger, sadness nor joy, and needless to say she was wife to Ismael now.

We would sleep those first nights on the roof of Saadiya's tiny house but Jared was uneasy, not liking this, and to my surprise he dug deep into his saddle bags to bring out mosquito netting that I'd not known he possessed. "Why?" I asked. "You'll see," he said, and see I did, for as it grew dark and the steady hot wind faltered he lit a match to show me the netting thick with mosquitoes.

"Too damn much water here," he said grimly. "Those palm trees sit in three inches of stagnant water—there's the rice field, too—and stagnant water breeds mosquitoes and mosquitoes mean malaria."

It had simply not occurred to me that there could be too much water in the desert. "But this is an oasis, not desert," he reminded me. "The desert's healthy. Tomorrow we'll look for a place outside of El Hagar to camp."

For this we set out at dawn, filling a guerba with water and borrowing two donkeys from Saadiya. Having come up from the south, we headed east in the direction of the sharp hills and cliffs that shaped one side of the depression. The heat was already building and a steady wind from the north stung our faces with sand. Half a mile from the village we saw three truncated pillars rising out of the ground and casting three shadows; we rode over to look at them.

"Roman—they have to be," Jared said, dismounting.

"They're marble!" I said in surprise,

glancing back at El Hagar's small mud huts.

"For all we know there could be a whole city buried under our feet," he said, examining them. "They're half buried by the sand as it is."

Bakuli and I had sometimes seen strange half-buried shapes in the desert, but there had been no one to explain them. "When were the Romans here?" I asked.

"Long ago, before Christ was born, and probably for a few centuries beyond. They've left ruins all through the Sahara and Egypt, forts and frontier posts and customs houses, and since the route from the Sudan passed here—the Forty Days Road—they would have been here, too. It must have looked very different in those times," he said, glancing around us at the inhospitable landscape. "I suspect El Hagar's artesian well was also built by them." He was eyeing the columns thoughtfully; what interested him, he said, was that two of them were of precisely the same height, being slightly taller than he was, and set six feet apart. "This is giving me an idea," he said, and pointed. "We could drop our mosquito netting over these two and make a tent, pinning down the net with stones."

"It would be very hot," I said doubtfully. "And without shade."

"It's hot in El Hagar," he reminded me. "As for shade"—he shrugged—"palm mats, a rug—better than being eaten alive by mosquitoes. People here don't understand that those worms wriggling in the water of the rice fields grow up to be malaria-bearing insects."

"Not even Onkeir?"

Jared smiled. "He listened politely when I mentioned it, but I think he was laughing at me."

We rode back into El Hagar, one idea excitedly begetting another. With Onkeir's help Jared laced palm trunks together just wide enough to insert as a floor between the two matching columns, and high enough hopefully to defeat snakes and scorpions. The mosquito netting, weighted at the top, formed a tent that fanned out well beyond the pillars and gave us luxurious space. Our blankets made a roof that cast a thin shade during the day and could be removed at night to see the stars. In the sand I buried dates to dry and season.

When our creation was finished two days later we both stood back and looked it over critically. "Could still use a few refinements," Jared said.

I couldn't help laughing. "It looks just like a playhouse that children build out of boxes and crates."

"Well, who's more inventive than a child?" he said with a grin.

The work having tired him, we spent the afternoon testing out our new home by lying on the platform with jugs of water beside us while I read more to him from his book about the explorer James Bruce in Abyssinia.

" 'The king,' " I read, " 'very often judges capital crimes himself. When the prisoner is condemned in capital cases he is not again remitted to prison, which is thought cruel, but he is instantly carried away and the sentence executed. . . . The capital punishment is the cross. The next is flaying alive.' "

"This is not very restful," murmured Jared.

" 'Lapidation,' " I continued, " 'or stoning to death, is the next capital punishment. This is chiefly inflicted upon

strangers called *Franks,* for religious purposes.' Just see what you escaped," I re-
marked.

"Barely," he said. "The wonder of it is
that Bruce did."

Each day I watched Jared grow stronger.
I'm sure the villagers thought us mad to
camp beyond their oasis, but they were
not unfriendly. Apparently Onkeir had spoken to them of the fight with bandits and
how miraculously Jared had survived deep
wounds, Allah be praised, and how it was
believed—in the strange manner of foreign
people—that the sun could be healing.
Once settled in our camp, Jared occasionally joined Onkeir and the other men in the
village who sat for hours near the date
market drinking cups of coffee, talking and
observing the dates spread out like a car-
pet to dry. I would not part with my barracan, but during such visits Saadiya
showed me how to mend its holes and
often gave me goat's milk to carry back to
our tent. From the date market we bought
dates richer than any I'd ever eaten before,
and from Saadiya we bought flour with

which I made unleavened bread, burying it in the embers of our campfire at night to be crisply baked by dawn. But most of all Jared and I spent hours talking of our future. Land was cheap in Africa, Jared said, and was being settled, true, but how did I feel about Scotland?

"Does it have space and sky?" I asked.

"In the countryside, yes."

"Then I'd like country. Can you write books in the country?"

"Best place for it," he said. "Sheep, perhaps, and a garden?"

"I don't know anything about gardens," I told him, "do you?"

He laughed. "I grew up tending an acre of vegetables. If we'd not planted them every year there would have been some very hungry days in winter."

Such talk was as nourishing as our simple diet of dates, bread, water and goat's milk; wealth was strictly relative, as I had already discovered.

One evening, deepening a hole in the sand to build a better cooking fire, I found a round metal circle with a few letters barely discernible on it, and taking it to

Jared we examined it. "Obviously a coin," he said, "and surely Roman, but I can't make out the letters."

"I see a C-o-n," I announced proudly.

"Where?"

I pointed, and narrowing his eyes he said, "You're right, and over here there's t-u-i-s. Well, well," he added, pleased, "the Roman Emperor Constantius. Let's see what else we can find, we've certainly time enough. Let's go exploring."

We had heard of ruins not far from El Hagar, at a place called Dush where no one lived anymore. One day before dawn we set out with two camels and enough water to see us through the day, and traveling south, but east of the Forty Days Road, we found what remained of a temple, the entrance to the vanished building still intact, protected from the wind and sand by crumbling walls but its empty doorway leading only to the desert beyond. It was a silent place, full of ghosts and inhabited only by scorpions, but it was rich in pottery shards that we dug up before the sun grew noon-high. Our greatest discovery had the shape of a cup, and I

handled it reverently. "How old?" I whispered.

"Centuries old," said Jared, touching
its eroded surface.

"I wonder who it belonged to. I wonder how different from us they were."

Jared smiled. "Not very different, I'm
sure. They loved and hated and fought
wars and planted seeds and bore children
and, who knows, maybe they found relics
here, too, from an even more distant past."

I looked at him. "And stood here wondering about those other people just as
we're doing at this moment?" When he
nodded I said, "It's like a caravan then,
isn't it, a long line of people on the march,
one group passing out of sight and another
coming along. . . ."

"Until a century's passed—another
and another," he said "and here we are in
whatever year this is, 1913 or even 1914
by now, holding a cup someone made and
used nearly two thousand years ago."

I shivered. "That's a long time, Jared."

"With many changes."

"Will we change?" I asked.

"Everyone does, but you and I will

change *together,*" he said, "and that will make all the difference."

When we rode back later to camp it was with a handful of eroded coins, the ancient cup, a few shards, and the sun was setting so that we traveled under a sky exploding with riotous oranges, pinks and scarlets. And always waiting for us was night: if our days were rich in companionship the nights with Jared were heaven.

We had been two months at El Hagar when Saadiya's husband Ismael returned from guiding a caravan up the Forty Days Road, and with his arrival Jared said that it was time for us to think of leaving. "Time to travel south and dig up my gold before my pockets are empty, Caressa."

I felt a passing sadness to hear such words, for our days here in El Hagar had been the happiest of my life, but knowing that without the gold Scotland would be only a dream I said as cheerfully as I could, "All right, when do we start?"

"Hear me out," he said soberly, "for I've thought it through in my mind ever since we came here. I have to go alone, Caressa."

Dismayed, I cried, "Jared!"

"Where I'm going is no place for a woman," he said firmly, "and I'll want to travel fast. Now listen and try to realize the worry you'd be to me. I've talked of it with Onkeir—"

"With Onkeir!"

"Yes," he said calmly, "for it's needed sorting out for the sake of dividing what money remains, and thinking what's best and safest for you. There's a railway now as far south as Sennar, it goes by fits and starts but it goes, and in Sennar I can buy or hire a camel and be across the border in Teseney by the next full moon at the latest."

I said despairingly, "But if it takes nearly a month to get there, that means a month to come back? Oh Jared." I looked around me at the desert that had seemed like magic and I realized the magic had been in me, for I was suddenly seeing its isolation and its smallness. "That could be *two months.*"

"You won't stay here," he said, guessing my thoughts. "I've thought long and hard on this and I want you to wait for me with your own people. In Cairo."

"Cairo!" I cried. "I've no people there, Jared, why?"

"I mean there's an American Consulate there," he said. "You and Onkeir will go by train—it's only two days' travel—and Onkeir has once visited Cairo so he knows a little of the city. He'll deliver you to the Consulate, for I won't let you travel alone."

"But Jared—"

"Two months," he emphasized, "and then we'll take ship for England, Caressa, and this you'll explain to them in Cairo because, unfortunately, it's going to take all my remaining dollars for you and Onkeir to reach Cairo and for me to travel south. Because of this—and it goes hard with me to say it—you will have to present yourself to the Consulate as a Distressed Citizen. However," he added firmly, "you will carry with you a promissory note with my pledge that I'll repay all sums advanced for your expenses as soon as I join you in two months."

I said in astonishment, "You'll travel without Onkeir?"

He nodded. "I must." Opening up his sack of coins he emptied them on the floor. Seated cross-legged he picked out the two gold rings and said, "One of these goes to Onkeir, as promised in our contract. As for the other, it will take that much for you and Onkeir to go to Cairo by train." Pointing to the pile of Maria Theresa thalers he added, "And this much to see me travel second-class rail to Sennar." The pile had grown ominously small and separating what was left he added, "This will buy me food on the way, and a camel to cross into Abyssinia and recapture my gold from the earth."

"Jared, that's not much!"

He smiled. "That, love, is why it's time we leave this blessed place. We can only thank God for the railway opening up so far south, except that trains cost a hell of a lot of money."

"Jared, I want to go with you."

He shook his head. "I have nightmares, Caressa, about what could happen to you. These are rough times in the Sudan."

"I'm not inexperienced."

He smiled. "That I grant you, but I don't know what I'll meet with, nothing that a rifle can't handle but worrying about you being with me could stay my hand."

We argued fiercely about this for long hours, but he had me at a disadvantage: I might have acquired a small knowledge of a small part of the Sahara but I knew nothing of Nubia or the Sudan, or the few miles of Abyssinia that Jared would have to cross to reach his cairn. That was *his* knowledge, and I could not fight his calm and steady assertions that it was no place for a woman. Ultimately I had to accept this: the gold for our life in Scotland lay a month away and he could travel faster if he traveled alone.

And so it was that Onkeir, Jared and I, with Ismael as our guide, set out one day in the full heat of summer, for it was Ismael who knew the trail over the Dush Pass that would lead us across the desert to Esna and the railway. It was a punishing climb out of the depression and over the pass, and once we reached its peak it was to meet with savage winds and deep gullies that needed care in crossing, but cairns marked the trail, as well as potsherds and animal bones, and we moved on, leaning against the wind. After two days the trail divided and we headed to the northeast across a waterless plateau toward the Nile.

We reached Esna all too soon, for if the journey had been hard, what lay ahead was harder. We set up our tent outside the town and the next morning Jared made travel arrangements, trading one gold ring for the tickets that would separate us, and giving the other to Onkeir. I was now so tense with dread that of Esna I would remember only a town where men wore fat red turbans—Jared said they were Gubts, or Coptic Christians—but I would remember with haunting clarity our last night together in the tent that had been our home.

In the morning Jared silently packed money, rifles, ammunition, food and medicine kit into a sheepskin, rolled it up, tied it and laced it to his shoulders. There was a last ride on the camels when Ismael delivered us to the railway before setting out on his return trip to El Hager. Jared's train to the south would arrive an hour later than ours, and so we three stood numbly by the rail tracks and watched the train for Luxor and Cairo move inexorably toward us. It was now that I gave Jared the only object of value that I thought I owned: as the train came to a stop I slipped Jacob's old compass into his hand.

"To bring you back," I said.

"I'll need no compass for that," he said roughly, and I saw the pain in his eyes, and certainly there were tears in mine.

"Allah Kereem," said Onkeir.

"Inch'Allah," Jared said, and thus we parted.

nineteen

After living in the desert with its great silences and its solitude Cairo was an assault on the senses that almost stupefied me. Certainly it frightened me and I clung to Onkeir lest I lose him in the crowds. There was such noise it appeared that everyone must shout in the streets, while below this sounded the rumble of trains and omnibuses and a blowing of loud horns; a string of camels made its way past us braying pitifully; there were horse-drawn arabas here, too, as in Tripoli, but preceded by runners shouting, "Make way!

Make way!" It seemed a gray city to me from the houses and mosques that we passed, and it was hot. Only the cry of the muezzin was familiar.

Many times Onkeir stopped to ask directions until we reached a broader street with a few ragged palms. *"Hinehk,"* he said, pointing. *"Amreekehnee Qunsuleeya."*

The Consulate . . . American. Terrified, I shrugged off my ragged barracan and smoothed my new baggy trousers and gandoura, tidied my headscarf and said, "Onkeir, what do you think I—"

But Onkeir had vanished into the crowds and was nowhere to be seen. I nearly wept, made fragile by his disappearance, by the noise and by the strangeness of it all. Suffice to say that upon entering the Consulate I was regarded with horror and told to leave at once—until I spoke more words in English, clearly startling the man who had received me. Following this I was directed to a hard wooden bench in a hallway and told to wait until someone was free to hear me. After an hour I progressed to a room where a young man sat behind a desk; he looked friendly, and if my clothes disconcerted him he suppressed his reactions and rose to shake my hand. He was clearly baffled, though, when I told him in English that I had come as an American and as a Distressed Citizen, but with a promissory note from Jared until he arrived in Cairo to pay my expenses.

"Promissory note? American? You have proof, of course, of your citizenship?" he said pleasantly.

I handed him the promissory note and explained that I had no proof or identification. "Which is why I'm a Distressed Citizen," I pointed out.

He laid Jared's note on his desk without looking at it, and his attitude was suddenly very official and not so friendly. "You must understand that we have very rigid laws," he said stiffly. "If you have no passport, no papers, no documents, no identification—" After a glance at my face he picked up his pen and added, "Shall we begin with your name, please?"

Struggling to be helpful I told him my name.

"Caressa Bowman," he repeated, frowning. "Bowman? Is that Boman or Bowman?"

"B-o-w-m-a-n," I assured him.

"And you said *Caressa?*"

I wondered if he was hard of hearing; certainly he seemed to be puzzled by my name. After he'd sat and stared at me, his scowl deepening, he said, "It has a familiar ring, you see, it—good God!" he gasped. "You're *Caressa Bowman?*"

Since I had already told him so I saw no point in replying.

"But I know you," he cried. "At least my sister— But you were killed in the desert, in Tripolitania, in the Fezzan. Three years ago, surely?"

Before I could sort this out he said, "We made inquiries for *months*—but Tripoli reported you dead, both you and your husband. My sister cried for days." He sat back and stared at me incredulously. "You must think me suddenly mad but my name's Bill Stanhope, does the name Stanhope mean anything to you?"

"Stanhope . . ." I said slowly, because it seemed so long ago, "I once had a friend Isabelle Stanhope. We met on the *Valeria,* sailing from Marseille, at least I think it was the *Valeria,* and—"

His eyes had widened in amazement.

"You just walked in here, not mentioning this—resurrected from the dead after all this time? It didn't occur to you—my God!" he said.

"Well, you see," I told him, *"I've* known I wasn't dead. Is Isabelle well?"

He laughed. "She's right here in Cairo." He shook his head dazedly. "You're going to be the talk of the city when *this* news gets out. You'll stay with us, of course— Isabelle's keeping house for me and a marvel at giving parties."

I said, "Oh no, I only want—my friend will soon be—"

He cut me off. *"Of course* you'll be Isabelle's guest and mine; I can't wait to see her face when she hears you're alive." He smiled at me boyishly. "I do wonder—yes, I think Rogers will want to interview you, and Damien ought to be told about you, too."

I was tired and I was bewildered, but for the next several hours I was made much of, interviewed by one man, queried and interrogated by another, and my years in the desert reduced to facts with no shape to them and then consigned to paper. What they learned I don't know but for myself I learned that this was June 14, 1914 and I was therefore twenty years old and would be twenty-one in a few months. Isabelle was summoned and arrived breathlessly to end the interrogations at last. "I can't believe it!" she repeated over and over again, half-laughing, half-crying. "You're alive, Caressa, you're *alive!*"

I thought, *How untouched she looks,* and for just a moment this collision of worlds left me dizzy, and then she hugged and kissed me, which I found very brave of her because I was certainly dirty and she was elegant and clean and smelled of lavender.

"What you must have gone through!" she cried, but seeing her brother frown warningly, she added, "But now it's time to forget it all. Oh do let me take her home now, may I?"

And now there began a time of loneliness more searing than any that I'd experienced in the past. Half of me remained, still, in the desert and all of me waited for Jared and yet I must talk, smile and conceal every thought; I must also learn to eat again with a knife, fork and spoon, to wear skirts and to sleep under a ceiling that hid the stars and pressed down on me hard.

How kind Isabelle was. She had not changed, she was as generous as I remembered her, as vivacious and as lovely, but it was I who had changed. Through her eyes I could see the Caressa I'd been so long ago, and that girl was a stranger to me. But Isabelle saw no change, I was still the sixteen-year-old confidante for whom she'd hoped to give a ball, and to this was added the attraction of my being heroine-of-the-moment. She moved between pity for me, and admiration of my endurance, but there was also envy of the attention the newspapers were giving me and awe at the invitations that it inspired.

What was bleakest of all was my realization that I couldn't speak to her of Jared. There was no intimacy between us, although fortunately she didn't see this, for I understood soon enough how different a world I'd entered, full of rules and mores I'd forgotten or never known. I saw that Isabelle would be appalled—revolted, even —if she learned that I had lived with a man to whom I wasn't married; in her eyes I would be labeled a fallen woman and no circumstances could forgive this. Hating myself for doing so, I reduced Jared to a friend—as indeed he was—who had rescued me from the desert and had seen to it that I reached Cairo while he proceeded to Abyssinia before joining me in two months.

I was completely out of my element and I knew it; worse, I had been robbed of choice. I had expected the uncomplicated status of Distressed Citizen, I had assumed that Jared's promissory note would be honored and that I would be given a modest stipend for lodging and meals in a small room, from which I would emerge to explore the life of a city that I would later show to Jared. Above all, I had expected privacy. I don't think it ever occurred to Isabelle or to her brother that I didn't want to be their guest; they had no imagination. Whatever had happened in my years since the massacre was not to be talked about, and if at times I grew edgy or my thoughts wandered elsewhere, Isabelle took great pains to be forgiving.

Mercifully Cairo's interest in me was short-lived; I was replaced after two weeks by news of the assassination of an arch-

duke in Sarajevo, and the ensuing ultimatums and accusations between the
countries in Europe occupied the front
pages of the newspapers, which was a
great relief to me because the pace of Isabelle's social life was more than enough
stress to handle.

It was during my second week with
her that I found one person to whom I
could talk, who guessed my feelings and
skillfully drew them out of me, thus giving
evidence of becoming a friend. I met him in
my borrowed finery at the ball that inevita-
bly Isabelle gave for me, both to show me
off, she said gaily, and to introduce me to
Society. I had been aware of the man
watching me while I was introduced to an
endless number of people, all of whom regarded me with much curiosity as they
congratulated me on my survival. I noticed
the man because of his stillness, which
was conspicuous among so many people
who twittered like sparrows, although a
few struck me as more like vultures. I had
not been introduced to him but he was
waiting for me at the punch bowl, a tall
gray man in his fifties, and so distin-

guished-looking that I assumed him to be at least a consul or an ambassador.

Studying me, he said with a clipped British accent, "Your smile doesn't reach your eyes, Mrs. Bowman. Are you really to be congratulated at being among us or should sympathy be extended instead?" When I hesitated he said, "When you stop smiling you impress me as rather miserable."

I did not deny this, I merely looked at him appraisingly.

"You've not acquired the art of flirtation, Mrs. Bowman?"

"I've had no experience of it," I told him. "Nor of small talk either."

"No wonder you're miserable." He took my arm and led me to one of the alcoves set into the hall. "Half the people in this room have empty heads, but I confess I'd give a sovereign to know what your thoughts are this evening."

I was tempted to ask for the sovereign. "In Seguedine I was bought with four of them but my thoughts are my own."

"Exactly," he said, nodding, "so I will ask only for your company. I wonder if you'd do me the honor of having tea with me tomorrow at Shepheard's? I think you'd enjoy seeing the hotel and watching Cairo pass by its terrace."

The suddenness of this took me aback. I said bluntly, "I don't know either you or your name."

He smiled faintly at this. "Quite. But I think Isabelle will vouch for me, I'll just have a word with her. I'm Linton Teal."

"*Sir* Linton Teal," Isabelle said later in an awed voice. "Rich as Midas, Caressa, and a baronet. He's a collector—of magnificent things even museums can't afford to own, and rumor has it that in London he has three Rembrandts. Oh, you *must* have tea with him, Caressa."

I did not see why I must, but at least he seemed kind and more discerning than anyone I'd met, and it was in this manner that I met Sir Linton Teal and had tea with him on the following afternoon.

Shepheard's Hotel was a colossal building with jutting cornices and a great dome on top, but its interior nearly overwhelmed me since I had not yet adjusted to rich foods, either. The extravagance of it! It became a blur of opulence, of gold and pearl inlay and mosaics and Persian rugs and chandeliers, potted palms and everyone looking as rich as Sir Linton, whereas I was in a dress of Isabelle's, tucked and basted to fit, and my skin was a dark unfashionable brown. I felt better once we gained the terrace, and more comfortable still when we were seated in wicker chairs with lemonade, tea and macaroons in front of us, for here I could look out on the people in the street. It was like the front-row seat at a theater: a troop of Egyptian soldiers passed by in their blue and white uniforms; there was a flash of scarlet and two British soldiers rode by on donkeys; next came a string of complacent-looking camels led by a scruffy little man. There were men with trays of turquoises, and vendors selling stuffed crocodiles, and every other passerby seemed to be a woman bundled into black with only one eye showing to prove that she was inside.

When Sir Linton offered me another macaroon I returned my attention to him. "Tell me, Mrs. Bowman," he said with a smile, "I am frankly curious—impertinent, perhaps, as well—but after such astonishing experiences your reactions interest me.

How does it feel to come back from the dead?"

I said again, patiently, "But you see I *wasn't* dead—except to other people."

He nodded appreciatively. "Quite—so I'll rephrase that. What, then, is it like to not know from one day to the next whether you'll continue living or be still alive the next week or next month?"

I said dryly, "Stimulating."

"Ah . . ." he murmured. "Yes, I see. But in what way?"

I realized he was serious, that he was not making idle conversation but really wanted to know. "Well," I said, "looking back is not the same as it was at the time, is it? Sometimes there was—well, much despair. Sometimes hopelessness, sometimes fear, sometimes," I acknowledged, "the utter joy of another day."

"Joy," he repeated in an odd voice as if this was a word new to him. "But you were—you surely couldn't have managed entirely alone?"

I smiled. "There was first of all Bakuli for a very long time."

"Bakuli . . ." For some reason he looked pleased. "Tell me about Bakuli."

And so I told him, finding him easy to talk to, and I began to appreciate this man, or to be grateful to him for listening, and in spite of his air of remoteness—or perhaps because of it—he listened well. Actually I think I felt a little sorry for him; I gained the impression that in some strange way the juices of life had been sucked out of him a long time ago, leaving only curiosity and intellect, for there was something blood-less about him, about his pallor and his parchmentlike skin, as if he had spent his years indoors—perhaps collectors did—and I sensed that what I had to say inter-ested him because my life had been so very different from his. And so we talked—or I talked, answering many questions, un-til the tea grew cold.

As we rose to leave, "Have you seen the pyramids of Ghizeh yet?" he asked. "Perhaps I could entice you and Isabelle to visit them with me tomorrow . . . ?"

When I next saw him alone it seemed that he had inquired about me at the Con-sulate. "I have connections," he explained, seeing how startled I looked, and then, al-most idly, "Who is this Jared MacKay whose promissory note you brought to Cairo with you?"

I only smiled at this and shook my head. "A good friend," I said.

Nevertheless, within a matter of weeks he had skillfully drawn from me the meaning of Jared in my life, his whereabouts, and our plans, so that he knew of me not just the bits and pieces that had circulated around Cairo following my appearance, or the little Isabelle knew, but almost the whole of my story. "I hear that you visit the Consulate each morning to ask if there's a message from him," he said. "It's been only five weeks; do you really believe this Jared of yours could travel so quickly?"

I thought, *Oh yes—yes he could,* but I did not say this.

My naïveté and perhaps my feelings about Jared appeared to amuse Sir Linton for he continued to seek me out. "Why?" I asked him one day after we had visited Old Cairo and the bazaars and were again having tea on the terrace of Shepheard's Hotel.

"I cherish oddities," he told me with his ironic smile. "Being a mere spectator of life, I find philosophy a vast comfort; I enjoy speculating about life, having been denied it in the sense that you've lived it. And we have become friends, have we not?"

"You've been very kind to me," I said. "Yes."

That was August 2, I remember, and when I woke up the next morning my only concern was that it was August 3, and nine weeks now since Jared had left for Abyssinia; he had promised to be in Cairo in two months and he was a week overdue.

That was early morning; by noon I learned that Germany had declared war on Russia, and when I woke up on the following day England had declared war on Germany and I was stunned to hear that suddenly Africa was at war now, too. Feverishly I went to my maps again, pinpointing Abyssinia, which was next to British East Africa, which in turn was next to German East Africa, suddenly enemies now—I had not understood this—and coinciding with this terrible news came the realization that I could no longer overlook my queasiness each morning or my growing suspicion that I might be pregnant: I *was* pregnant, and had been so for more than three months, and where was Jared?

In Cairo, Germans and Austrians were interned or mysteriously vanished, and martial law was declared. In Berlin it was announced the Turks were going to attack and reoccupy Egypt and gain the Suez Canal, and I began to devour the newspapers: in the Uganda and British East Africa Protectorates—and, oh God, both countries bordered on Abyssinia—appeals were going out for volunteers to fight with the King's African Rifles. . . . Horses were desperately needed and were being rushed from Abyssinia to Nairobi for service against the enemy in German East Africa. . . . The Emperor of Abyssinia, it was reported, was cooperating in every way. Had Jared reached Abyssinia safely, and had he left it safely? Had he met with delays and been swept up by the war? He was a British citizen, after all; had he been commandeered to deliver some of those horses to Nairobi? Where was he now, and why was there no message from him if he was still alive?

I find I have little interest in recording the days that followed. I moved through them, I breathed, I smiled, I arranged the expression on my face carefully, like a mannequin; I wept frequently in dark corners and cried passionately and bitterly when alone at night. By mid-August the British had opened hostilities in German East Africa by bombarding the coast towns of Bagamoyo and Dar es Salaam, and an armored train was patroling the three hundred miles of track between Nairobi and Mombasa. In late August in Europe, the Germans entered Brussels and three days later the Battle of Mons was fought between the English and the Germans until the English were forced to fall back to the Marne. . . .

September came and I tried to think of ways to leave Isabelle and sustain myself on the streets of Cairo while I waited for Jared. Lacking so much as a sixpence for flight I considered a juggling act, or picking pockets again, until I realized I was too well-known by now, I would be conspicuous, and the Consulate upon which I depended for news of Jared would take steps to stop me; worse, I might even be deported ignominiously to America where Jared could never find me.

In desperation I turned to Sir Linton. "How can I find Jared?" I pleaded. "I can't stay in Cairo any longer. Before the war moves closer I've *got* to go south and look for him, I *must.* Can you help me? Have you influence?''

"My dear Caressa," he said, "there's a war being fought. The railroads are under guard and soldiers given top priority, and in this country women *never* travel alone, it's unheard of.''

"There might be people I could travel south with," I pointed out.

"You would need permission," he said, "and I can only assure you, my dear child, that at the Consulate no one would give you permission. They would be appalled at even the thought of it and you wouldn't know where to look now in any case. May I ask what's behind this sudden panic? Does Cairo bore you so much?''

"I'm pregnant," I blurted out, "I'm going to have a baby.''

"Ah—I see," he said, his eyes widening at this. "Yes—yes I see. . . .'' There was an odd expression on his face; I waited for him to tell me how shocked he was but instead he leaned back in his chair and said conversationally, "Tell me, Caressa, what do you think your life would have been if, having met Jacob, you had said no to his proposal of marriage?"

I thought about this and shrugged. "A typewritist, I suppose, or typist as they're called now."

He nodded. "And married a clerk, no doubt, and lived a small life with him and had half a dozen children. What, then, do you suppose your life would have been like if your mother had not had such lofty ambitions for you at this Whistle—"

"Thistle."

"All right, Thistlethwaite School and you had remained in the carnival?"

I said impatiently, "What does it matter? A magician, probably."

"You were already that," he reminded me, and his words were so like what Grams had told me that I gave him a quick startled glance.

"Instead—" he began.

"Instead," I said angrily, "I am penniless and pregnant. Are you about to draw some bookish conclusion from all this that makes me a metaphor of something?"

He smiled. "No, I was about to ask you if you would marry me. You have survived so much already at such a tender age that you just might survive marriage to me. And your child will need a name."

Now it was my turn to be shocked. Not very tactfully I said, "But I'm waiting for Jared! I'm going to have his child."

"Quite so, but he's already a month overdue, is he not? If I may ask so delicate a question, how far along is your pregnancy?"

"Four months or more," I admitted.

He nodded. "To have a child, to be ostracized by society because you're not married, would be calamitous for you, Caressa. The Victorian era still throws its shadow, even though the Queen, bless her, is long since dead. My dear girl, I am offering you the protection you will very much need soon."

I said grudgingly, "I don't understand. You surely have to be mad to suggest such a thing. I don't love you, and you've already pointed out the circumstances of my life, whereas you—"

"Ah, but I also know what you have become," he said. "I told you I am a collector. Your beauty is returning and is quite breathtaking and there is nothing insipid about you; life has accomplished that for you—and you have lived. I envy that. It would be interesting to see if my humdrum life would kill the life in you or whether some of it would infect me and give meaning to what has become a rather dull existence. I might also—"

I said again, doggedly, "We have become friends, it's true, but I have to point out again that I don't love you, Sir Linton."

He nodded. "And I was going to point out that you have waited in Cairo for nearly four months now, and for how long can you wait? Women in this world don't even walk on the street unaccompanied."

"You're telling me I have no choice?"

He lifted an eyebrow. "Have you?"

"Like Jacob," I said bitterly.

"Oh no," he said, smiling, *"not* like Jacob, for I take very good care of my collections. You will do me credit and honor, Caressa, for you have grace, beauty and above all experience. You're the only woman I've met whom I'd like—"

"To own?"

"No," he said simply, "to cherish."

Oh God, I thought, *where are you*

Jared? For here was Sir Linton Teal determined to make an honest woman of me . . . except there was nothing honest about Linton, as I would discover.

twenty

~~~~~~~

It was 1914 and women wore long skirts and were divided into Good Women and Bad Women, and good women did not have children out of wedlock; in America they didn't even have the vote yet, and in Cairo women wore veils and rarely left their homes. At the Consulate they had grown increasingly skeptical about Jared's return so that I feared deportation, and certainly I had overstayed my welcome at Isabelle's. I was penniless, but without a proper visa from the Egyptian authorities there were no jobs for which I could apply, and Cairo's streets were already full of pickpockets and jugglers. If Jared was unable to send even a message to me the implications of this were terrifying: I had to confront the fact that if he had met with some accident the child I carried might be all that I would ever have of him, and it was the child I must think of now. My situation had become desperate.

And so, after three more weeks of fruitless waiting—for want of choice and to give my child a name—I became Caressa, Lady Teal, wife of Sir Linton. We were married in a private ceremony in Cairo, after which I was tactfully whisked away to England before the war made travel more difficult and before my pregnancy became conspicuous. I left behind Jared and the desert and three years of my life, and with the abandonment of so many dreams I was left with only hope to nurture me; there was panic in me, too, as I went into exile, and certainly once in London there was nothing to make me feel less a captive. The life that Linton inserted me into, like a letter into an envelope, was rigid and sunless and full of rules. If in Cairo he had been kind in his attentions and understanding, it was pride of possession that triumphed now; with the stroke of a pen I had become his, an object to mold and to change, and he was a stern teacher, so relentless that sometimes I wondered if he thought that by changing my clothes, manners, accent, posture and simple tastes he could change my heart as well and never lose me to Jared. Wealth, after all, can be another form of seduction. Or perhaps he knew that every day I waited for the mails to arrive, hoping always for news of Jared from the Consulate in Cairo.

But there came no news of him and so, still lacking choice, I resigned myself to the chic gowns and the diamonds that Linton saw to it I wore, and learned from him to discuss graciously and intelligently the various crises of the political world, to speak Impeccable English and to live in a pale brick Georgian house.

And none of it felt real; the stars in the English sky were dim and the sky at noon a lackluster blue. I lived with sticks of elegant furniture surrounding and stifling me and there were no campfires, no space to rest the eyes but walls everywhere I looked, confining me.

I sleep where night overtakes me . . .
my house will not crumble. . . .

Oh God yes.

One small encounter was real: shopping in the West End one day I saw an old man, a black man and a beggar standing helplessly and patiently in the shadow of a wall. I might have passed him by but for the tribal scars on his face and the pattern of the shawl he wore under his ragged coat; I stopped to stare at him and blurted out in Bakuli's Bemba, *"Mwapolêni!"*

He was as astonished as I. "Thou *sosa* Bemba? *Mwapo leni!"* he cried, his face coming to life.

"You are far from home," I said. *"Cifulo?"*

"A a a," he moaned, "I am *mfwila."*

Well, I thought, *I too am* mfwila—*a person in mourning,* but I only nodded.

He said sadly, gesturing toward the sky, "There be no *Cipinda bushiku*—Milky Way, no *Mulanga*—Morning Star—in this place."

"Or Southern Cross," I added, but he didn't know such English words. I gave him all the money I had with me, I asked his name and wrote on a slip of paper where he might go for help: to a shelter—a *nsaka,* I explained, where he would be fed. I knew the shelter, for I gave as much time to it as I could. He would be safe there and when I had more money I would see to it that he was given passage home. This I told him, and he said with dignity, "Thou be *cisungusho.*"

"A miracle I am not," I told him gravely, "but I have known a few, *ee.*"

Watching him pull his ragged coat more closely about him and walk away I turned to find that one of Linton's friends had been passing and had stopped. "Lady Teal," he said in a startled voice, "you were speaking to that beggar *in another language!*"

The mask I was learning to wear slipped easily back into place. "Nonsense, he's African," I said, laughing at him. "How on earth would I have learned his language?"

How indeed.

Deborah was born and she was Jared's child and mine, but there were moments when I would think—and I confess this—that if not for her I might somehow have remained in Cairo where Jared could find me. In horror I would push these thoughts deep, stricken with guilt, but once Deborah was old enough to talk it no longer mattered very much, because Linton took a great interest in her; increasingly she became his child, and perhaps rightly, because he had lost me. Irrevocably.

He lost me on a day when Deborah was four years old and when the Great War had been ended for a year and was a slowly dimming nightmare, its victories already illusory. The day and the moment are engraved in me forever: it was the season of *Ganni Wazuwirn,* which the Tuareg call the autumn moon, but it was morning and there was a fog. Surprisingly there are days in London that would remind me of the desert, and if this seems impossible then you've never seen the dust carried along by the harmattan—or the gibleh, as it was called in Tripoli—until it forms a curtain of haze of the same texture as a London fog. I was gazing at this from the window of the library and perhaps there was sadness in my face when I heard Linton's step and turned, for his voice was curt. "I see you've gone through the mail already—as usual," he said.

I nodded. "Yes," and then, "I wonder, Linton, now that the war's over and Deborah older, would it be possible for me to go away for a few weeks?"

"It's not impossible. Where did you think of going?"

I shrugged. "Somewhere warm. Cairo, perhaps."

His eyes glittered like pale gray marbles. "So you can look for Jared?"

I didn't deny this. "Make inquiries, perhaps. After all, he's Deborah's father."

His voice matched the coldness in his eyes. "There's no need to make inquiries, I took care of that years ago." He said flatly, "He's not coming back."

Puzzled I said, "You sound so sure, how can you possibly be that certain?"

"Because," he said evenly, meeting my glance, "I have seen to it that he'll never come back."

I felt suddenly chilled and struck with foreboding. For a second I had trouble breathing but I said politely, "Oh? Just how could you manage that?"

"With money," he said. "A great deal of money and a pair of Arabs named

Eyoub and Hammed, to whom I gave orders to find him and kill.''

Kill . . . The word had vibrations and reverberations alien to this civilized and formal room. He had said it so calmly, too, not kill *him*, just kill, like an animal, except he couldn't mean Jared—*Oh please, God, not Jared,* I thought—because to kill Jared was to kill me, too. I stared in shock at this man with whom I'd lived for nearly five years, and I saw that he knew this, I saw the triumph in his eyes as he exacted revenge on me for loving Jared, but although the chill inside of me met with a terrible rage, I allowed no emotion to show, and this struck me as so familiar a reaction that I hesitated before I spoke, wondering at it, until I remembered a young Caressa who sat and waited in the desert with the dead all around her, steeling herself to show no terror; my terror now had the same taste to it. I said carefully, ''That scarcely seems a way to encourage love.''

He smiled then, and it was a cruel smile. ''No, but it can encourage hate, which is more bearable than indifference.''

I scarcely heard him, I was only wait-

ing to ask, "And did they find and kill
him?"

"Of course."

"How do you know that, how can you
be sure?" I asked this almost idly but my
hands had curled into fists.

Linton walked across the room to his
desk, drew open a drawer and brought out
a small object, handing it to me.

It was a worn pewter compass, the
initials on it almost ground away by sand
but still decipherable: JLB. It was the compass I'd given to Jared long ago in Esna.

I stood there, cold and still while I died
inside, silently screaming at the pain of it.
"When? *When?*"

"Not long after meeting you in Cairo,"
he said. "When I learned that I had a rival.
After I learned his name and where he was
going and that you waited for him."

"That long ago—that soon?" I
gasped. "When all the time you knew—
But how reckless of you to tell me," I said.
"Don't you realize I could put a spell on
you, a sorcerer's spell?"

He only laughed at this and went out.

I stood by the window for a long time
staring blindly into the fog, and then I went

upstairs and from the recesses of my closet I drew out a cardboard clothes box. From it I removed the ragged barracan I'd worn for so many desert years, and from its pockets I brought out a crimson head-scarf, a worn finger puppet with the face of a clown, the green glass stone, the carved muffin man and the handful of red poison seeds.

I counted the seeds: there were twelve.

I too could kill.

Bakuli had said, "Swallow like that, no harm. Crush and—*Kai!* die fast and no-body know. *Nobody.*"

Crushed into powder these could be dropped into Linton's glass of afterdinner port; if too coarse they could be mixed into a pudding with raisins or nuts. It could be done, and I had the means.

I smiled and I'm sure it was not a pretty smile, but we all wear masks, don't we? Linton had worn one; how smooth and charming he'd been, and during all those weeks in Cairo when I'd counted him as a friend he had been cold-bloodedly arranging the murder of Jared.

Swallow like that, no harm. Crush and —Kai! *die fast and nobody know. Nobody.*

Dear Bakuli, with his loving and generous heart, so steadfast as a companion. My *ndume,* I remembered, and my smile softened, but against the memory of him I placed the thought of how often in my life I'd been swept along without choice as I obediently followed Mum's dreams, married Jacob, married Linton.

I had choice now.

It's when we're given choice that we sit with the gods and design ourselves: this was the moment to learn who I was and what I'd become; I closed my eyes and became very still, seeing Bakuli and his radiant smile, seeing the great cliffs of the Tibesti and the desert stretching before me to a distant blue horizon; I saw the five stars of the Southern Cross in the night sky and a certain tent in Seguedine and the miracle of knowing Jared; I thought too of Amina and the sacred Hausa shrine and of the *iko* I'd first experienced there, and I pictured Isa and Shehu and the face of Mohammed when he gave me the Hand of Fatima. As my mind emptied itself of hate the gods in me answered, and I understood who and what I was and the gifts I'd been given in this life, and although I counted the red poison seeds again I knew that I couldn't kill Linton. It was unfortunate but I would have to pity him instead.

Grief never welcomes spring, and summer is too bright; autumn brings wood smoke and dying flowers to match a sad heart, a respite for me before the glittering social life of Linton's winters. A young Churchill dined with us—he was colonial secretary then—and once Bertrand Russell. I was called an innovative hostess and my work at the shelter noble, which I thought ironic, and Deborah began to learn how to read some of the words in her picture books. My only refuge was the garden, where I would pace restlessly up and down its paths each summer morning and some-times late into the night, the words of Amy Lowell's "Patterns" keeping step with me and explaining to me my future:

> In summer and in Winter I shall walk
> Up and down
> The patterned garden-paths

In my stiff brocaded gown.
The squills and daffodils
Will give place to pillared roses,
and to asters, and to snow.

I shall go
Up and down
In my gown.
Gorgeously arrayed,
Boned and stayed.
And the softness of my body will be
*   guarded from embrace*
By each button, hook and lace.
For the man who should loose me is
*   dead.**

Dead is such a final word.

And   yet . . . and   yet . . . There came that strange day when Deborah was six years old, a full decade before Linton had the grace to die: it was late summer, when the chrysanthemums blazed with color, and I was in the garden when Bertram came looking for me. I stopped my pacing and watched him move slowly and ponderously along the paths, never for a

* Amy Lowell (1874–1925).

moment losing his dignity, not even when he tripped over a stone; it would never have occurred to him to lift his voice and call to me.

He stopped in my shadow, cleared his throat and spoke. "There is, Madame, a—" He paused, his nostrils pinched. "A somewhat—a man at the door asking to see you, insisting that you have met before."

How carefully Bertram avoided the word "gentleman"; amused I said, "Tell him I'm busy, Bertram."

"Yes, Madame. I'm sorry, Madame, I thought he'd come about the gardener's vacancy but he refuses to go to the rear gate."

"It's all right, Bertram," I told him, and remembering that I had work to do I turned and strolled with him toward the French doors to the library. "But if we'd met before why didn't he give his name?"

He opened the door and stood back for me to enter. "He did give a name, Madame, but considering his appearance—he wears a patch over one eye and his clothes are rather disreputable."

I looked at the litter of papers on

my desk—bills, appeals, invitations—and winced. Impatiently I said, "Then what was his name?"

"A Mr. Jared someone, Madame, I did not catch the last name."

I grasped the back of the desk chair and steadied myself. *There are other Jareds in the world,* I told myself, *and the Jared I loved is dead, Linton said so,* but my heart plunged and then jumped and for a second I feared that it would stop and never beat again. I said quickly, "I'll see him after all, Bertram. Please show him in."

When he stared at me in disbelief I added sharply, "At once, Bertram."

And waited, clinging to the back of the chair; it seemed that only my death could defeat my hopes for I was trembling. In the hall I heard Bertram's voice: "She'll see you now. This way, please."

The suspense was intolerable and my hand tightened on the chair. The door opened and I gasped, for it was Jared standing tall in the doorway, only a little changed: leaner, darker, his hair bleached nearly white, and one of his blesséd green eyes hidden under a patch of black.

"Jared," I whispered incredulously. *"Jared?"*

Neither of us moved. My voice, breaking on a sob, cried out, "But he said you were dead. Two years ago he told me. He'd sent men to kill you."

"They did their best," he said, watching me from the doorway. "They robbed me of one eye and all my gold and left me for dead."

"But—not dead," I whispered. *"Not dead?"*

Words, meaningless words, while all the time our eyes were devouring each other, speaking and answering a thousand questions until at last I understood that he was neither ghost nor hallucination and flew across the room into his arms.

What was it Shakespeare wrote of love not being love which alters when it alteration finds? Jared had sold all his possessions to come to England and search for me. Linton's assassins had nearly killed him, and once recovered he'd been commandeered as a scout for the King's African Rifles and then he had been a prisoner of the Germans . . . all those years! . . . but I had known a Bakuli who taught me

that trees cry when they're wounded and
that rocks and stones have spirits, and I
had learned that what endures is not visible to the eye, and so I saw only poetry
and triumph where Bertram had seen poverty: I saw Jared.

"I thought you'd never leave that
chair," he said, smiling his magic smile so
full of warmth and tenderness.

"I thought I would faint," I told him. "I
nearly did. Jared, hold me tight."

"I am holding you tight."

"Tighter," I said.

"With pleasure, but Caressa—"

"Yes?"

His face was grave. "God only knows
I mourn what happened to separate us,
but there's something I have to say—it
goes hard for me to say it but there's no
changing things, Caressa. I can't carry you
off to the Sahara or to Scotland, no matter
how I dreamed for years of doing it. I've
lost both my gold and the best of my
youth, but when I found myself still alive
with empty years to fill I knew they had to
be lived near you. *Had* to be. If I could only
find you."

"Thank God yes," I said, kissing the

patch over his blind eye and his seeing eye. *Not dead,* my heart sang, *not dead.* "Nothing matters but seeing you again. Jared, did you know that you and I have a daughter?"

"No," he said in astonishment, and with a cry of pain, "Oh God, what I've missed. So that's why—"

"Yes, for her sake. Her name is Deborah—your mother's name—and she'll be back in a few hours, she's six years old and I want you to see her."

He shook his head. "Not yet, Caressa, not like this." He glanced down ruefully at his clothes. "I'm only off the boat, you see, I couldn't wait. I need to find a room somewhere, and buy a few clothes."

"Have you money?" I asked.

"Enough," he said. "From Cairo I wrote to a London publisher who sent a small advance after seeing the first chapter of my book on Africa."

"Jared, it's *happening?*"

"I think so," he said almost shyly. "I plan to find some sort of job—I won't need much, only a room and the time to write— and if once in a while, Caressa, just once in a while—"

"Yes," I said, and suddenly I was re-membering Bertram. Taking a deep breath I said, "Jared, the butler mistook you for— can you grow flowers as well as vegeta-bles?"

He looked down at me, very still and alert; he said quietly, "I've done that, yes. He thought I'd come about a gardener's job, hadn't he."

I nodded. "We need one, you see. There's a lovely little cottage behind the greenhouse, very private, a wonderfully quiet place for writing."

"I don't think I could bear to see you with him, not you and—"

I stared at him in astonishment. "Do you think for a moment I forget that I share this house with a murderer, Jared? We live polite and separate lives, Linton and I. This week he's in Paris hunting down a Velás-quez and it's up to me to find a gardener. Come and see the cottage," I told him. "It is a place," I added deliberately, "where we can have a little time alone together. No one goes there. Will you look at it?"

And so I led him out through the French doors into the still-fragrant garden and we walked down the paths that I had so feverishly paced, we passed the fountain and the greenhouse and reached the little cottage in the rear, and when the door closed behind us we came together with a fierceness born of too many years apart. And the cottage became Jared's home for the rest of his life.

Deborah has interrupted my writing with a hysterical phone call, something about Sara, but Deborah is often hysterical about her daughter. I cannot understand what she's saying except that Sara is planning to leave her.

"She's twenty-five," I remind her, "and she's a very sensible young woman."

"Sensible!" cries Deborah. "She hasn't a sensible bone in her body." Turning from the phone she calls, "Sara? Sara, come here—*you* tell her."

I hear Sara's light voice saying, "Grams, can I come and talk?"

She will be here in half an hour.

She has Jared's green eyes and my dark hair and if, as they say, she looks like me, then I must acknowledge that once I was beautiful, yes, for she is all of that, as well as tender and confiding. She arrives breathlessly, as always, and even Bertram's solemn butler-face holds traces of a smile as he ushers her into the library.

"Oh, Grams," she says ruefully, "I've done it again, I simply can't please Mother, I've left her in shock, and—Grams, I don't want to hurt you too." She flings herself on the floor next to my chair and looks up at me with a troubled face. "He wants me to go with him," she tells me. "Peter. It's why you've not seen me lately, it's become terrifyingly serious. He wants me to go with him and Mother's so *upset.*"

"Don't scowl, Sara," I tell her automatically. "Go where?"

"To the Sahara."

"The Sahara!" I echo incredulously.

She nods. "He's the American I brought to meet you, the one who calls petrol 'gasoline' just as you do. He's an engineer, he works for an oil company and they're sending him out to the Sahara where there's all that oil, and Mother's shocked—you know what a snob she can be. It's too far, she says, and—oh Grams, you look shocked too."

"Not shocked," I tell her dryly. "Do you love him?"

"Yes," she says simply, "but Grams, you do look strange, you've gone all pale suddenly."

"Startled perhaps," I tell her. "Envious. Astonished, certainly, at the rounding of a circle."

She laughs. "Rounding of a circle! Envious? Grams, what does that mean?"

I realize that it's time—past time—to tell her what she needs to know now to fortify and free her; it is the very least that I can do. I say, "Because your mother was conceived in the desert, Sara, very near to the Sahara, which is a place that I am very familiar with, incidentally. You've never known this, nor has she, but I tell it now. Privately."

She smiles but she's puzzled. "Isn't your geography a little confused, Grams? It was in Cairo that you and Grandfather Linton met, isn't it?"

I nod. "True, yes."

"Well then?"

"But you see," I tell her gently, "I was already carrying a child—your mother—when I came to Cairo."

She gasps. "But this is unbelievable, are you serious?" Gleefully she adds, "You mean Linton wasn't my real grandfather, and Mother—" She giggles. "You're not trying to tell me that Mother—Mother of all people—is illegitimate? My staid and very proper mother?"

"It skips a generation," I tell her dryly. "She doesn't know and you won't tell her. She'll learn of it after I'm gone because of certain details, practical ones, that she'll need to know. But illegitimate, no—thanks to Linton."

"But Grams," she says delightedly, "who was he? What happened? Oh, no wonder you've always seemed so—so different."

"It's a long story, my dear, and not very important now," I tell her. "It's you who are important."

She brushes this aside. "But who was he, my real grandfather? A desert shaykh? Oh please!"

"An Englishman," I say. "A traveler, a hunter." It's as good a description as any, I suppose.

"But why didn't you marry, Grams? Did he die, was he killed?"

My thoughts veer back in time and I hear Linton's voice saying, *With money and a pair of Arabs named Eyoub and Hammed, to whom I gave orders to kill. . . .* but there is also Bertram's voice, *Madame, there is a—a somewhat—a man at the door asking to see you, saying that you've met before. . . .*

"What is it?" Sara asks. "You've been remembering him, I can see that, but you're keeping me in suspense."

"I'm sorry," I tell her. "Suspense?"

"Yes, I asked what happened to him, Grams. Did he die?"

I smile at Sara and tell her that we'll talk of this another day, that Peter must be waiting for her, that already it's teatime and I'm a little tired. I long to tell her that he's dead now, yes, but until he died in my arms four years ago he lived safely in the gardener's cottage and she knew him as John—what better revenge upon Linton, who had sent two hired assassins into the desert to find and kill him?—and that each morning he brought roses to me from the greenhouse. With humor and with love. And Linton never guessed.

I wish, too, that I might tell her who it

was that she talked with for hours as a child, drawing much comfort from him, which appalled her mother, and that she has read all of the books that Jared wrote under another name—I need only lift my eyes to see them in the bookcase near me: *Abyssinian Tales, Hunting in the African Bush, King Menelek the Second, Trekking in the Deserts and Mountains of Africa*— but as Grams used to say, everyone's life is a story full of chapters and some chapters are for telling and some for concealing, and for the sake of Deborah, Linton and Jared the strange events of my past have been firmly locked away. Until Sara startled me—but she has left now to meet Peter—and except as I have placed on paper who I have been and what I have seen and why I possess a muffin man carved out of stone that is centuries old and once belonged to a desert queen.

Perhaps Marcus Aurelius is right and the causes of a life are from all eternity spinning the threads of our being and our destinies prepared for us long before we're born, but I'm no philosopher. I know only that here is my story, as true as I can tell it, or as Omar Khayyám has written, *A hair, perhaps, divides the False and True.*

But he has also written, *The stars are setting and the Caravan starts for the dawn of nothing—oh, make haste!*

For this I am ready; the words I write have lately become difficult to place on paper, I grow tired but how glorious it's been to feel again, and even more glorious to unmask this proper Lady Teal whose mask bears the weight of years. I inform on myself, ready now for the next Caravan and wherever it may take me, but I know this: if there be another life beyond this one I would pray to Amina's Giver of Breath and Life, and to Bakuli's Christian God, and to the Allah of the Muslims that I be given a trick or two of magic again, a tent under the stars and Jared in my bed each night.

This I pray: I, Caressa Horvath, also known as Missy, Little Bowman, Stranger from the North, *bako* to Amina and to the Hausa and their shrine spirits, widow of Sir Linton Teal and beloved of Jared.

Iyaka ya kare—it is finished.

Shī kē nan—that's it, there is no more.